Knight and Daye

By Sherrie DeMorrow

Published 2016 by

Lightning Source (UK) Ltd
Chapter House,
Pitfield,
Kiln Farm,
Milton Keynes
MK11 3LW,
UK

Cover Art Design by Sam Wall

samwall.com

To LL for help and support.

To LO, RR, JG, CH, and especially AC and MC for
inspiration, courage and strength in helping me write this in the
first place.

PREFACE

Fakespeare

There is a conflicting nature throughout the book as the author is showing the main characters of Daye and Lear as polar opposites of one another, especially coming from different time periods and experiences. The conflict is also shown in regard to how most of the human characters talk, i.e., old world/old school style vs. modern; British vs. American. They slip back and forth into these modes frequently. There is a poetic nature to the story and combined with the prose, she thinks it makes for interesting reading.

The author has always been keen on poetry and one cannot get better than Shakespeare. However, with a bit of tweaking, she came up with a style which resembles his, and has jokingly termed it as 'Fakespeare' (it is her own, **based** on the style of Shakespeare). Do bear with it, and though it may seem a bit edgy, it does work in a lot of places (and it is intended as such).

There are references to Shakespeare's Richard III and some of the characters therein. However, a few of the names were changed slightly and none of them reflect the actual historical figures nor their Shakespearean counterparts. This is NOT a story about Richard III himself, nor any of his contemporaries. It is a space/fantasy story set in the future, of different time periods and on various planets. However, it does explore an alternative ending to the actual Richard III story.

Other references include a 1960s bit, ecological, sexual and religious themes.

Asperger's

Both characters of Daye and Lear have Asperger's. One was treated for it and had known about it for much of her life (Daye). The other one (Lear) has not been treated and only found out later in her life. This made the character an angry soul, who decided to get back at her family and humanity for all the trouble they put her through, as remembered in flashback sequences and reprobation scenes. Asperger's is considered by most to be a very high end of the Autistic Spectrum Disorder range, and it gives the sufferer an interesting point of view (i.e., it looks like the sufferer is in our world, but not quite fully). One sees things differently than others and possibly with a more acute sense of being.

There can be allowances made by others toward consideration of the sufferer, or the whole condition can be ignored and the sufferer just suffers quietly in a back corner. This makes for difficult living, and it is best to allow the sufferer to experience and feel the fullness of what life can offer. Usually, this should be good, sometimes it is not. This story shows the extreme responses of each of these characters respectively experiencing their own conditions and how they would affect others.

Old School/Classical Actors

The author puts much emphasis on various classical actors in the story and makes mention of them by name or character, in whole or in part. One is not going to give a list of the who's who of that scene from long ago. They are technically figures of fantasy due to their being deceased. However, it cannot stop one from imagining an alternative experience for them. They are muses to be recognised for the value and experience they had once shared with their audiences. These fellows now can enjoy another role or two to play, as an homage to their once spectacular talents.

Latin Names for Aliens

It is noted that the aliens in this story have Italian/Latin-style names. The author had an acquaintance long ago who had a very psychologically unstable and unhappy childhood and on which the Lear character is based. There was an Italian father involved whom she had lost due to horrific circumstances and as a result, she was left to pick up the pieces of her lost heritage throughout her adult life. Hence, the aliens having Italian based names is a reflection of that loss and the fact her very own heritage has been alien to her as she had been alienated from it.

Chapter I

(Circa AD 3200)
PRESENT DAY

It was a nice calm day,
Hardly a cloud, like an English summer sky.
A light breeze blew some rubbish out of its Complacency,
But it wasn't always like that.
The late War was reflected by the Many
To be one of THE most devastating experiences
Ever to be had over a period of ten centuries.
As the lights of life flicker'd in and out,
Much rubbish was collected to defeat an alien enemy......

* * * * *

I was walking along a path toward a hotel where it had been scheduled for me to attend a conference. It was a sublime morning so far, possibly allowing for a captivating day, weather permitting.

I finally reached the Hotel Klaaxon which loomed large in a space with many people milling around. Inside, it had an ancient art deco look about it. Plain, yet elegant, like a dowdy girl in a glittery dress wearing no makeup. A quaint place to stay at, perhaps, with planning or necessity.

Someone approached me, probably for security reasons.

He said, 'Badge, please?'

I grabbed my badge from my backpack. 'Here ye go.'

'Ah, Cynthia Daye,' he read aloud, perusing the information, 'Okay, third room to your right, down that corridor,' he pointed outward showing the way.

'Thank ye, sir.'

'Most welcome.'

I went to the room where directed. A sign beside the door read '250th Annual Librarian's Conference'. Looked correct, I thought and I walked in.

There was a couple of hours worth of lectures with people taking notes and the like. As this was my first conference, I tried to listen to the speeches. Unfortunately I found it slightly boring and too in depth for the layman. I felt isolated amongst the more seasoned pillars of people around me, nay, 'twas quite intimidating. Why did I go? I thought, would it help me or my career? Perhaps, and although I had a degree, I had started my way at the bottom as a bookshelver. Most people would find this work hellishly boring, yet I took to it with relish atop a sausage in a bun.

It was lovely and I had access to many a work, especially in the closed area of books where patrons were inadmissible. It felt like a goldmine to me and, as those books were being used, they needed to be returned to their place. It was fantastic and something that I thought could last forever. My restless spirit gnawed inside me as I could not wait 'til the coming break. Still, I had all day to attend, and then, to my knowledge, I'll go home to a much looked forward to bath.

At last, the refreshment break was announced and I moved toward the food and drinks counter when I spotted the most beautiful hominid creature I had ever seen.   I was nervous....should I approach, I asked myself.....oooh, with such a delicious countenance, I bet he's married, or ga--I stopped myself. No, Christ perish the thought! The creature I spotted was clearing away cups and dishes and waiting on people for food orders unavailable at the tables. Gosh, he looks busy. I've got to see him before this damn break ends.

Someone called out from behind the table, 'Tea, coffee anyone?'

I took the liberty to order some tea. Was this last orders like at a pub, i.e., 'Time Gentlefolk...', alas!

A lady addressed me, 'How would you like your tea, dear?'

'Umm....milk with two sugars, thanks.'

The cup was made and I took a sip. 'Cheers,' I complimented the staff and walked away.

That porcelain dish, currently at rest and tuxedoed behind his stand, was waiting for the next rush......oooh...here is my chance. Don't blow it, UGH! (These are reasons being a girl is so trying at times.)

With another sip, I gathered my wits (what wits?!), courage (doubt that on order!) and headed over to the gentleman.

'Hi, I'm Cynthia, Cynthia Daye,' so clumsy, I thought......grrrr!

'Ah, nice to meet you. I am Brian Alexander Woodes-Hastings.'

I think I had a rabbit in my pants.

'What's a man with a name like that doing in such a place as this?'

'Working. It's just a name I've been christened with. 'Tis of no consequence,' he dryly replied, dismissing the matter.

God, he's humble.....and cute.....wonder if....I thought, getting nowhere fast.....

'Please excuse me, I've to attend. Stay there,' he said.

'Okay, sir,' I mumbled, but with the hope of a submerged log bouncing back atop the water.

He walked away for a time, leaving me alone with my cup and backpack. They certainly were not interesting company! Making friends has never been easy for me, nay, it was frightening at times.....all due to having Asperger's. It is something I daren't discuss in public for fear of ridicule or blushing embarrassment (on my part). I try to act dignified as possible, using examples from those I had taken an interest in over the years. However, most people here did not know who I was and they hadn't a clue about me. So it was quite mutual to all.

This Woodes-Hastings fellow was the most intriguing bit of being at this conference and oddly enough, he had nothing to do with it! I was searching for him, yet, alas, break-time was over and everyone was recalled to the lecture room.....torture room, more like. My interest gets piqued and BAM! 'Tis the way of me, I guess....I sighed. Where is that sweet piece of someone I only just met and spoken to?

The afternoon wore on like a fading garment on an old skeleton. It did prove interesting, but I think overall, I will stick to shelving. Someone at work had encouraged me to attend, and thinking it may progress toward advancement, I did. However, my current status proved more satisfactory and I hated positions of serious responsibility.

As the programme wound down, there were rumours of snowy weather heading for our region of Sydmouth. Snow? I don't think so. Nevertheless, upon reflection, I remembered the War had done its damage to this fair planet of Novaterra. The resulting climate changes here allowed for freak storms like this to hit, even out of season. (Out of touch, more like, but I could not argue with nature, nor would I.)

Shortly after the programme finished, there were crowds of people gathered at reception in the lobby, clamouring in near panic for night-time accommodation. My eyes opened wide looking out of a nearby window. This was no rumour, for the snow had arrived, gathering upon the ground in all innocence and grace. Yet, it had its cruel side when the wind gets involved and that innocence is thrown about everywhere quite viciously. It looks like Christmas, I thought loudly, but in midsummer? I wondered where this Woodes-Hastings went off to. I bet he panicked like the rest of us! I thought again, nah, he seems to cool to do such a dumb-ass thing.

I walked away from the crowd and went snooping out for him. I prayed he would remember me, though our encounter was all but brief. My nerves got the better of me, but my conscious shouted NO! I fought on, long and hard to find him. Gosh, he's an elusive bugger, especially when there's a crisis afoot. I stumbled across the kitchen area when I heard a terse voice from behind me.

It asked, 'Where do you think you're going?'

I gasped and felt I got caught out as I turned 'round. Lo and behold, 'twas that......ahhhh......fellow....my…my prize; the hunted became the hunter at once, his blue eyes piercing into my soul.

'I....I..,' I tried to speak.

'No need. You are looking for something, then? Why aren't you with that group I saw you with?'

'It was not a group, it was just a conference. I attended alone, sir.'

'I trust you require to remain the night.'

'Yes,' I replied. He was good, I thought....I wondered if he could read fear in a person.

He read something else, though, 'You do not like crowds, do you?'

Now how did he know THAT?

'Umm, no I do not,' I replied meekly.

'I can tell, you know. It came with my military training a long time ago. Human psychology and all its spectrums, including spectrum disorders,' he admitted.

Does he know my secret? I dared myself not to broach the subject.....not yet....let me get to know him first....please God, let me get to know him!!!!

'Don't worry, I will not hurt you nor tell anyone, if there is anything to tell. I apologise for not showing earlier after asking you to wait for me. I know 'twas not fair of me. I want to make it up to you.'

'I am not going anywhere in a hurry. It seems impossible outside....'

Woodes-Hastings's eyes widened, finishing the sentence, '....and it is getting much worse. Come, let me take you to where you will be safe.'

He extended his hand out and led me to a room nearby. I was nervous again...more so, yet, I had to trust in this nasty hour.

I looked up and took a good view of him. Well chiselled, tall, thin framed, middle aged, warm, yet expressive eyes, full lips, full head of sandy light brown hair, lightly greying in spots. Oooh, what a hunk.....I think I had another rabbit in my pants. He sensed the nervous giddiness on my part, but did not venture to comment.

'I've a friend named Richard who is staying here for the night. He owes me a favour, so I think it is high time to level with him, eh?'

'Okay,' I replied, thinking I hope he's not a crazed maniac one hears about in the media. In my off days, I was, and still am, rubbish with people.....awkward, frustrated, and the like. Could it be different now, with meeting Woodes-Hastings and now this Richard person? I think I hit the target on a dunking board, so it couldn't be all that bad.

'Ah, here we are,' Woodes-Hastings came to the room in question and knocked on the door.

A rash answer came forth, 'Who's there?'

'It's me, Alec, I need to talk to you.'

'Hang on.' There was rustling about and then the door opened.

A man came out, a bit shorter than Woodes-Hastings, longish dark hair, brown eyes, hawkish nose, thin lips, overall comely frame and appearance.

'Cynthia, this is my old friend, Richard Laurence Tarquinne, III; Richard, this is Cynthia Daye. I wondered if I could ask a favour from you,' he turned away from me to confer with Richard, who seemed reluctant, yet as there was no one else screaming for his 'precious' space, he allowed us in the room. They still conferred at the doorway and I sat down on one of the chairs. At long last, it seemed, they made an agreement and shook hands.

'But only this once,' Richard demanded.

'Why of course,' Woodes-Hastings ensured, 'No sooner said than done.'

I did not know what went on between them, but I knew not to pry, as it was not my business. It seemed like they knew each other for many years though with such banter and familiarity.

'Cynthia, I will leave you in good hands here. Enjoy your stay,' Woodes-Hastings said.

'Do I owe you anything for the stay here? I have--,' I was curtly interrupted.

'No,' he said, 'I've worked it out with Richard. I will bring you breakfast in the morning, if you'd like.'

I interjected, 'Gosh, yes please!'

Richard suspired sharply as Woodes-Hastings waved goodbye to me and closed the door.

'Okay, you.....' Richard said, glaring at me.

'What?'

'I am doing this as a pure favour for a friend, so no funny business, you hear?'

'I know and understand that. I would not dream of such a thing.'

'You wouldn't, would you now?'

He looked at me with careful eyes, 'So what are you here for?'

'I attended a librarian conference.'

'Oh, a librarian are you?'

'Well, I have a degree, but at the moment, I am shelving books.'

He stared at me with intensity and asked, 'Why?'

'Starting at the bottom, sir,' my brown eyes stared at the floor.

Richard interjected, 'God, I hate being called 'sir'. Please call me Richard.'

I perked up, 'Okay Richard,' I smirked, then turned serious, 'anyway, jobs are scarce at the moment. I am lucky to get this much. I was hoping to attend this conference for betterment, for advancement or such like.'

'Uh huh,' he grunted. Typical male! 'How long do you work for?'

'Part time, just mornings for now.'

'I see.'

'So what is your profession?'

'A solicitor,' he paused, 'would you like a drink?'

Ummm, I thought. 'Any tea, then?'

'There are a few here on the tray,' he summoned me to the table to choose.

I looked at the packets. There was an excellent assortment of flavours.

'Vanilla chai, please,' I decided.

'And so it is,' Richard said as he prepared my cup, 'How do you take it?'

'Milk, two sugars,' I answered.

'Just like me, then, how about that?!'

He gave me the cup and made his own. We sat at the table and chair set up next to the window opposite the double bed.

I asked him, 'So why are you here?'

'Break, quick holiday. I was supposed to return to the office later when---,' he ended his sentence observing the violent snow outside then continued, 'When the weather got tempestuous. I booked an extra night as soon as I heard about it.'

He saw my backpack and looked concerned, 'Is that all you have with you today?'

'Yes,' I said, 'I was not planning on staying here. I had meant to leave by now.' I took another sip of tea. God, it was delicious.

'Well, you are free to sleep on the sofa or even on the floor.'

'But you've got a double!!!'

Richard stated harshly, defending his territory, 'Yes, and I intend to use it ALONE!'

I sighed heavily, a huge pile of defeat tumbling down the proverbial mountain. Richard looked at my expression, looked outward, then back at me.

'Okay, okay, you can have one side of the double. I was actually joking earlier. I would not have expected you to sleep anywhere else,' Richard confessed.

That made me mad, but thankfully at least he is letting me use his bed. (Personally, I do not take well to joking, especially in serious matters such as these.)

Richard got up from the chair and went into the en-suite. He brought the basket of toiletries out for me to see.

'You are a lucky lady. Although you will have to wear your clothes if you have no changes, and from what I see, you have none, at least you can use these for your comfort,' he showed me the basket contents. The usual bits were in there like shampoo and soap, but there was also toothpaste and toothbrushes, wrapped in plastic.

'Oh thank you,' I got up to kiss and give him a hug. I finished the tea and decided to have a shower instead of that bath I had earlier thought about.

The night passed tidily on. Richard was on his bed with a small laptop typing out one of his legal drafts and I, wrapped in towels, sat to watch the telly. There was nothing really to watch, but it was reported the storm had subsided somewhat and was heading to the nearby region of Gielby. I thought about recent events. It had been very nice of Richard and Woodes-Hastings to help me out. It was like the knights of old helping damsels in distress for whatever-the-reason.

Richard looked at his travel alarm clock and asked, 'Have ye eaten yet? It is getting late.'

I thought about it, 'No,' I replied, 'I'd forgotten all about that.'

'I'll ring out, shall I?' he took the phone and dialled a number to have some foodstuffs brought into the room.

About a quarter of an hour had passed when a knock was heard, and Richard answered the door, 'Thanks, Alec, I owe you one,' he said.

Woodes-Hastings smiled greedily, giving him a food tray, nodded and walked away.

Richard closed the door and carried the tray to the table where we had the tea earlier. We ate our sandwich and chips meal, along with other finger foods when Richard asked me, 'What would you have done, if not for tonight?'

'Go home, stay home, have a bath, watch telly, be boring.'

'That is no life for a young girl like you.....by the way, how old are you anyway?'

'Thirty-seven.'

'Uuummmm,' Richard pondered.

'And you, si---,' I stopped, remembering to drop the formality.

'Forty-eight.'

'Not a cruel distance, then.'

'No, not at all.'

'Married?'

'No,' he reflected, 'I spent my time on career. Never had time for those sort of things. And you?'

'Still looking, unfortunately.' I suddenly caught an air of curiosity and asked, 'Were you involved in the War?'

'Yes, I was in the Whadjataat Squadron,' he smiled at the memory of comradeship.

'Shooting the aliens? Freeing humanity?'

'Of course, and got rewarded for it too.'

'Oh?'

'I got knighted, along with others in the squadron. I do not like to use the status though. 'Tis a mere title,' he scoffed.

'It sounds to me more like an accomplishment.'

'Yea, well, there were many of us. I am still in touch with some of them, like Woodes-Hastings (whom you've already met), Buckingham, Nay-Smith, Brackbury (or Bracks), Cateliffe, and Clearance, who was the lucky dustman. Oh, Heavens, who else?'

Boy did I meet Woodes-Hastings, I thought, but I needed to ask, 'Why was Clearance a 'lucky dustman'?'

'He did not have to go out and fight off aliens like we did. He collected the rubbish that we threw back at them,' Richard then offered, 'Maybe I will take you out to meet my old mates.'

'Thank you, I would like that very much.'

'Good. Buckingham works in my office, so he and myself meet regularly.'

'Is he a fellow solicitor?'

'No, he's my scrivener.'

'Eh?'

'My clerk!'

'Ah.'

'I could use another. The business is expanding. You like typing?'

My eyes popped out, 'Yes, I am quite good at a computer.'

'Filing, organising, the sort?'

'Yes.'

'You said you were part-time, mornings, eh?'

'Yes, I did.'

'How would you like spending the afternoons with myself and Buckingham?'

'Oooh, yes, please...,' it seemed like an eager ambition, but one never knows.

'Here is my card,' Richard thumbed in his wallet to fetch a thin paper and handed it to me which I put it in my backpack straightaway.

'Thank you Richard.'

'You're most welcome,' he said smiling at me, then yawned, 'It's getting late and I need to be in early tomorrow, if possible.'

'Weather permitting,' I added.

'Yes. I think we should turn in, no?'

After some time for oblations, we abedded for the night. The oddball weather started to subside by this time, returning to flurries, and then to nothingness. Inside, the bed was warm and I realised I did not bring anything to wear. I decided to sleep in my underpants and tucked myself under the covers. Richard was already on the other side, sleeping soundly; he too, with just pants on. We obviously had not bargained to spend the night here!

Morning came lustily, reassuring the current senses. The storm had passed as midsummer reasserted itself with the flutter of birds chirping in adjacent trees outside. The sun beams shone through the window via a slit in the curtains made by myself. During the night, I went to the toilet and opened the curtain slightly due to intense loathing of darkness in a room, especially in a strange room.

I awoke early. It was 6 o'clock. I got dressed back in yesterday's clothes, mostly for modesty, and went up to Richard. I gave him a kiss, hopefully to stir the ravenous creature within.

'Morning,' I cooed.

He turned to me, 'Hello, my dear. Do please excuse me,' he climbed out of the bed, heading for the toilet. I looked out the window and much of the snow had been shovelled aside overnight by working-crews run by a local company called Nay-Smith. A van with its logo was parked as workers were doing their final rounds. The summer sun shall get rid of that white shit by midday, I thought, uummmm, I wonder if that Nay-Smith is the same......nah, I'll not wonder too much here.

Richard came out of the bathroom and gave me a hug. I enjoyed it and turned round to kiss him gingerly round the mouth, tongue-in-cheek style. It aroused something.

He whispered, 'Would you like breakfast, or me first?'

I never had been asked such a question. It seemed not unreasonable, considering he DID share his room with me for the night, unplanned even. Not to say I am a loose sausage, I always carry a strip of contraception pills in my backpack, just for these crazy-ass emergencies. Lucky I took today's sample whilst doing my morning usuals.

'I.....I....,' the stuttering began.

'You do not have to, if you do not wish to,' he said.

I hesitated for a quick moment when my consciousness screamed and hit me proverbially upside the head.

It was a situation that may not repeat itself again and I thought, go for it!

I changed my mind forthwith and put my arms around Richard. We landed on the bed as our natural rhythms kicked in (and for a change, they did not kick me in the arse!). We shared a few moments together. Life proved itself short, especially in recent decades, I thought. We have been through total global devastation in the War; he being in the skies with comrades, and as for myself, I landed a position in a stupid bottle recycling factory.

We felt completion as we respectively gathered up our emotions.

He asked, 'Good for you?'

'Quite so.'

'Brekkie, then?'

'Oooh, yes, please.'

He got up and went to the phone. He dialled a number and ordered that breakfast Woodes-Hastings promised.

Soon enough, as Richard was nearly done dressing, Woodes-Hastings arrived with the goods on a trolley.

'Made especially for you,' he said, winking at me.

'Thank you,' I had a quick look, 'Gosh, it's lovely.'

'Enjoy it,' he said, leaving the room.

I thanked him and took the trolley over to the table. Richard finally finished dressing; he looked extremely handsome in his suit. I did not know which feast to go after, the suited one, or the edible one.

We tucked in and ate heartily. The tea was lovely amid the very full English we enjoyed. The sausages reminded me of the even more full English I enjoyed. I smiled at this and giggled.

Richard wondered, 'What's so funny?'

'Nothing,' I had a difficult time containing the hysterics.

'Come on, tell me,' he insisted.

'Okay then,' I took a sausage and put my tongue all over it as if it were a.......

He chuffed, 'Okay, I get it Cynthia, please stop!'

I then chomped at its end.

'CYNTHIA!'

I laughed as the rest of the moment passed without much fuss. 'Twas frivolous anyway, I thought.

'Still, mustn't wait, I need to go shortly,' Richard's tone was serious.

I was despondent. The time flew faster than a starship in an air tunnel.

'Darn, it was so lovely being here,' I whinged and pouted.

He finished his tea. 'Well, that is the problem with hotels. They are a temporary fix to a permanent matter.'

'Eh?'

'One must sleep, m'dear, then one must GO!' He emphasised the last word.

I felt slightly taken aback by this, but I hoped he did not mean it. I used to take things dead-seriously in the past, but since the War, I have learned not to. One could not take life too fastidiously, for it could end at any time, I thought. One never knows and sometimes it is not worth the question to ask.

'I did not mean it like that, silly,' he apologised, putting his arm around me.

Phew, I got scared. I swore I took him for an arsehole a second ago. Remembering my previous thoughts on life, I forgave Richard for his brusque comment.

'That's okay. I was probably asking for it,' I sulked.

'No, seriously, I need to wrap things up at this end. Take your things and go, and please contact me when you return home and I will see where I can fit you in the office. Okay?'

'Yes, I will. I look forward to the prospect of working with you and meeting your friends.'

Considering I hardly had ANY friends, I thought the opportunity was too good to pass up.

I kissed him goodbye, thanked him further and left the room. I went down round the corner to a nearby fire exit. It was also near the kitchen area where Woodes-Hastings was working. There was a quick hope to try and find him, however, I did not wish to linger too long as I saw staff flitting round like butterflies to feed the masses that stayed overnight.

I started to walk away when a familiar voice caressed the air.

'Cynthia?'

It was Woodes-Hastings.

'Hello, I did not want to disturb you. I see you're busy, and.....,' I muttered apologetically.

'Don't worry, luv. You're alright. How was the stay for you?'

'Very nice. Never thought I would be treated so kindly. I loved that breakfast you made up.'

'Thank you, my lady,' he bowed to me, in mock fashion, 'Are ye lost?'

'Yes, I am looking for the exit. I see there is a fire exit, but....'

'Oh, that's okay. It is not alarmed at the moment, let me take you through.'

'Are you sure I do not owe you anything for this? You really put yourself out for me.'

'We will discuss that another time, if need be. Sometimes, it is worth helping one's neighbour, you know, especially one such as you.'

I blushed as he walked me to that exit I saw earlier.

He called out as I left the building, 'Here ye go. A safe journey for thee, my dear!'

I turned round to wave at him, which he returned. The door shut fast afterward. There was no knob on that door on the outside and one had to get in with a key. I guess there was no turning back now.

The moments of the past twenty-four hours caught up with me so fast, I found it difficult to walk; I hailed a taxi and took myself home for a good long rest.

Chapter II

The next day, after I had finished my few hours at the library, I rang the number on my mobile from the card Richard had given to me.

Several rings later, an unfamiliar voice answered, 'Tarquinne Legal Services, how may I help?'

It was Buckingham, his clerk.

'Hi, Richard gave me a card with this number on it.'

'You're Cynthia, aren't you? Richard told me to expect your call. Come round, we're having lunch now.'

'Okay,' I further confirmed the address with Buckingham and rang off.

I went to 69 Druelcote Lane, Sydmouth. It was a converted Victorian-style semi with the respective signage up. I walked in. The high ceilings complemented the foyer, with a lovely tiled floor and separate rooms housing the various offices in the building. The business looked small, but efficient. It may take some getting used to, if I am accepted into employment. This is a long way from just being on your own with books for company.

A short stocky fellow came up to me. He was a shirt, tie, and trousers sort, probably with a cardigan on a cold day. His dark eyes were expressive and I noticed a receding hairline.

'Will you come with me, Richard and I are in the back room.'

'You must be Buckingham.'

'Aye, 'tis me.'

'Odd way to talk, no?'

'Nah, just messing with you.'

We walked off to the back where I was given an interview. I told Richard, formally this time, of my work and abilities. I wanted to inform him of the Asperger's issue, but....I hesitated. I knew it would need to be declared and after all I had been through with him......so I told him.

'How long did you know this?'

'I was diagnosed at three and known about it most of my life. I had support over the years, yet I do not like to discuss it with most people.'

Richard, as an aside, asked, 'Why did you not share this with me at the hotel?'

'You did not ask and I do not like to divulge as it would've ruined a beautiful moment.'

'I see,' he said, pausing to think, then added, 'I will discuss the matter with Buckingham. Could you please wait in the foyer and give us some time?'

'Will do, sir,' I replied, figuring in this case, the 'Sir' would be needed.

Richard smiled at me and winked, leading me back to the foyer.

It was about ten or so minutes before I heard anything.

'Do come in, please,' Richard beckoned.

I returned to the room where I had the interview with Buckingham and Richard. My nervous nature came through pretty fast and it showed.

'There is no need to be frightened, dear,' Buckingham stated.

Richard whispered something in his ear. He acknowledged the issue and moved on.

'We will take you on board, Cynthia, and try you out for now, is that alright with you?'

'Fine, sir.'

'You will start after lunch tomorrow and work in the afternoon. Buckingham will show you what to do.'

I was hired. Wow....now I have two jobs.....it seemed convenient for me, considering all I would do in the afternoons is bugger-all or nothing, and bugger-all seemed more fun. The money would come in handy for me as well so I would not have to keep dipping into my savings all the time.

So that was the beginning of my time with Richard and Buckingham. Working with them was fun and they allotted for my condition by keeping the stress level down as best they could.

It had been several days on, when Richard asked me, 'Would you like to meet some of my comrades I told you about back at the hotel?'

'Oooh, yes, I would. Thank you,' I gloried in the prospect.
Well, it beat nothing at all, I guess.

'Okay, well, after work, we will go over to the arcade for our
rendezvous.'

'Splendid.' I could not wait.

We later left the office to hang out at the games arcade.
Buckingham left a bit earlier, leaving me alone with Richard. I
looked round and felt the buzz going on amongst the wood
panelling and exposed stone fireplace. The early evening
sunshine touched gently against the large latticed window that
had a small coat of arms lying therein.

It did not feel like a games arcade, (it was more like a pub), but
as this is an era where everything is possible, and anything
goes. Restoration was the order of the day and most people,
who either peeked in or stayed for a tipple at the drinks
counter, had found the arcade most appealing. However, it was
a very heady atmosphere with people winning and losing all
the time. At least it felt like that.

Richard slowly wandered over to an old spitfire game where
Buckingham was playing. It was a shooter style game that
Buckingham liked reverently, as he was an eager enthusiast
and an ex-fighter pilot who served in the War.

Buckingham turned to Richard, 'Ah, how are you, again, old
boy? Can't stop now....trying to defeat the enemy.' His gaze
went straight back to the plane in question.

'At it again? You never change your guard, do you?!'

'Must keep up; never know when one's needed!'

Richard sighed heavily, 'Dude, the War is over!'

BLAM--Buckingham shot down a winner. He whooped with exuberance and a clenched fist, which relaxed after the fleeting 'victory'. He calmed down enough to ask Richard, 'Wish to stay for drinks, then?'

'Yes, please,' Richard replied and he and Buckingham went over to the counter to order. Buckingham saw me and motioned me over.

He chimed, 'My dear girl, we're over there,' he pointed to an area where Clearance and Woodes-Hastings sat quietly, drinking and waiting.

'Thanks,' I answered, waving at Buckingham, then moving in said pointed direction. I introduced myself to the awaiting company and realised there was someone there I had met before.

'Hello again.'

Woodes-Hastings glanced at me, then did a double-take, 'Ah, my old girl, Cynthia. The one who I met at the hotel? You remember the snowstorm that night?'

Clearance was snoozing, a bit high on his wine, but recovered quickly.

'Hotel? Snowstorm?' he enquired, jolting from inactivity.

I recalled that Woodes-Hastings had served as a caterer at the Klaaxon that night when Richard and I got stranded due to the weather.

'Yes, I do remember,' I said to Woodes-Hastings, 'And you had arranged for me to stay with Richard. '

'Umm, umm,' he nodded, smiling.

'Oooh, I see,' Clearance acknowledged. He took a sip of wine and he chided, in a dirty-old-man way of thought, 'so you're Richard's bit of fluff, eh?'

I protested with a grin, 'I am NOT Richard's bit of fluff!' Then I further added, whispering into his ear, 'I currently work in his office.'

Clearance intoned affably, 'Do you now?'

At that point, Buckingham and Richard had joined us.

'Ah, sit here old chap,' Buckingham instructed Richard.

'Thank you,' he replied.

Woodes-Hastings enquired, 'So, how was that spitfire game?'

'Quite good ol' boy, quite good,' Buckingham proudly exclaimed, continuing, 'of course it took me awhile to get the hang of piloting again, but it did not take too long. If it did, I would have lost. I nearly did, however, but I got in a shot.'

Woodes-Hastings sneered teasingly, not expecting an answer, 'How many coins did it take you to get that shot?'

Buckingham sneered back at Woodes-Hastings, blew him a raspberry. We laughed at the joke.

I commented, 'He's really a good shot. He got the enemy and flew him off the screen. I could not do that. I'm rubbish at those sort of games.'

Woodes-Hastings disagreed, 'Don't be silly, I am sure you are very good at something.' He changed topic, 'So what did you do in the War, then, my girl, hmm?' He glowered in anticipation. Was he flirting with me or looking to spread his seed without the wait?

I thought about his question. The WAR. The crazy-ass time we were all in. When people were fighting for depleting resources, a bit of freedom and reusable bottles to fill storage tanks.

'I collected and processed bottles, sir.'

'Stop calling me sir. Call me Alec.'

'Okay, smart Alec,' I giggled.

'No. Seriously. Plastic or glass?'

'Plastic but I was put on glass for a short while. My fingers were did in pretty bad.' I showed him my hand.

'Erm, not too bad. Many had far greater war wounds that that.'

'I know. I am sure 'tis the case. Furthermore, I lost my family in the fighting, and I have no one else, sir,' I reverted to 'sir' on recalling the pain of loss and lost our gained familiarity.

Alec stopped his train of thought, 'Oh, I do apologise. Such condolences should ne'er be brought upon one so young and sweet.' He took my hand, 'I do hope you consider us family.'

' 'Tis very kind of ye to say such a thing to me,' I answered, not expecting all the warmth I was shown.

The prospect was beautiful. A retired version of the fab four sitting right in front of me (not to be confuddled with a musical group which was quite popular in an earlier day). I smiled and leaned over to give a small kiss on Alec's cheek.

He was slightly abashed, but thought....oooh..... and asked me, 'Are you married, dear girl?'

I replied, 'No, and yourself?'

'No. I currently live with Buckingham.'

'Are you ga-?' I hesitated in asking.

He anticipated the question and stated, 'We are not in a serious relationship, if that is what worries you. We just live together and whatever happens between us, is just that; it happens. I do, however, like a bit of the fairer sex as well,' he winked at me.

Ah, so there is a possible hint of availability here, I thought. Although I had enjoyed my time so far with Richard, Alec seemed to be quite a dish to simmer with. Alec's persuasion had not bothered me in the least bit. After all, he admitted to liking women!

'Cynthia, you're not drinking anything,' Buckingham said to me, 'We must remedy that.' He got up and asked 'What's your pleasure, then?'

Heavens! I had not thought about a drink. I've been too busy socialising with Richard's mates that it eluded me.

'Tea, please, with two sugars and crème liqueur,' I answered.

'Now you're talking,' he smiled, 'I thought you were one of those religious tee-total types.'

'I am deeply devotional, but I know how to have a good time, sir.'

Familiarity overcame Buckingham, too, 'Oh stop calling me 'sir', call me Ralph, please.' He then turned to Richard, ' 'Sir' sounds so pretentious, doesn't it ol' boy?'

Richard looked up, 'Quite so. I will have to remember to give Cynthia a good hiding,' he winked at me.

Ha-ha, I thought and then carried on aloud, 'You are men of many means and abilities. You fought in the war, and thus you all earned respectability.'

'Just because of our respectability, as you so nobly put it, does not mean that 'we' don't know how to have a good time,' Alec replied dryly.

I smelt the playful mock snobbery in him. It was not bad, it was just 'his' style. Since my time with Richard, I'd felt I've been admitted into the 'old boy' clique.....and boy, did THEY clique!

Ralph went to fetch my tea and returned with a warm and most inviting medium sized vessel.

I welcomed the drink heartily, 'Thank you,' I said, taking a sip.

'Most welcome. How is it?'

'Lovely,' I purred, soothed by the liquor. I stared at Richard and got closer. 'Nice bunch you have here,' I whispered.

'I know. We've been thru a lot together during the War,' he replied.

'Bet the aliens were better than you!'

'Nah, they couldn't beat us. We were ace pilots.'

'I say, Rich,' Ralph protested, 'I am still a pilot.'

Richard scoffed, 'In your dreams, Buckingham!'   He realised his outburst, 'Do forgive me. I let go.' He leant toward me, 'He'd been mostly gaming for many years since. He would play the same game over and over, variations on a simulation, same result.'

'BOOM! The enemy explodes its wrath o'er the skies,' Ralph concluded, in mock-poetics.

'Oh, you give it a rest,' Woodes-Hastings murmured, 'You're just a silly ol' fool who loves to relive the glory.'

Ralph cried standing up, 'Yea, and it IS the glory, Woodes-Hastings! You do not know the excitement of being up there in the Heavens....'

'In outer space, more like,' Woodes-Hastings interrupted.

'Yes, well, that....but to find oneself shooting at th'enemy with a blow that no one's ever seen. That is living!'

He mocked, 'What did you do, put a cap in their arse?'

'No, sir! I shot a flame up their arse and blew them out of space, dear boy.'

I sighed, taking it all in. What these fellas needed was a good fuck, but it was not for me to decide whether they get one.....such pompous silly-tarts!

Woodes-Hastings asked, 'So what are you doing this evening, Richard?'

'Dunno,' came his answer. He looked at me. 'Maybe take in a bit of theatre. I hear Shakespeare's on tonight.'

'My boy, that sounds like you're about to switch on the telly,' Ralph stated amusingly.

'Yea, well,' Richard hesitated, 'It's the play Richard III. Cynthia's been bugging me to see it.'

'Oh, I did not know you were keen on history,' Ralph said to me.

'Well,' I began, 'I do like a bit of medieval antiquity....kings and things, present company excepted, of course.'

Ralph made a face at me, then continued, 'Then, you're in for a treat, there's that fellow, oh, what was his name...ah, Sir Cedric Wolfe-Harris. I heard he is very good. Marvellous, even. A right honourable rave-up, if you know what I mean.'

I thought of the prospect, silently drooling in the mind. Sir Cedric was the best Shakespearian, ever. Still going, doing other trades in his day, but the old school Bard is what he does, and loves, best. I heard he did an amazing modern version of Othello in the 'hip-hop' genre to get younger audiences keen. It was so popular, it was made into a film, entitled 'Yo, Des!'. However, dear Sir Cedric loved and preferred his classical way with words and performed them as such.

It was also revealed that he had another life during the War, working in the bottle factories, like me. He was much older, but still contributed to the war effort. I had seen him in passing, not properly meeting one another.....and definitely not to imagine his transformation into the actor's life.

We talked a bit longer, then Richard said, 'I'm off,' and turning to me and holding his hand out, said, 'Come, my friend.' I got up and took it and held his hand.

Buckingham asked, 'So you two are going?'

'Yep, we need to prepare to go out tonight,' Richard answered.

'Ah, it takes awhile for one to go out, then,' Buckingham laughed and turned to me, 'Especially for you, my dear.'

'Ha ha,' I snorted back and gave him a quick kiss on the cheek.

'You take care and enjoy the show.'

'We will.'

Richard and I bade our respective farewells and left the group.

Buckingham carried on with his drink, Woodes-Hastings took his mobile out to have a go at the puzzles and Clearance relaxed, nearly nodding off.

'You look tired, Art,' Buckingham stated to Clearance.

Clearance stirred, 'Yea, you are quite correct. Must be the drink; 'tis so relaxing.'

'Do you wish to leave, then?'

'I think a taxi should be sufficient,' Clearance answered, eyes slightly closed.

Buckingham went into command mode. 'Woodes-Hastings, you've a phone,' he said.

'Already on it,' Woodes-Hastings paused his interlude to ring for a cab. The other end picked up, 'Hello,' he began, 'Ah yes, I am in need of a taxi for a friend living at,' he then paused and turned to Clearance, who was more alert than before, and asked, 'your address, please?'

'118 Guinness Park Lane,' came the reply.

Woodes-Hastings went back into the phone conversation, '118 Guinness Park Lane. Okay, yes. We're at the arcade on Cushing Row. Right. See you in a few minutes. Thank you. Bye,' he rang off. 'They will be arriving soon,' he announced.

Buckingham was relieved at last his friend would be taken care of.

'So what are your plans for the evening?' Woodes-Hastings continued to Buckingham.

'Might stay here a bit more, play cards,' he said, 'I know I've a pack of them round somewhere.' He patted himself down toward an inner liner pocket, 'Ah, here they are.'

Woodes-Hastings retorted, 'Oh, that is so archaic, Ralph!'

'Well one has to maintain the traditional in the midst of all this eyepoppin' claptrap,' Buckingham gestured around him, 'It is also quieter. Sometimes, one likes the space of things without all the racket, you know.'

Woodes-Hastings grinned, closing up his game, 'You're on! Sometimes it would be nice to see a real crossword for a change.'

Buckingham returned the favour with a twinkle in his eye, 'I do know what you mean,' he answered, dealing the cards.

A moment later, a member of staff approached, 'Someone call for a taxi?'

Buckingham perked up, 'Yes. It is for this gentleman.' He prodded Clearance, who nodded off again, 'Wake up, your ride is here to take you home.'

Clearance stirred, 'Eh? Ah, good,' he said, getting up. 'I will be seeing you later, then.' He paused and realised the group got smaller. 'Where is Richard and that lovely girl we met?'

'Already gone away,' Woodes-Hastings replied, unflinching with a set of cards in his hand.

'Gracious, I had not realised it was so late,' Clearance replied with an air of sadness.

'They're going to the theatre,' Buckingham revealed.

'Aye, that should be fun for them. Well, cheerio, then,' Clearance departed to the awaiting ride.

Buckingham and Woodes-Hastings remained, playing their respective hands.

'Nice pleasantries, that,' Buckingham mused.

'Ummm…..lovely girl, Cynthia,' Woodes-Hastings thought aloud, dreamily.

'Yea, so she was,' came the reply, ' And a good worker too.'

'Wouldn't mind a dalliance with her, though,' Woodes-Hastings continued, dreaming.

Buckingham played his hand, agreeing, 'Yes, she was quite nice and possibly Richard's girl. They're gone to the theatre together on a date.'

'Serious?'

'Ask him. He might say no,' Buckingham teased.

The tension tugged a string with Woodes-Hastings. 'No, I do not think our Richard can be that cruel.'

'Wanna bet? Long ago, there was a King of England, called Richard who was once thought to be the cruellest of them all, but not these days.'

'I know that, but our Richard is not a King!'

'Ah, but my dear Woodes-Hastings, he can still have our heads.'

'How?'

Buckingham laughed wittingly, 'If we advance ourselves toward his friend, who knows what he might think?'

The teasing was too much for Woodes-Hastings. He stated in a most determined manner, 'Well, I will ask our Richard if he is serious with Cynthia, and if he is not, well, then, 'I' will court her!'

'Well, I would be more subtle if I were you. What if Richard is serious, umm? One does not want to be overtly fond over such a thing,' Buckingham soothed.

Woodes-Hastings' eyes widened and he came closer to Buckingham, 'It would be 'so' worth it, just to kiss her.'

'Well, I wouldn't do that here; that should be done in private,' Buckingham responded, understanding where he was coming from, 'Actually, I would not mind a bit of her, myself.'

Woodes-Hastings was astonished, 'What? Then, let lead us on, forthwith!'

Buckingham hesitated. He did not want to hurt Richard and he knew there was time spent together. 'Well, we will see,' he said, laying his cards down, 'I win. You really need to concentrate on the game, my dear Alec, or the lady will surely have your head.'

Woodes-Hastings laughed. 'Okay. I am a fair loser, but I will bet you that I shall have her, if only for a moment.'

Buckingham settled, 'You're on!' It has been awhile since the rivalries kicked in again. He put his cards away and suggested, 'Want to go eat?'

'Yea, why not,' Woodes-Hastings replied, 'Not that there is much to return home to.'

With that, they departed the arcade.

Chapter III

Richard and I attended the Leechrist Theatre that night for the performance of Richard III, long awaited by me. It was an unusual place as there was no stage in the traditional sense. The stage as it were, was more circular, with the audience surrounding it, so one can see the action from a different angle or perspective. The hidey holes leading to the dressing rooms and staff only areas, were behind black coded doors, depending on the play. In this instance, they were coats of arms, blazoned in a soft neon so instead of a curtain, there would be a gentle dimming, cum blackout with a soft candlelit-style light remaining so as to not scare the audience.

As the play unfolded, I noticed similarities to an old film version I saw many years ago, however, there were parts which were re-written by Sir Cedric himself (in the light of the late King's actual rediscovery in the 21st century back on Earth). In this version, Richard defeated the upstart Tudor fellow, took a new lady for his wife and queen (his first wife, Anne, died of illness), and reigned into the period, which, (in reality), the Tudor successor's son, Henry VIII, had been wooing, winning and killing many a wife.

The issue with the princes was carried out simply; Richard had them separated and smuggled abroad. They were raised and tutored in a foreign land. No one knows where, except Richard, for reasons of state. He does not intend to reveal it, nor will he this side of the grave (or any side for that matter!). By now, they would be ruling their own principalities, and having their own families, maybe happily, maybe with difficulty.

The final scene played out. Both Tudor and King Richard were heavily clad in battle armour, their arms displayed wildly about their person in pretentious pride. Their swords flaying in the air, clashing with a ferocity that would scare the best of souls.

'Take that, yon Tudor, or I will cut thy soul down like grass!'

'No, my counterfeit-liege, I will have thee off thy throne by thine arse!'

'Marry, my lord!'

'I shall not marry in thy presence, sir, thou'st put me to shame.'

'The shame of a whoreson yet to be!'

There were further clashing of swords and endless fighting, with fake blood emerging upon bodies wounded, and a pointed sword having missed the young Tudor by a pinch. The glaring coats of arms and embattlements decorated the stage and actors thereupon.

'I will have thee swinging by your convictions, Tudor, and thou wilt ne'er seest a penny spent in thine honour.'

' 'Tis as well, thou unholy One, for the only penny anyone would spend on thee is on a postage stamp!'

'I will hang thee faster than you can say portrait gallery.'

King Richard swung in for the kill.

'I will have thee, by the throat, and prevent thy blood from spoiling fair England, ever!' He lunged at the boy, 'killing' Tudor, who then fell, gasping, 'A kingdom, a kingdom, a kingdom for a purse!' He then died.

Richard smirked and so smug he was with himself, turned to his men, 'We have won the day. The White Boar shall reign supreme and into the next century, so shall it be!'

The lights went out and paused, switching back on again. There was a standing ovation for the cast and they did their bowing for a few seconds, then departed the stage. I was enthralled and clapped profusely. My Richard did as well, sensing the same satisfaction I felt.

I whispered to Richard, 'Is it possible to meet Sir Cedric? I think I remember him from the War.'

'It may take some doing,' he replied, exhaling, 'I will go and ask but if we do meet the fellow, please do not be childish. If we do not, I want no bemoaning from you. He is quite popular, you know.'

'I won't, either way,' I promised. I did want to congratulate him on his reinterpretation, however.

As the remnants of the audience filed out, we stood by own seats and waited. The crew were cleaning up the stage for the next night and oddly enough, the grand actor was humbly collecting personal bits and bobs he used as props. He saw us and asked, 'Can I be of any assistance?'

Spoken like a true king, I thought. Richard said to me, 'Let me do the talking.' To Sir Cedric, he said, 'Ah, we wanted to wait for the crowd to disperse. My lady here has Asperger's and she hates crowds. I pray your forgiveness.'

'Ah,' he chuckled, 'I understand. Asperger's, eh? Oh well. Still, you came tonight and that is what matters. I do hope you enjoyed the play, nonetheless.'

I could no longer contain myself and had to blunder in, 'I really enjoyed your performance and the play, sir. If you are not too busy, I would love to discuss it with you.'

'Oh, I think I can spare a few minutes for you, my girl. Thank you and I am pleased you enjoyed the play,' he smiled and peered at me as if he had a recollection. 'Hang on, didn't you used to work in one of the bottle factories during the War?'

'Yes,' I said, 'I think you were a supervisor or something of that nature.'

'A superintendent, actually,' he paused and recalled, his eyes widening with intent to carry on the conversation, 'Well, hold me breath, just a moment.' He exited to the back with his props to be put away for the next performance.

Richard looked at me with a 'you lucky bitch' look on his face. I got worried.

I asked innocently, 'You're not mad at me are you?'

'Nah. However, it was fortunate you got to meet him. Odd that he came out though.'

'Maybe he had those props for years which needed extra care.'

Richard scoffed, 'Or maybe the clean up crew was one short.' He then stuck his tongue out at me. I giggled, taking it as good fun.

Sir Cedric then reappeared from the darkness of the rear exit.

'I am so sorry to have kept you waiting. I do remember you..... what was your name again?'

'Cynthia, Cynthia Daye.'

'Yes,' he smiled at me, dwelling on the memory, 'God, that was so long ago.'

'I am curious regarding your reinterpretation. How did people react to the change of Richard's perspective?'

'People were sceptical at first. Who in their right mind has the nerve to rearrange and/or change the Bard? We had our people research the newer evidence which puts Richard in a greater light, much better than what he was originally thought of. We then pitched and performed it to various theatres, most were impressed. I am thinking of having it committed to film shortly.'

'Like your Othello?'

'Yes. Did you see it?'

I hesitated, 'Umm, don't think I have, no. Sorry. From what I saw, it was not really to my taste. I preferred the traditional version.'

'As do I, my dear, but we must move with the times. Life is full of change and sometimes the common needs to transform into something unexpected.'

I looked at Cedric, who was still in costume during our interlude together. 'You do realise you still stand as a King, sir.'

'I do not mind. It puts a little fantasy into one's everyday, no?'

'I'll say it does.'

Cedric glanced and saw I had company. 'Who's your friend, then?'

Richard came up and introduced himself, 'I am Richard Laurence Tarquinne, III.'

'With a name like that, who needs people like me,' Cedric chuckled again. 'It is lovely to meet you both.'

'This is a great theatre. I like the way the stage is set. Quite different from the norm,' Richard commented.

'I agree,' Cedric paused then continued, 'the relationship between the audience and players is ever so important. It is best one can see the action from all sides, almost like cinema. You can get really good shots from various perspectives and with this play, which I partly re-wrote, it makes it all the more important to show the sides of Richard that one cannot see from just a one sided view.'

'I take it that most people have that view,' I stated.

'Afraid so, my dear,' Cedric said sadly, pausing, then continued, 'please give me a few minutes, as I need to change and I have something I want to give you.'

The time looked uncompromising, but I was a greedy soul and wanted to see more of this fellow. I pleaded with Richard to remain. He felt obliged and gave me a 'yes, alright' look. I smiled.

'We will wait then,' I said to Cedric, walking Richard toward the front row seats to relax whilst waiting.

'That's grand, Cynthia. Won't be a moment,' Cedric said, taking my hand to kiss it. Richard was bemused.

Once the actor went into the darkness where the dressing rooms were, Richard said to me, 'I wonder what he'll give you. Sure is a saucy fellow, that.' He gave me a near dagger look, yet done in jest.

'You are not jealous, are you?'

'Nah, just playing. I know he is a favourite of yours and it is apparent that you have known him for a long time.'

'Well, I only knew him in passing during the War. It is not as if I put 'bonnie prince' Cedric photos on my wall, silly,' I said mockingly, giving him a raspberry.

'Hmmmm,' Richard reflected, 'You probably do, though, so I should talk. Compared to him, we've only just met.'

I took mild offence to the comment, as it was none of anyone's business whose photos I hang on my wall.

'Yea. He was not a bad bloke. I only remember him as a supervisor, a head of department or the like, and not a scrummy button of an actor one would dream to get into bed with, or to even have a lavish conversation about one's life.'

We fell silent. The theatre had an eerie glow to it as the security-dim-lighting was on. I took Richard's hand and held it. I looked at him, wanting a kiss. He read the thought and complied.

He backed away after a minute, 'I thought he was your dish?'

'Can be. Let us see how it floats, eh?' I smiled and continued the embrace.

Our position was interrupted by the reappearance of Cedric, dressed in his boring best. (Well, compared to the garments of King Richard, anything would look tat.)

'Jesus, I am so sorry for keeping you waiting, I did not mean....oh,' Cedric apologised then stopped, realising Richard and I were kissing.

'No, 'tis alright,' Richard replied, pulling away from me, 'She was just thanking me for a wonderful evening out.'

'Well, erm, here's to a lovely, successful evening. Oh, I have something for you, Cynthia dear,' Cedric handed me a flat 10x8 folio.

'Ah, thank you,' I said, facing Cedric. His appearance had not changed much since our factory days, but he glowed with the experience of one much older. Without all the make-up, his face revealed bags of character, especially round the eyes.

'Look, we need to run,' Cedric warned, they will be locking up the building soon. I had told the staff of our delay, so we've only a few moments to depart before the alarms kick on.'

Without hesitating, Richard said, 'Well, let's go then.'

We got up to walk out, and as we headed toward the back exit, my mind was gnawing with desire as an animal with its prey. I pressed the envelope further.

I boldly asked, 'Can we go for a drink before bed, sir?'

'Oooh, what a splendid idea,' Cedric exclaimed.

'Could use one meself,' Richard agreed.

We finally left the grounds of the Leechrist into the night air. There was a pub nearby, a few minutes walk, called The Cunning Planne. Mercifully, it was still open, as they had extended hours into the wee of the night.

Going inside, it had a small resemblance to the arcade we hung out in earlier. In fact, the same architect, Lorne Seymour, who built the pub, also did the arcade, in a style reminiscent of the medieval buildings from old Earth. It had since gained listing status due to it being a few centuries old already.

A small group sat at a table and oh my word, it was our gang, Woodes-Hastings, Buckingham, and Clearance, sitting at a table and having drinks.

'We should not be meeting like this. People will talk,' I softly whispered to Buckingham.

He turned his head round, and smiled. 'Cynthia, what an honour it is for you to grace our path again. We must do this more often.'

Woodes-Hastings jerked up suddenly from his phone, exclaiming with surprise, 'Good gosh, Cynthia!'

'Still playing your games, then?' I grinned toward him.

'Why yes, it feeds the mind,' he said, 'Oh, I see you have brought some fair company.'

'Fresh from the Middle Ages,' Cedric bellowed, taking a near seat.

They all talked amongst each other whilst I suddenly realised I had that folio Cedric had given to me back at the theatre.

I opened it carefully and there were bits and bobs to sort out within. There was some delightful literature regarding this latest production of Richard III, along with an autographed photo of Cedric as the dear King, at his most dishiest. I quietly drooled, then read the description.

'For Cynthia, Lovely as you are, you will always be my Queen. Love to you, Sir Cedric Wolfe-Harris'.

You will always be my dream, I thought. Then, I saw a small card inside. It was a business card….Cedric's own professional business card. Wow, with his phone number too. Shit!

I flipped over the card and there was a continued message to me, *'With love, do be in touch.'* I returned it to the folio, with the other papers and photo and put it all in my bag neatly. I felt elated and sinfully embarrassed. I was flattered he thought so highly of me, even bothering to remember me from all those years back.

I nearly fainted with glee, when Woodes-Hastings had noticed my giddiness and asked, 'You alright, dear?'

'Yes, more than alright, thank you,' I confessed. I wanted to share this with him, but was hesitant. It was a personal message to me, and I respected it as such. My mind was spinning faster than an airship's motor flown during the War.

Cedric quietly smiled to himself, knowing what discoveries I had just made. 'Perhaps the little one would want a drink. You look awfully flushed, my dear,' he said to me.

I accepted the offer, 'Quite, sir, yes. Umm..' I paused to think, 'Advocaat, if you please.'

'But of course,' Cedric got up to the bar for my order.

'So how was that play of yours, then? Do tell us about it,' Woodes-Hastings stared directly at me.

'Oooh, it was wonderful, whimsical, wish you were in it, cool,' I said, slipping a gag at him.

'Ha, I am no actor, Cynthia,' he dismissed.

I winked at him, 'Aren't you?'

He laughed, 'No, I am not. I am a jack of all trades and generally a know-all, but ne'er on the stage.'

'More's the pity, then,' I said sadly, 'Your talents look unbounded.'

'Yes, well, ummmm.....,' he blushed, not knowing how to take the compliment.

'So you enjoyed it,' Buckingham said.

'Ah yes, I did,' I replied.

'Richard?'

He responded, 'It was better than I thought. I liked the new additions to it. I do not wish to spoil it for you by telling you what goes on therein.'

Buckingham nodded in agreement. He saw Cedric approaching, 'Your drink's here, Cynthia.'

I turned, 'Why thank you,' I said as Cedric put the drink down onto my part of the table, then putting the change away in his pocket.

'So how are you flyboys then,' Cedric addressed all, referring to their time during the War.

'I had a good kip,' Clearance spoke up, knowing he was not a 'flyboy' then.

'Too much of the wine, eh,' Cedric chortled.

'Well, yea,' he calmly dreamt of his former career as a haulier.

'It is age, too,' Buckingham revealed, 'Isn't it, Art?' He gave a laugh.

'Could be,' Clearance said, calmly, 'but does one wish to admit to age.'

There was a pause.

Richard then turned to me, 'So, what did our Cedric give to you?' He referred to the personalised collection I glanced at a few moments ago.

I gave the folio to him, as I had nothing to hide. Well, I could have hidden the card in my pocket, but it felt better not to. Relationships are tricky creatures at the best of times and I did not wish to be devoured by one.

Richard went through the folio, finding the card at first glance. There was a quick tinge to my cheeks as he read it to himself.

'Oooh, so you are planning a date now?'

'Maybe,' I replied sardonically.

He then returned the card to the folio and found that autographed photo. Oh shit, here we go, I thought. I wondered if that 'Queen' comment might put him off, or make him jealous??!

'*For Cynthia,*' he read aloud, '*Lovely as you are, you will always be my Queen. Love...*' his voice quivered and paused.

A quick surge flashed between us.

'You're not thinking....,' Richard intoned.

I gasped, 'Yea, right. In 'your' dreams, sir!'

Richard smiled and chuffed away the recurring formality. I took another needed sip of that Advocaat, and felt the warmth with a slight pinch going down my gullet.

'Ahh,' I sighed aloud, not meaning to.

Woodes-Hastings asked me, 'Feeling good, then?'

'Yes Alec,' I said, smiling.

The night dallied on and discussions and drinks were running dry.

'Alright,' Buckingham exclaimed, rubbing his hands, 'Who's for bed, then?'

Everyone, including myself, sat up, astonished at the proposal.

'Just kidding,' he laughed, 'But 'tis getting on a bit, don't you agree?'

He was right. The last orders had been called and my mind was whizzing with delicious curiosity regarding my companions. Although Richard and I were very good friends, we were not really serious.

We still had to go home to bed, however, as Buckingham advised.

He asked me quietly, 'You have a place, Cynthia?'

'Yes, I have a flat but I live alone.'

'Pity, because we were wondering, umm.....,' Buckingham thought, licked his lips and continued, 'If you care for some more company? Alec and myself are sharing.'

'Yea, Alec told me about your relationship last time,' I said nonchalantly.

He said reassuringly, 'Our door is always open to a pretty young thing like you.'

'I am not THAT young!'

'Ah, but compared to us, you are. You look it! It is what most women would kill for.'

I never thought of it like that. Of course, if they want to kill me for it, it would look as if they would have much difficulty with this lot abound.

I collected my things and said goodbye to Richard, 'I'm staying with Ralph and Alec tonight, is that alright?'

'Sure, whatever you fancy,' Richard gave me a smile but was dispirited it was not him.

'So you are not mad at me?'

'My dear, life is too short for that. I know I will have you again. Another time, perhaps.' He came up to me and kissed me firmly on the lips. 'No offence taken.'

Phew, I thought, as I followed Buckingham and Woodes-Hastings out, bidding farewells to all.

Cedric walked up to me, 'Don't forget,' he then kissed me atop my head.

'I won't. I saw the card. You are a card, you know.'

'I know. Wild and unpredictable, but harmless. You never thought I would be doing this after all these years?'

'Not in a thrillion light years!'

'Well, goodnight, my love, and be careful.'

'I will.'

The company departed, all going their separate ways.

Woodes-Hastings, Buckingham and I grabbed a cab in the rank outside, heading for their place.

Buckingham, out of concern, asked me, 'Do you want to pick anything up for yourself?'

I was not far from the pub, just a few streets down.

'Yes, that sounds like a plan,' I replied, 'Cheers for that.'

The taxi went to my place first where the driver and fellows had waited for me. I slipped into the back and got inside.

Buckingham schemed, 'Cor, what a lovely girl.'

'Yea, quite,' Woodes-Hastings replied, 'We're not going to....?'

'Nah, give 'er time, luv. Come on, we're knights; we cannot do that sort of thing! It would be so common, eyyecchh!'

'She ain't common, though,' Woodes-Hastings bemused, 'So, she is staying with us?'

'Yea, I sensed her loneliness. True, Richard's a friend, but I had a feeling he would not mind. Besides, I overheard them discussing it and no blows were struck.'

'Oh, thank God,' Woodes-Hastings said excitingly.

At that moment, I came out with a small suitcase. The folio was put away in a safe place in my bedroom. It will be dealt with on the morrow, I thought.

'Hi,' I smiled at the two men waiting for me.

'Hi, get in,' Buckingham said, making space. The driver took my suitcase and placed it in the boot of the vehicle. We drove off together into the night.

We arrived at the house, a two bedroom semi on the outskirts of Sydmouth. Not too far, yet not disgustingly urban.

'Looks nice,' I said, getting out of the taxi.

'It works,' Woodes-Hastings said, 'We've been here many years.'

'Oh?'

'Yea,' Buckingham recalled, 'What is it, 10, 15 years. Good heavens, I cannot remember.'

I asked, 'You've been friends for that long?'

'For longer,' Buckingham explained, 'However, we have lived together for round the time we moved here.'

'Same place?'

'Same place.'

'Gosh. Did you ever invite other women before?'

'Yes,' Woodes-Hastings recalled, 'but none that could match us.'

I confirmed, 'And you think I do?'

'We know you do!'

Daaaamn! I thought. They were so racy, yet, it was best if I was heading for bed.

Walking inside, I saw a little black and white cat at the door.

'Oooh, you've got a cat,' I crouched down to let it sniff my hand and be accepted for petting, 'Is it a boy or girl?'

'Ah, a boy. Wilfin,' Buckingham stated.

'Cute,' I said. The cat stood purring away then walked around to follow us. I then continued, 'Housebound?'

'Sometimes Wilf goes out, but mostly remains indoors.'

I had no animals in my home. My cat died a year ago and I still have not gotten over it. Thankfully, it is easier on one's social life, as one did not have to worry about the caring side, if an opportunity like this knocks at the door.

I wondered, 'So you both are turning in, then?'

Buckingham remembered, 'Yea, 'tis the weekend, is it not?'

Ah right, tomorrow was Saturday. Nothing doing at the front, then.

I further asked, 'So where am I to sleep?'

'Well,' Buckingham looked at Woodes-Hastings and back to me, 'You can either sleep with us, or on the sofa bed. We use the other bedroom as a library.'

'Oooh, you've got a sofa bed?"

'For always in those 'just in case' situations. Last second sort, you know,' Buckingham said.

'So, if I can't sleep or get lonely, may I.....,' I proposed.

Woodes-Hastings finished my sentence, 'Join us? We would be delighted and we promise to be good and respect you.'

Wow, bit of a twist, I'd say! I would have to think about this. We have only met in recent weeks, but their personalities meshed so well with mine that it feels like I have known them in perpetuity.

We all got ready for bed, Buckingham and Woodes-Hastings tucked me in, kissing me goodnight. They walked into their room and closed the door. I was thinking of serious deliciousness, and happily, I fell asleep.

In the morning, the sun streamed through the net curtains in the window; a soft breeze arrived, making the lounge quite luxurious amongst the books, papers and other bits and bobs surrounding my temporary domain. Did I hear a lark, perchance, whistling in the wind? I imagined its flight from tree to tree, finding food, finding comfort and finding freedom. As I became more consciously attuned to my surroundings, it had not been a lark after all, but Wilfin, looking for food.

Then, I heard the sound of water running and stopping.

'Hello,' I called out.

It was Woodes-Hastings, the other 'lark'. He came out wearing a pale cream monochrome loose fitting waist-high shift with trouser bottoms. He beamed at me, 'Ah, Cynthia, good morrow to you. How art thou, my darling?'

'Cool, sir, quite cool.'

'Good. Were you comfortable? Sofa-beds are not for the faint hearted, you know.'

'Yes. I snuggled in well.' Well, it was temporary. I did not mind.

Wilfin saw his master and jumped onto the bed for attention.

Woodes-Hastings asked, 'Wilf, my boy, do you want something?'

The cat meowed, nudged against him and purred. He then jumped down and headed toward the kitchen area.

'He is always like this,' Woodes-Hastings explained.

'That is nothing. I used to get a paw in the face whilst still in bed!'

He laughed, 'Ah, your cat must have been very insistent then. I am curious, what was his name?'

'Brian Mulberry.'

'Umm...inventive, imaginative. My Christian names are Brian Alexander, as I told you back at the hotel.'

'Yea, I remember.'

He glanced toward the kitchen, and saw the urgency in the cat's body language, 'Hang on, let me feed the little one and I will join you soon. Alright?'

'Can I join you, sir?'

'Ah, yes you can. Please remember, for you, it is Alec, not sir. We are good friends now, eh?'

'Right.' I cussed myself, forgetting my manners, in reverse this time. There was no longer a formality amongst us. He was comfortable with letting me into his circle and addressing him on first name terms.

I then got out of bed and followed Alec into the kitchen.

'Do you always feed Wilfin?'

'Yes, well, we take turns, Ralph and I, but I do it mostly. Ralph likes to sleep in.'

'I see. So you are a morning person?'

'Yes.' He put kibble into the small bowl and led the cat to his feeding mat. 'There you go, Wilfin.' Wilfin went straight to it and tucked in.

'Yum yum,' I said, with an air of silliness.

'Yea, let us leave him to it.' Alec led me to a settee and we sat down to talk.

'Do you enjoy working at the hotel?'

'Yes, but I don't keep jobs long. I get bored easily, bit of a drifter. I really liked it back in the War when we flew fighter jets into space against those aliens pursuing us. God, that was fun. Can't really top it now. All is so mundane compared to personal flight, even if it was for the purpose of survival.'

'About the simulations on your phone, do you try to re-enact your memories of the War in your game-playing in the same way Buckingham does?'

'Yes, but not as passionately as he, if I can find a game to fit the screen. Most of them do not. Then, I just resort to word based games, for the need to exercise the mind. We are not getting any younger, you know.'

I looked at him carefully and began to get to know him. He was quite comely for his age and he showed no signs of deterioration, for now.

'Forgive me for being forward, but, erm...,' I hesitated at my embarrassment, 'Um....'

'What, my dear?'

'You look really good for a fellow of your sort....um....God, you're hot...' I braked myself and covered my face, blushing.

He was not bothered. 'That is fine, Cynthia. You are quite a fancy yourself. Don't worry about it and please, for heaven's sake, don't be embarrassed.'

He made direct eye contact with me so as to mean what he said. He reached for my hand and continued, 'I think you are....,' his face reached for mine as I realised what he was going for. I went for it and embraced him, kissing for as long as I can hold my breath. It felt lovely and comforting, warm and a bit wet.

Oooh, I thought, feeling a bit odd down below. The kiss sent waves of passion through me and I put my hand under his shift. Feeling his bare skin underneath, I held him tightly.

He whispered seductively, 'Do you want more of this?'

'Yes, please.' I allowed the moment to happen. I took my contraceptive earlier, with knowledge this would happen. (And to tell the truth, I wanted it to happen. So there, nyahh!)

Alec began to remove the shift, 'Well, if an arousal is achieved, one must loosen up a bit, ' he purred.

We leaned back together on the sofa-bed which was still as a bed and continued kissing one another, firmly but gently. It felt so good. It was too soon to tell whether or not I was falling in love. At the hotel, I thought Richard was heaven's dish; Alec, however, is a mean contender and could be a sure-fire winner.

My hands caressed his back and he responded willingly. I probed at his skin in exploratory motions, feeling the soft texture of his flesh. I exhaled sharply as I was getting more and more aroused. It just felt delightful to be with someone.

Whilst we were 'at it', Buckingham woke up to go to the loo. When he came out, more alert, he asked, 'Room for one more?'

Alec looked up, slightly unnerved at the interruption, but forgave his friend. He wanted to be the centre of attention at that moment but to share is the price one pays when one is together with a partner.

With slight begrudgement, he said, 'Sure.'

'Our bed's bigger, if it helps,' Buckingham indicated toward their shared bedroom.

'Do you want to.....,' Alec asked me, nodding his head toward their room.

I saw his argument. It would be cumbersome with three on a sofa-bed.

'Yea, let us carry on in your room,' I agreed.

Alec took my hand, got me up and we went into the bedroom with Buckingham.

I had the time of my life after that but cannot express how odd it felt as a ménage a trois. I had never thought to indulge in such a practice and it was interesting to get used to. Yet, it was fun. It seemed the only way to accomplish this was to be surrounded and to succumb to the pleasure therein.

After much dalliance, Alec politely excused himself, leaving Buckingham and myself alone.

Buckingham asked me, 'So, how are you enjoying this?'

'Yea.. um, interesting, erm....well, it is a first,' I said, bit awkwardly, as I never 'shared' men before.

I looked at Buckingham and noticed an odd sight round his mouth, a whitish scarry like outline on the bottom lip area. I never thought to ask him as I had never been this close to him before. I fingered the outer rim of his mouth where the scar was visible.

'So what happened here, pray tell, sir?'

Buckingham explained, 'Ah, the war wound…it happened during a battle. It was not supposed to be a battle, as we were on a routine mission carrying a convoy of weapons when we were ambushed by oncoming aliens. They came upon us like mosquitoes. I was hit, but not down. The heat, however, scorched my pilot's mask and well, you can see what happened after.'

Poor Buckingham, at least he survived the onslaught.

'I trust many of you did not make it, then,' I assumed.

'No, quite a lot didn't.'

'Did the convoy arrive to where it was needed?'

'The convoy did make it successfully and never fell into alien hands. Also, please remember, you are a friend. It is Ralph for you.'

I felt regretful, 'I am sorry I brought it up. I pray I had not displeased you in any way.'

'Not to worry dear,' he said, kissing me firmly.

Alec returned. He is such a babe, I wanted him more….and more and more, until I realised I was falling in love with him.

'Forgive me,' I said, to no one in particular. I went to Alec and began further kissing and whatever came next.

Ralph was astonished, but understood. He was the older of the pair and felt Alec had a better chance with me than he, but not all was lost. He got the attention craved at the time and felt good for it.

Time passed. Alec and I were exhausted with pleasure and Ralph resumed his morning routines. I felt quite numb and it took awhile for me to come round from the euphoria.

' 'Tis getting late, my dear. Better get dressed,' Alec suggested.

I got up and in passing him, gave him a further kiss before I found my case to rummage for the day's outfit.

'I confess I enjoyed you a lot. Are you busy later, Alec?' I pleaded.

'Maybe, maybe not. We will see. I will give you my number before you leave.'

'Sure. That would be lovely, thank you.'

Ralph asked, 'Would you like breakfast here or out?'

I pondered, 'You have anything round?'

'Not really. One needs to do a shop again. Do you wish to join us out?'

I honestly felt famished, tired and happy at the same time.

'Yea, let us so do,' I replied.

Alec gave me a quick hug, then disappeared into the bedroom where Ralph was finishing his dressing. I got myself ready and once all was completed, we left together to a nearby pub for a nice late 'brekkie'.

After much time together, we parted company and I went home, suitcase in hand, feeling satisfied. I was already looking forward to another meeting, especially with Alec, who gave me his mobile number on the back of a business card he had knocking about his wallet.

Chapter IV

A few days later, I rang up Alec, taking up his offer to meet again. We each had a lot to do during the interlude between our last time together. The pain of waiting for our temporal engagement, I hoped, will be well worth it.

'Hello,' came the response.

'Hi, Alec, it is Cynthia. I was hoping we can get together again. I saw ye last at the pub with Ralph and stayed over at your place. I was thinking....um....,' I drifted off.

'Ah yes, I remember,' he smiled, 'What a fond memory. Perhaps tomorrow. We can make a day of it, you and I.'

I swooned, 'Fab. See you then. Will ye be arriving at mine, then?'

'Yea, sweetness, to thine.'

'Bye for now.'

'Fare thee well,' he rang off.

Gosh, that was nice. I stood alone in my flat, wondering if it was possible....thinking....eh, doubt it. I do not wish to break up his situation with Ralph, but it will be a matter to be discussed another time.

It was difficult for me to sleep that night, eagerly awaiting the next day to come. I thought about Richard and how I was hoping it would elapse into 'more than a friendship'. I was even unsure if I were right for the ol' fellow. My heart, though, was gravitating toward Alec like a magnet on a suicide mission to the sun. It was bright, yet it burned. Well, that is for the morrow and a long morrow, at that, I thought. I fell asleep, praying for all to be well.

Morning arrived and I found myself with a big lump 'sleeping' next to me. Was it a live cat? No, I do not have one. Was it a man? In one's dreams, yeah right! I looked closer, oh, it was an oversized plush cat I cuddle with. 'Shit, it is inanimate,' I said aloud, dreamily. Bugger. Can't wait 'til Alec arrives.

A beeping sound permeated the air. There was a message for me on the mobile. The text read, 'Hope you're ready. Will be there in an hour. Alec xxxx.'

Good. It is still on. Phew. I thought he had cancelled. I sometimes get paranoid about these things and I silently praised Heaven for the saved day and carried on with my oblations and breakfast.

After all was done, the hour was nearly up. I got my bits together when I heard the doorbell chime.

I looked through the window. It was Alec. Sigh. Potential……
…oh, never mind. Stupid thought, girl, anyway. Then, I opened the door.

'Hello sweetness,' he said, 'I told you I would be here.'

I let myself out and locked the door, 'And ever so willing?'

'Oh yes,' he grinned, 'Come on, our train leaves in half an hour.'

'Train?'

'Why, how else will we get to Brightpoole?'

'Ah, a trip to the seaside,' I was delighted at the outset.

'Mmmm….I am sure you will love it.'

We headed for the station where we immediately boarded the waiting train, paid the conductor (like on a bus, but it's a train and a convenience for people who are in a hurry, which is most of the time) and we took two seats for ourselves, facing each other, relaxing our way to the seaside.

Alec looked out the window. It was sunny outside, green of pleasant pastures, endless animals grazing and no one alarmed at anything. He then took his mobile out to resume one of his mind-teaser games. I took out my music device and plugged it into my ears.

It was a half-hour journey to the sea and suddenly the scenery around us had changed. It had become beachy and cooler, with birds flying overhead in the distance. People were on the sand in deckchairs of various sorts, lolling about, with a few souls who were keen enough to brave the cold sea for a dip. I also noted some tents set up as well and some other people therein dressed up in medieval gear. I thought, Could it be a re-enactment, perhaps?

I reached for my tasty morsel on the phone. 'Alec.....,' I said.

'Ummm,' he responded, face still in his phone.

'Look yonder, I think we've picked an exciting day to visit.'

'So we have,' he finally looked up, smiled and went back to his game.

'You know what is going on, don't you and you will not tell me!'

'Surprises are best left undiscovered until the last moment of time,' he explained, still in his ruddy phone.

Oooh, you muse of deceit, I thought slyly. Well, he is not of a devilish nature, but God, I hate secrets, especially if it could involve myself.

We arrived at Brightpoole as the train came to a stop. Steam plunged out of its orifices when we departed and it was quite thick at times.

'Oooh,' I said, waving my hand about.

'Don't worry, my dear, it thins out naturally.'

We walked out of the station toward the pier where all the tents were.

He asked, 'Shall we?'

'Twas so tempting, but I was eager to satisfy myself with his company, for now. I really did not want to hang about the beach all day.

'Nah, I just wish to remain here,' I said. The crowd looked quite daunting.

'Ah yes. You do not like crowds, do you? My poor angel. I remember from that time at the Klaaxon,' he said as I shook my head in agreement. Most of them having appeared whilst we were still aboard the train.

There was a small pause. 'We can watch a bit from here,' he decided.

'Actually, I don't care much about what's doing down there,' I said, pointing to the tents, 'I would much rather spend time with you instead. Perhaps we can come along later?'

He smiled, 'You want me, don't you? Well, then…' He came closer to kiss me. 'It will go on all day anyway. They will not finish 'til evenfall.'

Oh scrummy, I thought. Suddenly, I heard loud squawking noises and looked up. A colossal dark grey bird was flying overhead, with a resemblance of the old reptilian creatures one read about years ago. It looked as big as an aeroplane, with its wings out, and probably just as fierce, when catching prey.

'Alec, look up there, what a massive bird!'

He glanced up, recalling old history, 'Ah yes, one of the many creatures whose DNA was taken from a fossil found in the Earth several centuries ago, at the time of the evacuations. It is referred to now as the 'Zippaurus Mallanus', as its original name was unknown. They are not the most pleasant of creatures when one runs into them, though, but they are most graceful and magnificent to look at, from a distance, of course.'

The winged creature swirled around to get its bearings and began its search for food. Gliding high in the sky, it was like watching aircraft formations, but far more fanciful. It spotted a small mammal scurrying about and it viciously grabbed the creature in a blink and flew away with it.

The great bird then saw a ledge to stoop on to have its meal. There, it tore apart the mammal in its bestial way and ate it in a savage manner. Once the bird was satisfied, it flicked what was left of the carcass onto the ground.

A passer-by saw the corpse and walked around it with a face that reflected repulsion therefrom.

The bird then winged its way back into the sky, surveying its territory and carrying on its merciless search for food and adventure.

The breeze was light and firm. I sighed at the sight, reached for Alec's hand and leant against the pier.

'It is so fetching here,' I exhaled.

He carried on like a storyteller, 'The fresh air made it an agreeable place to go to, especially in the olden times, midway through the War. When our Earth was dying and the surviving inhabitants relocated here to Novaterra, people needed to escape the calamity and loss. Some of them had founded Brightpoole and made it into a spa town, similar to those on Earth, when a spring was discovered in the vicinity. People thus came here for their health because of the atmosphere as well as partake to the waters.'

'You mean the sea?'

'Yea, and the nearby spas. They are still running, you know.'

An idea flashed within my mind, 'Can we visit one? They did not become museums, did they?'

'Good heavens, no, child, they are not museums,' Alec explained. 'We can visit one. The pumps are in full operation and have been for hundreds of years. It took a lot of man-power, I'll tell you! This is one of the oldest replicated spa towns on the planet.'

I thought about a visit to the spa, but realised I had no kit with me. I relayed this to Alec.

'Well, for a small fee, they will provide.'

Bloody hell, I thought. This was going to be interesting.

'I do not believe in all my years, to be going to a spa town, let alone a working historical spa,' I commented.

'With respective mod-cons, of course,' he answered cleverly.

We looked at a nearby map to confirm our route. 'I have visited here before, luv, but it has been some time. Much has changed,' he admitted.

He continued to study the map and looked keenly at a small area. 'Ah, that's it. There is a place I wish to show you first.'

I could not venture a guess. 'Okay. What is it?'

' 'Tis a church, my lady; another stop on our wee historic excursion.'

'Ancient or modern?'

'Ancient, in the style of the Saxon churches harking back to the old days of England.'

I thought this would be a nice take in, 'Cool. Can we go? Have you been there for worship?'

'Yes. In my day, I have spent time there in communal prayer with the local folk. Although its numbers have dwindled in the past few decades, there is a resurgence of faith in the air.'

The church was stubby and small compared to the enormous ones with piercing spires in the sky that one is used to.

'Ah, here we are,' Alec beckoned.

The wooden door was open and there was a calm odour about it. The main sanctuary was ornate, tastefully done, with its wooden pews intact. I loved the lattice windows surrounding each side of the building with some stained glass figures therein. The altar proudly showed off its sacrifice as the image of Christ welcomed all.

'God, I love old churches,' I said, 'Especially in the ceremonial sense.'

Alec found a pew to sit in to further explain, 'Yes, well, as I said earlier, much has changed since I was last here, you see. They were High Church, but the style of worship was toned down a bit.'

'You mean to Low Church?'

'Yes, precisely.'

There was a pause. I longed for the Spa, but being here made me think.

'Please excuse me, I...' I said pointing to the cushions.

Alec knew what I was after, 'By all means, my dear.'

I rummaged for a cushion and knelt down, thinking:

Crash landing into the face of God in prayer,
And in thinking what to further believe in,
I realised my place was in faith.
One knew there was betterment and delight somewhere.

Even the grass was greener, softer.....elsewhere.
Oooh, Alec, I thought, Richard is cool, and a kind soul,
But thou, my love, art reaching a fanciful height.

Alec went for a cushion as well and did likewise:

There is so much soul searching, praying
And silent contemplation to be had.
In a dim light of a church,
Whose small coloured window is
The only light shining through.
One's soul dives in to a pool of thought,
Of freedom sought that no one else could ever see or feel.

After a moment's silence and reflection, we got up.

'Thank you,' I said.

'For what, my love?'

'For caring. You seem to take this seriously, as do I.'

He smiled, 'That's right, I do. If it pleases the Lord to show one
cares, I try to do my best.'

'Let us go to that spa, then.'

'Ah yes. Come,' he extended his hand for me to hold.

We filed out of the church. Alec put some loose change into
the coin box and looked up.

'For luck and your upkeep,' he said.

Alec and I walked out and through the churchyard; the sun mingling in the grass. We got past the gate and onto the adjourning footpath. I was curious about the headstones.

' 'Tis not for now,' he said, 'Another time, maybe.'

We had plenty of time, but as we had made a plan, it was best not to deviate away from it. He walked slowly along the path, past the houses and various buildings around us. We passed an antique shop that had many bits and bobs in the window as well as a small portrait facing outward.

I exclaimed, 'Christ, Alec, that looks just like you!'

'Oh?' he said with a smile. He looked carefully at the portrait. 'No, the resemblance is comely, but not a good likeness,' he showed his face to me.

'Still noble enough, sir; could have fooled me.'

'Are we back on the 'sir' again?'

'Sorry, cannot help it,' I apologised. Damn, there I go again. Can't do anything right. Must be the Asperger's, I thought.

We carried on walking toward the spa. Shortly thereafter, I noticed the sign above displaying a name which read, 'AJ Buckingham'.

I pointed to the sign, 'That is funny, you think?'

'Well, the coincidence is striking, ol' girl,' he chuffed, looking at me and creasing with laughter. We thought about our friend Buckingham and how ironic it was to come across his name in such a place as this.

I dared, 'Should we enquire?'

'Best not. Could be a distant ancestor or a forgotten cousin. Or it could be neither. Let us move on.'

We carried on to the spa. It was a lovely building, austere in style but luxurious therein. We paid the fee and got some towels, when I realised....

'Umm, we're going to be separated, aren't we?'

'Not necessarily. In the old days, yea, one had to. Decorum and all that; but now, we can remain together, if ye want.'

'Oooh, I'd like that, please.'

We changed out of our outer clothes and covered ourselves up in towels, though I had a racy thought of removing one of Alec's which covered his loins. He looked at me suddenly, knowing my intention as if he had read my mind.

'Now, now, my youthful friend,' he scolded, wagging his finger at me, deflecting the temptation. I felt discouraged then, because I could not 'get' him at that moment.

We locked our gear up and spent the next couple of hours getting pampered via steam baths, plunge pools (a la ancient Rome) and a lovely stress relieving massage done by the staff. Secretly, I had wished it were Alec, but it is best to leave this sort of thing to professionals.

He went up to me and asked, 'Alright?'

'Oh yes,' I said, grinning, thinking to ask if he could do a massage on me one day.

He looked suspicious. 'Why are you grinning?' He thought for a moment, 'Let me see….ah, I know. You enjoyed that massage, didn't you?'

'I did,' I admitted, boldly, 'And I had wished fervently that it was 'you' who did it!'

He laughed at the thought as we went to get changed.

I asked, 'I think we should eat, no?'

He agreed with a nod, towelling himself off and putting his clothes back on.

'God, that was great. Thank you for taking me.'

'Why you are most welcome,' he said giving me a kiss.

I felt warm inside, wishing that would continue. I looked around. Damn, not a worthwhile chance, in case we're barged in upon. Yet, it seemed not a bad idea if it was done with haste.

Alec wondered, 'What is my little lady thinking of now?'

I grinned ecstatically, 'Just wishing.'

'Wishing for what, pray?'

'Ummmm...wishing I was able to remove your towel earlier and…,' I could no longer contain myself. I gave him a kiss.

'Ah, starters, then….and you will see my loins again soon enough,' he winked and continued the kiss for a bit, then stopped. Not to be mean, of course, but one has to maintain…..

We left the spa and went out for lunch. Afterwards, we headed for that pier where the tents were. They were still standing and there was much activity.

Alec proposed, 'I say we should go in a bit further, shall we?'

'Onto the sand?'

'For a closer look.'

'Okay.'

We went down the decorative iron staircase without much fuss when we were spotted by one of our own, who waved to us. As it turned out, it was not a re-enactment as I thought. I glanced at Alec, who smiled to himself...of course, he knew better (the devil!). It was a bit of filming and there was much to be seen. Many of the deck chaired patrons of the sand had been cleared 'way by this point, and in their place were our dear friends, Richard, Buckingham, Clearance, and Cedric, plus scores of costumed extras. We did not know what scene was being filmed, so we stayed back to watch.

We could not hear much as the main players were at the edge of the shoreline. A horse galloped majestically through and I heard 'CUT' being shouted out. The rider stopped.

It was our Richard. He looked fantastic atop his horse, dressed in his battle armour, dressed as the King, defending his realm from invasion.

Cedric felt he was getting too old to go out and gallop about and his lower half was playing up.   He was more keen to direct, although he may have set aside a scene or two for himself. Our Richard was a mere double/stand-in for most of the scenes.

Alec and I carried on watching, when someone had crept up behind us.

'Fancy seeing you two here. Coincidence, eh?'

Alec looked up, 'Buckingham,' he greeted, with a kiss.

'I see you've brought the lovely Cynthia with you.'

'Yes. It was our day out together,' Alec said, then turned to me, grinning, 'I saved the best for last.'

' 'Tis nice to see you again. I did not know you were into acting or even re-enacting. I thought you were a stuffy old law clerk,' I said, clumsily.

'Nope, I'm more than just a stuffy-old-law-clerk as you so cruelly put it,' Buckingham winked, showing no offence to my odd comment, continuing, 'We all have our secrets; we all have our passions.'

'As you know, I enjoy a bit of history myself. This is a marvellous set-up you've created,' I replied, looking around.

'Well I did not create it. It was all Cedric's idea of putting his rewrite of Richard III to film.'

Oh, I thought, so he is going through with it. I hope it is as good as a version I saw, set in the medieval style, rather than a more recent version which was set in the early 20th century. The latter version, unfortunately, I did not enjoy as much, though it did have an interesting concept.

Alec asked, 'So what scene is being filmed, then?'

'Oh, the 'attempted' Tudor invasion. As you know, he tried twice to enter our realm, second time lucky. However, in this context, the second time becomes unlucky and he is thwarted for good, ne'er to return again.'

I blurted, 'Are you in it?'

'Yes, but not yet. That is why I grabbed the time to come over and see you,' Buckingham explained, 'Come, you have a better view down here.'

He led us unto the beach where the sand was warm and well trodden on. We walked over to some spare chairs and we were invited to sit back and enjoy. He then excused himself to make ready for the next shot.

I went up to him and gave him a kiss. 'For you, for luck and thank you.'

Buckingham smiled, returning the kiss and walked off.

'Wow, this is exciting,' I cried.

'Ummmm,' Alec responded, smiling at me.

'You knew.'

'Yes, I confess I did,' he admitted, then dryly suggested, 'Perhaps, you can be in it as well?'

I could not believe the wickedness of this man!

'Cheeky,' I called out.

'You never know. They are always looking for extras, you know.'

'On the spot, like this?'

'Never know...don't give up on it.'

I thought about it, but I figured there would be contracts to sign, money to be considered, and that dreaded word commitment. I was planning for a peaceful day with Alec. No excitement, just relaxation. I carried on thinking, wait, this is Alec, and with him and his friends, nothing is boring, even if they are stuffy old legal types, a jack of all trades, a retired dustman, or a squadron of ex-fighter pilots!

I did not ask further, and quietly watched, holding Alec's hand. I looked at him and kissed his cheek. He smiled warmly and returned the favour. Christ, I wanted him so badly.

'We couldn't, umm...,' I expressed.

'Ummm, what my dear?'

I whispered my intention to him.

He gave a me a startled glance and exclaimed, 'Good gracious, child!'

I quickly giggled at his stance, but he took it well. He thought it best to pass this by, for the moment. My thoughts soon after became forlorn and I wondered if he would really have me. I then deduced it was not worth lingering over. I will get him, I said to myself, I know I will. I shall have him and I will be the happiest lass in the land.

We saw Buckingham playing one of Richard's guardsmen. The numbers looked uneven, when I spotted Cedric approaching.

'Hi,' I said.

'Well, hello there. Fancy seeing you here,' Cedric beamed. 'I was wondering if you would like to share some limelight with us?'

I thought, Eh? 'Tis weird that he was asking 'me' to go out on set in shot? What if I ruin the camera??

'Go for it, kid, you might enjoy it, hehe,' laughed Alec.

'We could use you too, Alec.'

'Me? Oh God,' he chuffed, covering his mouth to stifle a giggle.

'Come on, we cannot wait all day,' Cedric beckoned.

I took Alec aside, 'Were you planning this?'

'I intended to take you here, but I did not think we would get called up! Looks like there will be more than just the two of us, then.'

We were led into a tent where we were measured for armour. The contracted legalities of this would be dealt with later. Cedric obviously wanted us.

It turned out we would also be in Richard's guard, like Buckingham, fighting for the defence of the realm. It sounded exciting. The armour would be full bodied, helmeted, but lightweight with light but realistic prop weaponry. It would not be for too long, so wearing all the gear in the sun would not be too trying.

We would not ride a horse due to insurance purposes, and I could not ride anyway. So, we were delegated to foot soldiering instead, covering and protecting the King.

A fellow hand stood by to assist in the armoury, one Stanley Nay-Smith. He was a tallish fellow (well, everyone was taller than me!), balding but with some longish hair at the sides and plain countenance overall. He was a great help as I found it awkward to put the kit on myself.

'I also assist with the horses,' he whispered in my ear, thinking of a quick flirt.

I responded, 'Doing what, pray tell?'

'Clearing up business,' he said.

Oh great, a shit shoveller! What would they think of next?!

'Ha-ha,' I said aloud, catching onto his line, 'I'm with Alec,' I pointed to the juicy metallicised morsel standing at the edge of the tent, waiting and ready to go on set.

I turned to Nay-Smith, 'Were your crews out there during the snowstorm a few weeks back. I was stranded at the Klaaxon and saw your van out the window.'

'Aye, 'tis my company. My crews were on duty that night and early morn.' He then looked Alec's way, 'I see you are quick with your armour,' he complemented.

'One tries one's best,' said Alec, then he turned to me, 'Told you I'm all sorts.'

I smiled and finished kitting up. I walked out with Alec.

'You look a right treat, kind sir,' I teased.

'I would rather see you as a princess, my dear, but I think a warrior stance suits you best,' he grinned.

I quickly glanced at a nearby mirror to see what he was on about. Damn him, he was right. My hair was piled atop my head and the armour made me look thinner and sassy. I was slightly uncomfortable walking around like a robot. I went along with it, being a bit of fun for all of us. Even if this had deterred from the main purpose of the day, a pleasant surprise cannot be trifled with, and when it lands, 'tis best to take its share of the fruition.

A costumed gent, Lovellby Cateliffe, entered, still in character.

'They're awaiting thee, anon,' he said.

I received my helmet, and turned to Alec, 'You ready?'

'Quite' he smiled, planting a kiss on the cheek.

We left the tent toward the rest of the afternoon, walking, posing, filming, and maybe getting a line or two in, if possible.

During my stint, Richard saw me and came up.

'How are you doing, luv; enjoying yourself?'

'Yes I am, but it is not what I expected.'

'No, suppose not. Still it is not every day one goes off to fight for one's King and Country,' he stared intently at me.

'Guess not,' I said awkwardly, 'It had been fun so far with Alec today.'

Richard harrumphed, 'Alec! So you've cast your lot with him, had you?'

'Look, we're friends,' I admitted, 'But we are getting closer and it is getting warm in some places.' I then blushed and felt embarrassed at the confession.

Richard considered and said, 'Well, thank you for your honesty, Cynthia.' He paused, looking over his shoulder, 'I want you to meet someone.'

He ran off into a crowded area. I grunted, and went looking for him, but gave up. Shortly, he emerged with a lady. A friend, perhaps? Oh dear. I felt I put my foot into more than just sand.

Richard came up to me with his companion. She was dark haired, dressed in the feminine medieval dress and reasonably attractive. Not drop dead gorgeous, thank Christ, or there would be another invasion to worry about.

'Cynthia, this is Joanna Portaclaire, Joanna, Cynthia Daye.'

'Hello,' Joanna said, sticking her hand out for me to shake.

'How ye do then,' I shook her hand, feeling a bit perturbed, but never mind. I was the one that had Alec, I thought.

'Nice to meet you, Cynthia. Richard has told me about you.'

I wondered what about….ah well, next time.

'I trust you are here for the script rewrites,' I assumed.

'Yes. Richard, in this version, defeats the Tudor scourge thanks to you lot and gets his new Queen in the end.'

'And you are she?'

'Yes...and as it is my name, it was all very convenient.'

All very convenient.....phooey, I wanted to be Queen, I thought. I glanced away and saw Alec coming toward us. My true King in armour....wha???? What was I thinking???

'So, I see you have met Joanna,' he said to me.

'Yes. Just as this story should have ended.' I tried to smile, but was slightly buffered due to my delegation to foot soldiering and not as the Hail Glorianna I dreamed myself to be.

Still, I had Alec, I thought. He gave me a kiss and walked back into the mock-foray on the beach.

Richard announced to me, 'We have to do a few more bits before we end the day. Everyone is going to the pub afterwards. Would you like to join us?'

I tried to break the reverie. 'Yes, alright,' I conceded. It would be a bad move to not join in, and choose to be alone...or just with Alec. Maybe Joanna will become part of our clique without too much offence. Maybe I am a jealous bitch at heart, but my heart was captured by a sweet nobleman and not a King after all. Maybe I am not good enough for a King. Maybe....I drifted into thought again. Damn my soul, why is love such a racy and flighty substance?!

Richard looked at me and started to worry. 'Zombied out, I see. What do you think, Jo?'

Joanna put her hand on my shoulder, 'You alright dear?'

I jittered in the armour thinking I could jump a million feet in the air then bounce back to land again.

'Christ, eons away…in another distance. God, I am sorry,' I apologised.

'That's okay,' she smiled, seeing my tension. 'Do you wish to carry on or let the men take over?'

'I think I've got metal fatigue. Please, have it removed. Do ye mind?'

'No, not at all. Most knights suffered metal fatigue in their day,' Richard said kindly, 'Anyway, we got enough shots with you, so you can stay here with Jo whilst we finish up. You may watch, too, if it is your pleasure.'

'I will. Thank you,' I said as the armour was slowly being removed from my body as if shedding one's skin.

I was finally back in my usual garments when Joanna came over with a cuppa.

'Thank you so much,' I said, taking the cup from her hand.

'I thought you would need one,' she said, joining me.

Shit, I thought, nice lady. Usually female packages of this sort come prickly. She was not one of them. We got on quite well, discussing things of the more feminine nature. This was perplexing, considering my preference for the company of men. On occasion, though, I get lucky and befriend one of my own sex who has similar qualities and interests to mine.

We discussed a lot of things, such as Richard, Alec, the bunch of us in general, even the War.

'So what did you do then?'

'Munitions,' she said, 'After all the materials were sorted, we created weaponry to use against the aliens.'

Wow, I thought, that was a dangerous job.

'You look good for someone working amongst explosive bits.'

'A lot of people did not make it. It only takes the wrong materials and whoosh!' She simulated an explosion.

What made 'her' so lucky? God? Nah.....I shan't go there. Why be nasty about it?

'I heard you arrived here with Alec,' she continued.

'Yes, I did. I had a lovely time with him as well. The day is far from over, now that we've run into our friends here.'

Some moments passed. Richard and his army were now fighting off Tudor with pikes, swords and brute force. I actually was glad not to continue on into the melee itself. I was thinking of Alec who took part in the fight scenes and beautifully he feigned the violence he portrayed. A true standing knight, I thought. I cannot wait for him to be alone with me again.

My mind drifted to happier, earlier hours with Alec. I was slightly grinning. Joanna looked at me concerned, as earlier when I had a trance, but she let go of the thought to disturb. Just as well, because I was swimming in delight.

I sipped my cup again. The sensation was welcoming like open arms when one needed them.

Now, it was Joanna's turn to do her shot.

'Good luck,' I called out to her.

'Thanks,' she said as she went over to the spotlight.

Cedric took her aside and gave her directions. The scene was a simple soliloquy, romantic and declaring her intentions for Richard. Joanna had to practise it and when she was ready, Cedric gave her the signal. It went like this:

I could feel my love beneath me and sometimes, above me,
(But for anyone else, oh, not really).
You caught me by sunlight
And paralysed me in your arms.
You gave me strength
And I want to marry you in style,
Being ever so close to you all the while.

You had your leg up and over your old pale situation
And took over life's pitiful woes.
Executing those round you,
Who threatened you,
And became your foes.
So like nature, pity....
But totally unnatural for you.

I was later your Queen,
Who woo'd you to the throne of life.
You stood by me; you would ne'er leave
And you will rule by me, ne'er to let me go.
Your chivalrous action was poised
Amongst all that was lost.

You gained more than you bargained for
In a tinplate covered in dust.
Your woolly, fuzzy material of uniform
Peers its inquisitive head
Beyond the metallic gauze you wore
When fighting for your Realm.

You are the true king
And saviour of Britain, through and through.
At last, you are what I came here to do,
To live for and prepare myself for you.

Everyone applauded and Cedric shook her hand.

'That was wonderful, my dear, simply wonderful,' he said.

Richard went up to her and gave her a huge hug and twirled her round, beaming.

I thought it was good too; so did Alec, but my intentions were getting more ferocious for him.

Shortly, the filming had finished for the day. The scenes needed were done, yet to be screened and edited. Alec came to me.

'Hi,' he said, 'I'll remove the armour and we'll go to the pub together, eh?' He gave me a hug.

'Love to,' I answered, kissing him, 'By the way, I enjoyed your stance out there. How did you know what to do, then?'

'Direction and imagination, my dear. I won't be long.'

I waited for a time whilst the production was closing down for the night.

I spotted Cedric who was putting bits away and asked sincerely, 'Can I help you?'

'Oh, my dear girl, we are alright here. I heard you wish to join us at the pub.'

'Gosh yes. Alec will be with me.'

'I heard you spent a fair bit of the day together,' Cedric presumed.

'Aye, we arrived this morning and strolled around. I wanted to spend time with him when you were filming. We did see the tents, but thought you can carry on as per.'

'Oh stuff of nonsense, you would have been most welcome anytime. Yet, I understood you wanted to get to know him.'

'Yes I did. He is quite a fellow, that.'

'I thought you were with Richard.'

'I was, but,' I hesitated, squirming in my thought.

'Too much on one plate, I see,' he raised an eyebrow.

I smiled embarrassingly, 'He did introduce me to Joanna. I figured...,' I could not finish the sentence.

He patted me on the shoulder, 'Ah, she was there for that last scene we shot.'

'Yes. We're just friends, Richard and I, but Alec...pwhaaoorr!'

'I can see his appeal upon you,' he looked at his watch, 'Well, I need to get on now. Will meet you at the pub, my dear.'

'Bye for now, sir.'

Cedric kissed my hand and departed. Alec then came up to me in his own clothes, without the metal bits.

'You ready?'

'Yep. Nothing for me to do here,' I said.

'Well, sorry to keep you tarrying. I was chatting and helping out a bit. You know how it is.'

'Yes,' I replied, realising we were alone. 'Alec…….,' I paused, nearly scared, but thankful. No one else was around. I gave him a hug, then went for a kiss. He complied, thank God, and we melted together for a short while.

'That was nice. Any reason?'

'Nope,' I paused again, to admit, 'I am rubbish at love, but I have very intense feelings for you, and….'

'Say no more, dear, I understand,' he lightly covered my mouth with his finger, 'I like you too and am hoping we can further this.'

'You are willing to take me on board?'

'Well, if you are not really serious about Richard.'

'We are just friends,' I interjected, realising that is what I was telling everybody.

Well, there was Joanna who, in that last shot scene, declared her love for him, even if it was only in a play. Personally, I do not believe Richard and I will go further and at this point, I do not think we will. Anyway, I believed firmly we would be better off as friends now.

I carried on, 'I met Joanna and would not be surprised, if...umm....,' I stopped, bearing in my mind the inevitable.

'Time will tell on that side of things. As for us, the same applies. Give it time and space.'

'Oh my space is ever so willing!'

Alec laughed, 'Oh, Cynthia! Come on, dearest.' He took my hand and led me toward that stairway where we were so many hours ago and ascended to the boardwalk above. The pub wasn't far, thankfully, just down the road.

We walked along and the beach's once crowded stance got sparser, especially now that the tents were removed. Everything seemed a blank canvas. The sun was still up, however, a little lower in this late hour, reflecting its mission against the nearby window panes to remind one it was still there.

I held Alec firmly. He put his arm around me.

'I verily love you,' I shouted out subconsciously.

He looked at me, 'You are really falling for me, aren't you?'

'Yes, either in love or in mud, cos I am probably making a right honourable pig's ear of it, aren't I?'

'No no, you are not, my darling,' he reassured, hugging me.

Buckingham rode along on a bike from the production company, passing us by.

He laughed, 'Last one in, loses one's head!'

Alec smirked and waved him on, 'He's got mileage.'

'He will beat us.'

'Yea, probably, but no matter.'

I wanted another kiss, 'Pardon my greed, but,' I leant in for the kill.

I surprised him but he took it in stride. Another handful of sand passed through glass fingers. I came up for air.

'I meant what I said earlier. I do not care if it sounds treasonous,' I proclaimed.

Alec went into hysterics, 'Treasonous? My God, you are a silly one!'

'Well, I thought, with Richard playing a King and your surname being Hastings, in part.'

'Yes, it is Woodes-Hastings. As our Richard is a bit younger than Cedric, it was decided he do the tricky bits during the filming.'

'Like the horse bits?'

'Yes.'

The reference made me think. 'Is that shit shoveller joining us, too?'

'Nay-Smith? Oh, I suppose so. We invited him.'

'So it will be our fellowship, some of the film extras, and the production hands, then?'

'Yes. Let's go, time's getting on.'

We walked some way further. The pub loomed in sight, The Cock and Grow. I giggled at the name.

Alec whispered, 'Stop tittering dear. Remember whose company you're in.'

I laughed loudly and harder, 'Yea, all cock!'

He came closer, 'Ahh, yet 'tis mine you truly desire,' he smiled wickedly at me.

My mouth watered, but he was right. Damn him, he was right. The feeling made me want to scream.

He resumed, 'I can sense your frustration and earlier disappointment. I was not trying to be cruel to you by foiling your attentions upon me beforehand. Now, don't you worry, if you really want, we can go to your place and spend the night. How does that sound?'

My eyes widened, 'I've only a single bed, sir!'

'Then it looks like we will have to widen it then, won't we?'

Ha-ha, I thought. I would be a bit of a squish but to be squished with him next to me would be…I dare not continue to think about it….there might be more rabbits abound.

I smiled at him as we approached the pub. Some of our lot were talking, smoking, and waiting for us.

'Ah, here they are,' Buckingham chimed to Cedric. He walked over to us, 'Welcome, come in my friends.'

'Thank you, kind sir,' I ribbed. I knew we were on first name terms but these folk have the look just begging to be called 'sir'.

'My dear girl,' Buckingham said to me, greeting me with a kiss, whispering, 'Did you have a good time with Alec today?'

'Oh my yes,' I said, 'It was fantastic. We took a train here and he took me on an informative walkabout before we saw you. I must admit, on our way, we saw a sign with your surname on it!'

'Was it AJ Buckingham? Oh, yes,' he laughed, 'Just a distant cousin of mine; I don't really know him well. I am aware of him though.'

'We were wondering, but...'

'Hush, now,' he whispered, 'I heard you two went to the spa nearby.'

I blushed, trying to hide a smile. Alec nodded to Buckingham, who fully understood.

Buckingham asked, seductively, 'Was it satisfying?'

I silently stared at him with knowing eyes, but I could not further my commentary as the memory of it was to precious to express to another.

'Well, we will discuss it later, perhaps,' he said as he led Alec and myself to a table where everyone congregated.

Cedric asked everyone round for drinks and went off to go order and do the usual oblations. Alec and I sat quietly together, soaking it all in.

He admired the surroundings, 'Nice atmosphere here, eh?'

I looked around. It had an old world, old wood feel about it, like that arcade and previous pub we'd been at. This place complemented the present company quite suitably.

'It is well and good for me,' I replied. I snuck my hand under the table to hold Alec's hand. He smiled and welcomed the moment, wishing I had dared further. I looked at him and wished the dare, too, but in polite company, we had to cool off.

Damn! I felt so famished without him, I thought and in reality, it had been an unexpectedly long day. I hoped the trains were still running, but who knows what will happen next with this folk?

A few barmen came over with the drinks and everyone had their share and chatted away.

A kind while passed when one of the company, a fellow called Andy Brackbury, whom I had not met before, had glanced at his watch, wherein the date lay, and said, 'Do you know what day it is today?'

'A bit late in the day for that, Bracks,' Buckingham chided.

Everyone thought for a moment and fell silent. I thought about it and definitely fell into mud. It was ancient anniversary when an ancestor of mine, Cynthia Lear, had allied herself with aliens who, with her assistance, attacked planet Earth and the Great Galactic Recycling Rubbish War commenced.

Her intense hatred of humanity led to the most chaotic and horrific circumstances in Man's history, which lasted about one thousand years. There were no other significant conflicts like this one or since.

' 'Twas the start of that War we were in,' Buckingham explained, 'Of course, I remember it well; we all fought in it, mind you!'

Yes, we know, Buckingham, based on your behaviour at the arcade in the previous week or so, I thought.

He continued, 'It all started when someone by the name of Cynthia joined up with an alien race.....,' he paused.

All eyes turned to me and I cried, 'Hey, that was centuries ago! I didn't do it!'

Alec looked at me, 'We know, but it is a coincidence the lady's name was Cynthia.' He raised an eyebrow at me and pierced me with the most bluest eyes of intent I've ever seen.

'Ummm......,' I hesitated, mentally grabbing straws, yet standing my ground, 'That was a long time ago.'

'But it led to centuries of conflict; we were all fighting for our lives,' remarked Richard.

'Yes, you probably were, but I do not go round forming alliances with blobs! I certainly do not hate mankind and I was in it too,' I said curtly.

Cedric piped up, 'Aye, you were a bottle sorter, my dear. Was that Cynthia really your ancestor?'

I felt ashamed at this, feeling it was the million pound question of the century. I should not have had to, but, here it is.

'Yes,' I admitted, 'Yes she was….on my mother's side.'

After a pregnant pause, Richard spoke, up, 'Christ! I vaguely remember reading an article written about the early stages of the conflict.' He looked round for a newspaper or something that would give a clue on the matter. He could not find one, so he went to the bar to enquire. Finally, he returned with a copy, thinking the anniversary would be mentioned in today's press.

He thumbed the paper through which shortly made its way onto the table spread for space.

'I found it,' he exclaimed, 'They've even reproduced the story published over a thousand years ago before the War started.'

He turned to a page which had written above, 'Cynthia's Story'. This commemorative piece runs thus:

A woman of human origin had been abducted by the Valastrons by the name of Cynthia Lear. She was living in England for many years, prior to the event in question, as a British Citizen. She was originally born on the East Coast of the New World and raised (then adopted) by maternal grandparents who were fifty years her senior because her natural parents were unable to look after her. Thus, she had a lamentable childhood.

Her natural mother, also born on the East Coast, had an impairing epileptic condition. Her natural father, originally from Lazio, Italy, had served in the Italian army, being posted where the mother was living.

He was discharged to settle down and eventually, he married the mother. After Cynthia was born, he was driven away by the maternal grandparents on the basis of religion. He was a Roman Catholic and the mother was Jewish, but from a family that **converted to the same only two generations back**.

This caused major conflict in Cynthia, who, in the end, left the grandparents and told them and their family to FUCK OFF. She forthwith left their respective religion as well and became an Anglican (or Anglo-Catholic). She was unaware of her Roman Catholic heritage and chose the Anglican way on the basis of her faith alone.

This left an emotional scar that **never healed** and Cynthia was left to various bouts of anger, unsettled sleep at night, and unnecessary flashbacks during her waking hours. She also suffered Asperger Syndrome, which the grandparents were unaware of. Because her behaviour was affected by said condition, they gave her much difficulty during her time with them.

As the years passed and her move to England was completed, the stress levels had eased, but the anger and violent desire for revenge had not. Thus, she was picked up by the Valastron race who saw to her health and well-being for the next several decades before she allied with them and other alien races to invade and eventually ruin the Earth and its inhabitants as 'her' revenge upon humanity. Her reason was that no one helped her during those difficult years and her revenge would be ecumenical, i.e. for all to suffer, like she did.

This led to the alien's attack upon Earth, and their consumption of the recycling and rubbish to use as weaponry against the humans. Humanity had to flee the Earth, as it was proving to be unfit for habitation, with all the past and present damage done. There were no longer resources, food or shelter for anyone.

The survivors of the attacks, like roaches, scurried to the farthest corners of the universe, and plagued new worlds with their presence. One of the planets, Novaterra, was inhabited by some of them.

There were human resistance movements which saved as much recycling as possible to create their own weapons on the distant worlds. The conflict lasted about one thousand years. It was only ended when the alien races agreed to let the humans be, as the one who really wanted the war, Cynthia Lear, had passed away of old age and all her progeny, which continued to fight in her name, had finally died out..........

Chapter V

(Circa AD 2100)

Somewhere in the outer regions of space, a minor conflict between the Valastrons and the humans had occurred. Due to a recent resurgence of human space exploration, there have been many expeditions beyond Earth whereby Man was stretching out into the boundaries of space, at last.

In one of these outer space exploration larks, a human space crew had stumbled upon a planet with slimy eggs riddled all over the surface. They did try to scan them to see what they were, but the eggs were made from a substance that was un-scannable and thus unknown. Pig-ignorance and fear had limited human understanding and so, regrettably, the humans destroyed the eggs. This action caused a great disturbance in the outer galaxy, for they had contained Valastrings, the Valastron young which needed to be maintained and hatched in certain temperatures. The planet was ideal for this, until human discovery and incompetence set in. As a result, the Valastrons waged a personal war against the humans for some time.

* * * * *

It was cold and damp on the ship, the Yakrey. Cynthia walked down the corridor where Spazio the Valastron stood watching the ringleaders of that expedition as they were being searched, stripped, categorised and eventually degraded.

The Valastron asked in his usual old raspy voice, 'Are they all accounted for Ms Lear?'

She said coldly, 'Yes. Are we ready for extermination?'

'You may proceed,' he said, slithering away, his 12 suctioned tentacles making the most annoying sounds.

Cynthia looked at the victims with glee, as she pressed the button that at once vaporised all within the room. No remorse was in her eyes or heart. However, in witnessing the execution, it made her think about her ex-family who did serious damage to her mind and soul.

Then, she had an idea……

'After all they did to ME!' she fumed to herself, then shouted, 'GUARD!'

'Yes, Cynthia,' said a puny stubby type named Uffizio.

'I want you to search all time and space, and find all remnants of the family directly related to me, without breaking the lineage. Have them brought here 'alive',' she commanded.

'As will be done,' he said and went out, tentacles a wee more quieter on this creature.

She thought inside, I shall have my revenge. You bastards will ne'er get away with what you've done to me. You swine! She then turned and walked away.

She did not care for humans in general. They were breeding and littering profusely and personally something needed to be done about it. She thought of destroying the Earth itself, but most of its resources there were already being depleted and have been for centuries. It was all down to the greedy human progress and she was disgusted by it. Some humans thought it would be a good idea to recycle things so as to not destroy too much of what Mother Earth provides.

However, after quite a few centuries, this proved infeasible. Damn them if they were doing it. They were such wasteful louts at the best of times. Not like me, she thought. Once upon a time, I tried to do good in the world and to help where I can. Yet what did I get for it? NOTHING! Now, 'I' will have something, she further thought.

She went to her chamber and took a seat. The intercom buzzed.

'Shit,' she said aloud. Who would disturb her at this hour?

It was Spazio. 'Ms Lear?'

Now, what did 'he' want?

She curtly replied, 'Yeah, what is it? I'm busy over here!'

'Your request has been granted. Your family has been traced and located. They are coming aboard straightaway.'

'Thank you. Put them in the Custodial Tower and hold them there 'til I am ready for them. I might be some time....in fact, a whole load of time, hahaha.'

'As you....,' the communiqué was hastily cut off.

'FUCK OFF!' she cried aloud, kicking in a chair. There was no one in the room and it was so cursedly lonely. This made her more angrier, more bitchier, and more nastier. She felt desperation and vulnerability. She was in no mood to face her family. They were casualties as far as she was concerned and casualties they will remain.....but they will not get away this time!

Those idiots, bigoted, egotistical, and horrible idiots, will pay for what was done. They took away my father, my God and religion, and my heritage, she remembered. The passion was so hot inside her, it burned into her heart.

She wrote part of it down in a poem:

The passion was so hot inside,
It made a near physical tattoo,
That one obviously cannot see.
But if one looks ever so closely,
One can see it there,
Encased, bejewelled
And pissed off with lava.

Ah, that felt better. Shame 'tis but a silly poem....there were loads, but here's a fresh one born to read and dwell upon.

She took a quick swill of a nearby drink in the chamber before she looked at the comm. system again. She paused for awhile, listening to a nearby radio which played soothing classical music. She was lost in another feel-good reverie, trying to break out of the hate and the deep-seated hurt she felt.

There was only one thing for it. She reached for the switch atop the unit.

'Get me my companion,' she snorted.

'Straightaway ma'am,' came the reply.

Her fingers tapped impatiently upon the table where she sat. Shortly thereafter, the nail biting occurred, not that there was much to chew off in the first place.

Long ago, she was afflicted by a drug her mother took whilst pregnant to stop pre-natal seizures due to epilepsy. As a result, her fingers and toes were not properly formed. Well, another tick into the box of well-butter'd hatred, she thought.

The doors whooshed open and a lean tall gentleman entered the room. He was about 6 foot, full head of greying hair with a remnant of sandy blonde, pale skin with a silvery tinge, blue eyes, and an overall swept back appearance. His long dark robe encased him in a dark contrast to his chiselled face, yet she preferred him naked, but what the hell!

He approached her, kneeling courteously, 'Cynthia, I am here. Do what you wish with me.'

She laughed, 'That is the WORST pick up line I ever heard! Silly Fal.'

He smiled and reached to kiss her hand, 'Oh my dear, but for a moment we can be together, for what you will have to do soon will be most tiresome.'

He was obviously aware of the approaching confrontation. She thought about it, he is right, you know. These had proved to be the most nasty and stressful of affairs. Not something to be taken lightly.

'Will you accompany me on this one, Fal?'

He grinned, 'Certainly. Don't I always?'

She swooned at him. Being nasty was never strong in the face of friendly opposition….especially one by the name of Spectrum Fallace.

'Stay awhile, I beg you. Thirty four years of life they and their despicable country have taken from me....let them stew in their own boggy filth,' she said, very bothered.

Fal came closer, lifted her head up and gave her a kiss. She is so depressed, he thought.

'I'll stay with you....for always,' he softly said to her.

'With you, life becomes better, simpler, easier....,' she droned in thought.....composing further poetic verse in her head:

Wet coldness surrounded my body in the bright winter sun.
It felt like spring, tho' upon us, was not quite there yet.
That delicate chest so cleansing to the touch.....
The flesh beneath, so uncallous'd,
Nay, hardened; just soft.
Supple yet firm, and lightly tanned.
You've been in the sun all day on your horse,
Bareback'd in the saddle and loving it.
I know when I saw you, I wanted to feel y'out so badly.
Lust became me, but I wanted love.
You did too and you gave it to me.
You were the only truth in my life that e'er happened.
That eternal soul, the cerebral flesh divine.
Your strong hands covered my upper body
And you kissed my head,
Then went down, further with me, to await a bed.
Entwin'd, we were, like a loose-fitting jigsaw puzzle,
I waited 'pon your pleasure.
All I wanted to do was kiss, cuddle, and fondle you.
And I hoped you would want it as much as I.

* * * * *

'You wish me to enter?'

'Do, please,' she begged.

They carried on loving. It was a vibrant night in the stars.... not being able to forsake, neglect, or pardon their feelings any longer. It was so strong, powerful, and natural, made complete with the feeling of aeroplane wind encompassing the moment. It felt fantastic as he withdrew his bit and excused himself to another room to clean off. Cynthia lay there, helpless in emotional frenzy, seeing that love won out again over the hate. She thought, damn, I am getting soft!

* * * * *

How did she get into these far spatial regions? In an olden day of the early 21st century, she was currently living in Salsford, England, and walking along a road in her neighbourhood. She soon felt an odd vibe somewhere. It could not be her, after all, as her vibes were sorely negative. The vibe got stronger, and a humming sound occurred.

A beam came out of nowhere, then she found herself teleported onto a large ship, many light years away from the neighbourhood block she once walked upon. She was due to pick up her son from school and make ready for her husband's arrival with dinner and a cuppa. At least she remembered to feed the cat. This seemed most inopportune. If I go missing, she wondered, will anybody care? Will anybody notice? Gosh, 'tis too late to ask now.

Strange beings surrounded her at this point, as they scanned her bio-signs. Let them carry on, she thought. Maybe this could be the lucky break needed for personal glory. After all, there was not much going on at 82 Greeneaway Lane.

This might be fun, she thought, being amongst alien life forms that EVERYONE back in the day had speculated upon, and here I am, hanging out with them!!!!

They were not friendly at first, thinking Cynthia might attack, but as she remained cool, yet excited to be in their presence, they felt those vibes she gave off and they relaxed round her.

'You will need to undergo experimentation, to see how your brain works and to make sure you are the specimen we need,' one of the aliens said.

'I'm probably crap but I pray you forgive the rubbish herein,' she said, patting her heart and head.

'That is why we brought you from your time period to here. Your emotional state is quite volatile and we are curious to see how you operate.'

She studied her surroundings more carefully, 'So this is the future, then?'

'I am afraid it is. You are in our time now, at least a century beyond your own. We have been having problems with your race and need assistance from someone like you who, we believe, has no love for them either. Is that correct?'

'Well, to me, they are a bunch of do-naught-tossers-about which need extirpating, if you want my true opinion.'

The alien smiled for the hope of his own race, 'That is what we were hoping for.' He extended his tentacle toward her for a handshake, which she heartily accepted.

There were several hours of this experimentation, examination, and understanding.

'I see you have a mental condition called Asperger Syndrome,' the alien discovered, 'Am I correct to assume you remain affected by the same?'

'Asperger's is for life, not just for Christmas,' she joked.

The alien did not understand the joke, nor did he care to ask.

After a time, he released Cynthia and (at last!) introduced himself and explained his intention toward her.

'I am Spazio, a Valastron. We note your planet has become disadvantaged and took you away from it to help us in our struggle against its inhabitants. They have conflicted with us in their recent explorations. They are, how can I put it, 'Getting in the way, and becoming a menace to the balance of the universe'. We note, through our experimentation, that your intelligence and anger levels show great versatility as well as volatility. You also show a greed for power, am I correct?'

Delusions of grandeur were a definite feature in Cynthia's bag. 'Yes,' she then sighed, 'being a mere housewife doesn't give one that Hail Glorianna feeling, does it?'

'No, I suppose not,' Spazio said.

'By the way, I apologise for not introducing myself. My name is Cynthia, Cynthia Lear.'

'We know. We scanned you on our star-charts before you were brought here.'

She thought…duh, they're aliens, they know who you are!

Spazio offered, 'How would you like to repose in your own chamber and relax?'

'I could do with some light refreshment, thank you,' she said.

'No sooner said than done. We have staff who pride themselves on tea and sandwich making.'

Good Lord, I could use one of those, she further thought.

She was led to a small room which resembled an old bedroom she had long ago. There was a bed, a dresser, nightstand with lamp, surrounding bookcases filled to the rim, similar to those she just left behind, and even a concocted window set up in which the sun was risen like on Earth in its daytime.

'We hope it can be of some comfort to you. Your tea stuffs will be ready shortly,' Spazio said, leaving her alone in the room.

A beat or two later, the tea arrived, and Cynthia was left with the loveliest set of crockery that she'd ever seen. She was hesitant to even touch the set due to her incessant clumsiness (due to her finger shortness - DAMN!). She tried anyway, concentrating very hard on the task in hand, and eventually, she mastered it. The pot was no longer full as such, so subsequent cups will be much easier to pour. She helped herself to the delicately razor cut, neat lined sandwiches even the Queen of England would be impressed with. They had fillings of many types of the usual fare. She ate happily, thinking this was much better.......

In regard to her counterpart, Spectrum Fallace, things for him were slightly different. His story went back to the late 20th century, nearly a year after Cynthia's actual birth.

His name at the time was Alexander Pennece DeMilo, the eccentric English thespian and historical researcher of the theatre.

He was lying in a hospital bed at this point, a late middle-aged man dying of cancer, not even sixty yet! His close knit family stood by, streaming tears all around him. It was a very painful experience. For him, there was so much to do, so much more… ah, nay again will I ever live to see…….his thought got cut short.

'Visiting hours are over. All visitors please report to the exit points and vacate immediately.'

'Fare thee well, my sweet DeeCyn,' Mr DeMilo said.

'My Penne, I shall ne'er forget thee,' she sobbed.

'Please pray for me,' he begged.

'I always will, even into your beyond.'

'Thank you, my darling soul, for I shan't ever forget thee, either.'

He kissed his wife gingerly, as if it were the final time, then she left with the children and grandchildren (after he hugged them).

When they filed out of the room, he lay there in his bed, thinking to himself. My life had not been a bad one, for I think I made the most of every minute I had of it, he thought.

He did what he loved, he had a family to spread his seed into the next generation and beyond. Ah, he liked that, but now, it was nearly over, as the curtain was drawn one last time for him.

He was struggling to breathe. It got painful and as the cancer ate away at his system, he began to cough and wheeze. He nearly pressed a button for assistance when suddenly, he was teleported onto the Yakrey.

Once aboard, the effects of the cancer began to slow down inside, almost reversing itself. He stood up, struggling to regain a semblance of order. He exhaled sharply, feeling no ill-effects from the cancer he reckoned had consumed him. He wondered, 'Am I dead? Is this the Paradise we were all preached about in church to believe in? It certainly does not look like Paradise, but it reminds me of...., ' he turned round suddenly when a hatchway slid open quite noisily and a figure emerged. It was Spazio.

In quiet and cool desperation, Mr DeMilo exclaimed, 'Who are you? What do you want with me?!'

'I trust your condition has eased itself,' Spazio assumed.

'Yea, it has, if you must know...wait, how did you know?'

'We know. That is all you can comprehend. If we explained it to you, you 'will' die of old age,' Spazio answered, chuckling to himself.

Mr DeMilo was not amused, 'If I am to die, then be it so!'

'And waste a human? I think not. You were, and still are, ever so dramatic. You may be a perfect specimen for someone who will become your counterpart.'

'What do you mean?'

'Again, to explain it would mean......'

' ....I'll die of old age, yea, very funny. NOW GET ME OUT OF HERE!'

'There is no going back, sir. You are in our time now, over a century and a half beyond your own. You will need to wait until the time is right and you will meet the counterpart we have chosen for you. Would you like some tea and sandwiches to refresh you?'

Mr DeMilo thought, These disgusting wretches serve tea? How queer!

'I will take you up on your offer....Mr...,' Mr DeMilo paused.

'Spazio. Just Spazio,' said the alien.

'Right…Spazio. Sounds Italian.'

'It is. It means 'space'. Rather fitting for an alien, no?'

'Ha-ha. My father was an Italian who came to England as a classical player on tour when he met my mother, and……,' he sighed at the memory.

'We know.'

'Lead on, then,' Mr DeMilo said, slightly losing patience with the alien being.

He was led to a room which was pleasant and comfortable.

Much like his study back home, it contained bookcases filled with volumes regarding his topic of interest. There was a desk with all its accessories, a large sofa, and a curious window feature which mimics the sun's course on Earth. He asked Spazio about this.

'That is due to humans not liking so much darkness round them,' came the alien's reply.

Ah, so that's it, Mr DeMilo thought. It makes perfect sense.

'Your tea stuffs will be prepared for you shortly,' Spazio left him alone in the room.

He perused the volumes carefully, wondering if he had read any of them in the past. They seemed intriguing enough as he took one from the shelf and flipped through the pages. Pleasant memories returned to his senses as he smiled to himself, reading his indulgences until the tea arrived.....

* * * * *

A few weeks had passed when the Valastrons decided the two Earth beings captured should finally meet one another. One was a famous actor, the other, a twee housewife. It was learned through experimentation that the housewife was a great fan of the actor and the aliens felt it would be nice for them to get together on a mutual basis.

However, they also knew that famed people and their respective fans could have issues upon meeting one another, so Cynthia was given calming drugs to relax her before the meeting. This is to ensure respect between them and not allow for too much over-enthusiasm on her part.

One of their names had to go......the actor....most people would have taken note of him. So it was decided Mr Alexander Pennece DeMilo will become Spectrum Fallace, or Fal for short. Cynthia's name went unchanged, as she was generally unknown. She was a 'screamer' with high expectations, which in time, with the Valastrons, will satisfy soon enough.

'So you've changed my name and now you will introduce me to a girl who is HOW MUCH YOUNGER??' Fal screamed at Spazio.

'Keep yourself together,' Spazio defended, 'She is near to your age now anyway, just of a more recent time, so you will have to get used to her. We think this will be a good match.'

'A match for what?'

Spazio grinned, 'All in good time, and the quirks between you both are quite compatible. Your mutual intelligence is high and you seem to be the type she would like to calm her down.'

Fal asked in near panic, 'Calm her down? What, um, who have you linked me with?'

'Someone who is very special and I hope you will think so too.'

Soon the door whooshed open and in came a short, young looking girl (who now was in her middle-age), brown eyes, comely features (she thought so at least), long, straight, dyed golden blonde hair with a fringe, and wearing a long blue and green coloured robe.

'This is the lady in question we discussed. I'll leave you to get to know her,' Spazio said, departing the room.

Fal spoke first, 'And you are?'

'Cynthia, Cynthia Lear. Et tu, Cut-ay?' Her eyes widened with delight, as she extended her hand toward him, checking him out.

'Ah, it is Brute, actually. At least, you know your Shakespeare,' he was impressed and greeted her likewise. 'I am Spectrum Fallace, formerly Alexander Pennece DeMilo, thespian, and historical researcher of the theatre,' he gently grasped her hand and kissed it.

Her emotions shot through the outer quadrants when she held his hand, realising with whom she was just conversing, yet staying as calm as she could, 'In my opinion, you are not a 'Brute', and I find you very dashing indeed, unlike some dumb-ass dorks I used to know,' she said.

'Dumb-ass dorks, you say? Come, pray, what do you mean?'

Cynthia rolled her eyes, forgetting he 'died' when she was very young and thus unaware of verbal colloquialisms of her generation.

'Well, it is like this....,' she began, faltering, trying to explain the meaning to him.

Her pausing made him realise its definition, if not exactly, and he took her aside, 'Are you saying I am better than those you have been used to?'

'DUH!!! You are a totally fab fellow to boot, delish, and the very source of hotness,' she then dropped the informalities, 'I also find you quite intelligent, a factor which has been very scarce in my day.'

Despite her attempts at self-control, her use of colloquialisms were getting to him. Then, he realised that she was a fan of his. He tried to compose himself for her, as elegantly as he could muster. If she is a fan, he thought, let us see what she remembers!

He felt the need to chastise her in regards to her speech, and remembering some work he did in the past, he began, 'Although, you seem a very affable counterpart and I look forward to many hours in your company, I will not have you cannibalise the English Language like that. Our mother tongue is very special, you know.'

Cynthia drew closer to him and stated excitedly, never-minding the chastisement, 'Yea, and I would LOVE that tongue all over me, please!!!'

The actor's eyes bulged out in horror. He never bargained for this, yet, this, this….who is she, then? What was she?

He broached the subject, 'What was your occupation before all this?'

'I was a housewife from Salsford, Mr DeMilo,' she answered, 'And, like yourself, I did some historical research, but as a hobby. My speciality was all about you. I am familiar with and earnestly appreciate most of your work, that is, whatever was available.'

'Put me under your microscope, have you? Call me Fal, please,' he said with an inviting tone.

Thus began a friendship that evolved into a close-knit relationship. They were very happy together, the Valastrons observed and they felt to leave it to them to sort things out for themselves.

The experimentation did not effect the Earthlings' relationship one bit and their love became stronger due to the affection now going both ways. The actor slowly understood her fascination with him as he remained close to her during this time. He learned much from her and she, him.

She smiled as she went with him to his quarters and they sat down together. She told him about her crummy-ass life, how things did not always work as they seemed and how she was not what she was led to believe, either.

'And I have scores to settle,' she concluded.

He wondered, 'Oh? With what or whom?'

'You will see,' she left it at that.

She then told him her family awaited her presence in the Custodial Tower and explained the depreciated relationship she had with them. Cynthia proved to be exceptional to the Valastrons, who knew she had issues and were willing to allow her to confront them head on, by giving her these choice opportunities.

They approached the cell, but did not enter. Fal listened near the door. He heard chatting voices expressing disbelief. The buggers were resilient, he thought, I can see where she gets her fire from.

'Cynthia,' Fal called.

She came over and stared straight into his eyes, mostly for comfort.

'Yes?'

'Are you sure you want to go through with this? I mean, I can see a pretty mean debacle coming.' He was good to sense these things. The problem was, Cynthia sensed them too.

She asked, half kidding, 'Would you like to do it in my stead?'

' 'Tis your decision, but it would be better for it to come from you.'

He was right again, damn him. She shuddered.

'I think this is something I must do,' she said.

His eyes widened, 'You think? You THINK?'

'Yea, that's right,' she paused, then exhaled sharply, 'Shall we dance?'

'Lead on, my dear; I will always be with you through it all.'

Heavens above, what a gentleman! No, wait, shit, we're in space, she thought. What a dumb-ass!

She took his hand and squeezed it firmly. He felt her pain inside through the handhold.

'Look, you needn't.....,' he said.

She ignored his concern and proceeded through the doorway......

Sometime after, Fal and Cynthia emerged away from the hot-cell for a breather. Fal went to a nearby console with a big red button and asked, 'Shall I?'

She was partially delirious from the experience, before she realised he was offering a way out of the painful situation. Was the pursuit of truth worth facing those noxious entities or is it better to let go, and utterly destroy the buggers?

'You have your answer. You found the truth. You got what you wanted with human reason and time dependency,' Fal continued as he gingerly fingered the red button, attempting to calm Cynthia's mind down to think of a better way, i.e., himself and the way toward love.

Here we go again, she thought, on my word, what is a girl to do?

'My love,' he cooed, letting go of the control temporarily for him to kiss her. God, it was so needed and so loving. She felt sorely tested, extremely miffed, and.......the kiss took a good hold over her.

'You do not have anything against me, then, now you see what I had to deal with in my early years, and what I had bitterly rejected.'

'Shhh....,' he put his finger over her lip, 'No, I have nought against you. In fact, in an odd way, through their trespasses, you overcame those despicable circumstances.'

'Say wha--?'

'They were tough on you, so you became tough. Problem is you are too hard on yourself. That is what I see. Oh my sweetness, let it end, and love me. In being with you, but for a short time thus far, I do love you.'

Her eyes widened. She could not speak further. Hearing someone say that he loved her blew her mind, especially if that someone was a person she really admired and loved personally herself. It made her wonder.

Alternatively, being in a room full of endlessly critical, bigoted and egotistical folk led to further disorientation and defeatism. Their ignorance about her true identity and medical condition did not help, either.

'I...I've a confession to make,' she said.

'Kneel, child,' Fal said bending down with her and holding her hands, 'What is it?'

She hesitated and started to well up in tears, 'I...I've got a condition, Asperger Syndrome, which is a form of autism. That is why I am so botched up and I get relapses and blank out at times. I doubt you have heard of this, because in your day, it was not well known. The bastards did not know I had it nor pursued the possibility thereof.'

'You do not seem to have too much difficulty with it,' he noted.

'I only got diagnosed several years ago, in my forties, before the abduction. Previously, I had lived with it unknowingly and struggled for much of the time.'

'Good God, are you going to tell them?'

'I do not know if I should. Do you think they deserve to know? 'Twas they who gave it to me in the first instance, as it is a hereditary condition. This is why I have a hard job of letting go of petty quarrels and moving on in life.'

'Crikey! In your heart of hearts, would you tell them?'

Cynthia regarded the question for a moment, then self-concurred, 'I would rather them stew in their darkness where they belong.'

'So that settles the matter; the answer is clear, my love.'

Fal got up and returned to that console with the big red button. The solution to everything stood protruding from the wall.

In case of emergency............

Cynthia rushed over and lunged herself where Fal stood. He grabbed her, seeing her intent.

'Shall we do this together? One step to finalise it all,' Fal recommended.

With both hands flat against each other, the inevitable happened.

The air in the cell began to recede and the room itself became overheated to boiling. The torturous process would take a while before a crescendo of screams were heard. Once completed, a light coming from the lower half of the doorway quickly flickered and vanished.

A light went on outside telling Fal and Cynthia that the elongated process had finished.

'Would you like further closure?' Fal leant upon the door, pried it open, and it was empty. The deed had been done. The whole group had been disintegrated and the room was left as immaculate as it was before their entry.

Cynthia looked aghast, but relieved. Extreme measures were most distasteful and hard to swallow. Still, in her twisted manner, she had to crack a joke to relieve the pain. She dug deep into the recesses of her mind for something he could relate to.

'My love?'

'Yes,' Fal stood ready.

She tried to compose herself at her best. Looking straight into his kindly eyes, she quipped, 'That, my dear sir, is how you pop corn!'

Fal laughed so hard, because it reminded him of those odd projects from long ago. I cannot believe she saw that tatty thing, he thought, she certainly knows my work!

However, he composed himself, and said in his thespianic best, ' 'Tis so futile to relate to those you thought had loved you and no longer so do.'

God, he was right again, she thought. His kindness overrode her anger and there was no more she can do now.

Cynthia and Fal walked through the corridor to his quarters.

He offered, 'Cup of tea, luv?'

'Yea, I do need one. Thank you.'

He had a tea set handy in his room, courtesy of the Valastrons, as there were times he wanted to do things for himself and entertain his lady. He made tea for two and put the cups on the table, alongside the milk and sugar.

'It is a wonder we have this here,' Cynthia commented, 'I bet in your wildest dreams, you would never imagine a cup of tea in space.'

'Oh you would be surprised what one can think of in this day and age when little miracles such as these can take place. This is way beyond what I would have comprehended in my day, I can assure you,' Fal remarked and went further, 'I know the Valastrons' secret. In trying to understand our human ways in making us more comfortable, they have hired a humanoid alien race, the Silardians, to handle the food and hospitality side of things.'

'Food and hospitality?'

'Aye, 'tis correct. Cooking, baking, concocting various ingredients and throwing them together only to call it dinner,' he chuckled, then got serious, 'I still do not understand why they specifically chose us in the grand scheme of things, but I am not disappointed in the result.'

She looked up at him, perplexed. He kissed her and proposed, 'Perhaps, as we have been together for some time, if this sounds good for you, we could get married.'

'Maa...marr....mmaaaa----,' Cynthia stuttered in shock, looking at the gold ring already on her third finger of her left hand. She'd been wearing the thing for years but so much time had passed since the abduction. Was it still valid, she thought? It was worn mostly out of habit now rather than out of true love.

He noticed the ring, and confirmed, 'You are married at the moment, aren't you? You stated earlier you were a housewife.'

'Yea....ye.......,' she further stuttered, 'um.....er.....'

'I'll stay by you, take your time.'

She looked at Fal who was more than a friend at this point. He was her companion, lover, and a damn good show off. She considered the possibility and remained true to her admiration of him.

'My husband and I were still together at the time I was sent to this ship. However, he became a transgender.'

Oh my God, the poor girl, Fal thought. First it was that accursed family, her autistic condition and now a marriage to a trans--what?

'At the time we married, he was a man. I did marry a MAN, but in the course of the marriage, he began to cross dress at night and later had come out with it, with intent toward completion. It was difficult to live with at the best of times, but he did so much for me throughout our marriage. I had dreaded every minute, and shrunk back into myself every time I looked at him with the girl-kit on.

'It was very awkward and I was living inside my mind at the time even more so. There was no support for me to discuss this matter as most people would have split up at the point of revelation. Nevertheless, I felt a sense of loyalty and supported his actions. I do not know what became of it.'

He figured it was all over, but, with a bout of optimism, asked anyway, 'Do you still love him? I know it had been some time.'

'Not as much as I love YOU, Spectrum Fallace!' She kissed him upon his lips and stayed there for the next couple of minutes before taking a breath.

Fal had to think fast. It was obvious he was in love with Cynthia and she was astronomically ballistic over him.

He, too, was married, but as it was thought he had died, most people would have assumed his match was over as well. He still needed to be certain and, although in outer space, he still wanted to do the right thing, as one would have done in his day.

'Let me speak to Spazio regarding this matter and we will further the plan if this proves affirmative,' he paused, 'Had you any children with this person?'

'Yes, before he came out, we had a son.'

'Only the one?'

'He is autistic, higher function. One of HIM is enough!'

'Ah yes, I do apologise.' Autism is hereditary, he recalled from a previous conversation. A wise move on her part. She might be a good match if all proves favourable. Her discretion was discerning.
He was walking toward the door to speak to the aliens.

'Hey,' Cynthia called out, 'One family is enough. Please stay, Fal.'

'Oh my love,' he ran toward her to kiss, nearly knocking her cup over. 'Sorry,' he put the cup aside.

'I was drinking that,' Cynthia said, slightly annoyed, but smiling.

'Okay,' he got up and sat in the other chair, taking a sip from his cup.

'Life, what is it worth now? Everything I ever knew was on that globe and now it is a complete storm,' Cynthia commented.

'Human nature can do the most dastardly of things,' Fal said dryly in a serious tone, 'It would not have mattered to me. Apparently, I was on my way out. One could imagine the afterlife, heaven and all. Then seeing a multi-limbed thing standing before me was most distressing, I could tell you.'

'That's right. You were dying or something, or it was reported as such,' she tried to recall, but her feelings for him made the recollection very painful for her.

'Aye, luv, of cancer.'

'Odd style of resurrection for you, then,' she joked, deadpan.

'I praise ye for the witticism, yet, I had not actually died! All I remember is taking what I thought was my last breath, when suddenly, I was aboard this ship and my ill-health began to revert itself. Everyone I left behind, however, thinks I am dead, or at least, that is what I would imagine.'

'All I know was I was on my way out to somewhere, forgot where by now, and like yourself, called up to this ship.'

'I was not sure about this at first, mostly due to our incredible age differences and you being a devout admirer of mine.'

'Apparently, I was given sedatives before our meeting, otherwise, I would have been more forthright with you. So, you do not find me undesirable, then?'

'Good God, of course not! You are a very endearing person and oddly enough to say, the ONLY person around,' he laughed.

They were the only two people from Earth the Valastrons wished to experiment with. All the other humans were too busy wrapped up in their respective messes to give a toss what an alien race thinks of them.

'I wish it were not so dark outside. Maybe someday, we could settle on a nearby planet and watch the sunrise, aeroplane manoeuvres, kites on strings, sunsets, take in some theatre (if other planets have that at all!),' Fal said.

She giggled, 'Or maybe settle upon a giant supernova?'

'Possibly, with a Bacchanalian twist,' he leant over to kiss her.

They laughed together and finished their tea.

Chapter VI

A few days later, Spazio arrived with the news of their respective pasts left behind. They were reasonably nervous, naturally, but took it all in their stride. It had been decades since the abductions so anything could have happened in the meantime.

'Cynthia,' Spazio said, 'I am afraid to say your transgendered other half had passed away a few years back. However, your son remains alive and well, living in sheltered housing with his wife, who currently looks after him.'

'So 'she' can wipe his butt now,' Cynthia sarcastically remarked.

Spazio ignored the remark, not understanding its intention anyway.

'Fallace, your wife has also passed on, but your family is happy and thriving. In fact, your grandson is a fellow thespian too, in the comedic sense with some serious roles thrown in. To further your joy, he had earned a very high Order of Recognition from your country.'

'My God....my God.... 'I' never was,' he reflected. He nearly cried and reached out for Cynthia who came up to him and held him tightly, mostly for support with a hint of seduction.

'You seem to be overwhelmed; and I thought it was me who was unstable,' she scoffed.

'The tears are not just for my grandchild, Cynthia, they are for us. This means we can marry.'

It dawned on her that she will undergo a new marriage ceremony. The previous one was fun, she remembered. It happened at a small church in a local village. Her husband (who was still male at that time) wore a kilt and she wore was a comely white gown. It was a very small affair, with a handful of attendees. It was a bit rainy that day too, but it did not dampen the spirits. A rainbow appeared that evening during the reception. It overall was a happy marriage, despite the ridiculous change her husband decided upon himself.

In the meantime, the Earth that Cynthia and Fal left behind had undergone further trauma, due to the endless demand upon its resources. Climate change had already began in some parts of the world and, in some of those areas, with devastating consequences. Many natural habitats were being ruined by rising sea levels and deforestation. It seemed hotter in some places, whereas in others, it just froze.

Dwindling resources meant the population needed to become more clever in making what they already had last longer. Yet, as predicted, they did not show that sort of spontaneity. Their greed also made the universal phrase, 'Love Thy Neighbour', absolutely redundant. Inflamed religious groups acted upon the unnecessarily vile social atmosphere. Other racial factions kicked off, just because they could, and chaos reigned everywhere.

Known third world countries had collapsed due to govern-mental incompetence, and the western countries were finally fed up with their digging for handouts without helping themselves. Most of Europe, however, remained stable, except in the eastern areas. There were some pockets of minority groups elsewhere, who had fled to join fellow freedom fighters in other countries, to act on their agendas from afar.

The New World territories of the Americas were the worst off, because most of the targeting and wastage occurred there. One of the main countries had gotten involved in the long-winded affairs of others and found themselves being the most scrutinised and hated.

However, within said place, many had called for action and defence, possibly leading to a revolution. There was much rioting and, despite anti-segregational laws, vast marginalising of various groups had occurred. Having too many people of differing cultures, races, and creeds had bred so much instability that it was rotting at the core. Everyone started to hate one another and all the 'peace on earth' talk became nonsense.

The Valastrons as well as other galactic peoples had noted all these happenings on Earth and humanity's potential downfall. They picked up on the vibe and found it to have possibilities for the future.

Cynthia found all these events irrevocably sad, yet, inevitable. I knew they were arseholes at the best of times, she thought, and I am the superior one. After all, 'twas ME that got abducted! However, she paused to thank God for her foresight to move to England and the Valastron's foresight to remove her completely from that miserable planet, before it all got too much. It was becoming unbearable there already, and now there will be no turning back.

Fal walked over to Cynthia, put his arm around her and gave her a hug. He looked out the window into space and said soothingly, pointing out into the starry sky, 'D'you want to spend time out there?'

She asked, 'What do you have in mind?'

'Ah, go for a ride in a small ship of our own, fly out for a few hours, check out a planet for ourselves, maybe?'

'Yea, this space shit is depressing me. One cannot tell night or day round here, can they?! Well, I'm game, for I am doing bugger all at the moment.'

'Good, so it is settled, then,' he stuck out his hand, 'Come, let us go and reach for the highest stars.'

'You are not an actor anymore, silly boy!'

'I like to reflect upon it now and again. Pray you won't mind,' he smiled.

'I do not mind; I find it very charming.'

He looked outward. He, too, thought about the Earth and said, 'Let them sort out their own business, and let us not think on it!' He turned away, and held her hand.

Cynthia realised it was time to move on and there were also plans for the wedding. She took that final step against her family and no one in space cared who or what she was. Alien curiosity is far lesser to that of a human.

They went to the docks and came across the guard Uffizio who moonlights as a mechanic. He was working on a ship.

'A mechanic too, what will they think of next?' Cynthia said to Uffizio.

'Well, I'm a jack of all trades sort. I heard you and Fal need a ship.'

'That is correct,' Fal said.

'Use that one,' the alien pointed to the next ship over, 'I have just finished it.' He then continued with his welding.

Fal walked over to the ship indicated and climbed in, helping Cynthia to follow. It was rather small, a two seater with controls, knobs, levers and fiddlers in the front.

Cynthia looked gob-smacked, 'I...I cannot work this thing out......,' she stuttered, 'Y--you can drive this?'

Fal looked at her, 'Might be fun to find out, eh? It reminds me of the old cars in my day. Can't be much different, no?'

'So, you are confident you can take this out without killing us?'

'If that is the case, this will be the shortest engagement, ever!'

'I pray not, sir,' she said, as she kissed his fleshy cheek.

He pulled a lever which switched on the engine and whoosh, it started to hover. A low hum emitted from the rear exhaust as Fal took the controls and led it past the hangar's exit port straight into space.

'Groovy, man,' she mocked, 'This is so cool!'

'My dear girl, I may have been a thespian, but a car is a car and in space, there is nought a difference.'

'Except you are bottomless,' she laughed.

'Try not to titter so, 'tis such a small vehicle.'

For a 'day out', this was not too bad.

Fal asked, 'Whither shall we goest?'

She reacted, 'Eh?' Then she thought, oh yes, the Shakespeare. Yea, Shakespeare in Space. She then remarked, 'Hahaha, very funny!'

'I was not joking when I had asked you, my lady.'

'Then I do not know. Do you know what is round these parts?'

'Let me look,' he fumbled for a map of some kind....any kind. Unfortunately, one would think they would be a paper map lurking in the compartments. It looks like the Valastrons have good memory of their environment so as to not need maps. He checked various switches that may give him a clue and, at last, he found a star-chart.

It was of the Crassus-Kerr system with eight planets revolving round a large sphere (a sun, perhaps?), similar to that of the Earth and its system. Most of them had life, but the furthest one, the Leevion, had not been researched yet as it was too far to do so. The previous attempt had to be aborted due to a beleaguered vessel running out of fuel and a tow-ship coming to its rescue. It was then thought of as not sustainable, due to the prohibitive distance.

Fal examined the screen, 'We can go here, my love,' he pointed to a planet not too far from the centre, Andros 4.

'It has a breathable atmosphere, nice scenery and a reasonable population. They are welcoming and friendly to visitors, however, no conquests, though,' he added as a joke.

Cynthia asked whimsically, 'Who, me?!!'

Fal chuffed and steered toward the planet.

'It is not like we want the place, is it? 'Tis just you and I, and that does not constitute an invasion party, does it?'

'Not unless one scouts the scene,' Fal answered.

She laughed as the ship descended to land.

She cried, reaching for her ears, 'Ow! This is no different than an aeroplane, either!'

'Hahaha, 'tis the same in all cases of air flight, my girl.'

When the ship landed, they walked out the hatchway to find themselves in a port. There were beings of many alien races here, similar to a film Cynthia once saw long ago. Some were blobby like the Valastrons, some were humanoid but for different features, and some were animal-like and bug-like.

It was a trip and a half, she thought, and all the Earth is missing out on this. Cynthia took Fal's hand as they walked together in the corridor in wonder and awe. No one could ever match this in a make-up job for the theatre, Fal thought, remembering the old days.

An odd character came up to them. Humanoid in stature, shorter than Fal and stout with a 'make-up job' as he would refer to, but, overall, a reasonable human-style look. He had a lime-green hue to his skin and clothing, which reflected the same, had swirling colours of white and yellow, embedded alongside the green. His hair was golden-orange, but rather thinning.

The new alien greeted them, 'Hello, you're new here, ain't ya?'

'Yea, just arrived. We are taking a day trip out from the monotony of the Valastron starship,' Fal said.

'Ah, yes. I've heard of them. Funny lot, but their staff make great teas, don't they?'

Fal rubbed his tummy, 'And much more too!'

'I see you have been well cared for.'

Cynthia interrupted as her feisty nature permitted, 'And you are, sir?'

'Oh gosh, sorry, yes. Buxby. Fizz Buxby.'

'Nice to make your acquaintance,' Fal introduced himself, 'I am Spectrum Fallace and this is Cynthia Lear, my intended.'

'Intended for what, might I ask?'

'Ah, we are getting married,' Fal answered him.

'Sounds lovely. Oh, wait a minute,' he paused, 'I vaguely remember hearing about a couple of Earthmen who were abducted by the Valastrons. The story has been all over the media. From what I can recall, you look Earthy; I trust you both are they?'

'Afraid so, yes, 'twas us,' Fal admitted.

'You Earthmen speak quite strangely.'

Cynthia giggled and revealed, 'Fal was an actor in his past life and....'

'I was a thespian, dearest,' Fal interrupted her, his nose slightly upturned in mock-snobbery.

'Okay, okay, forgive me,' Cynthia apologetically replied.

'Well, still an actor, I would say,' Buxby remarked, 'But never mind that. Let us go for some refreshment and we will talk .'

Cynthia was curious about Buxby, 'I never met a pure alien before. It must be different, your species and all.' This sounded bad, she thought, but hopefully he will not take offence.

'Well, to you I am an alien, to me, I am just ME,' Buxby laughed.

'No offence taken?'

'None whatsoever.'

Fal was concerned about the recent Earth conflict and how it will affect other parts of the galaxy.

Buxby groaned at this, 'Oh God, all the Earth is on fire at the moment, you know. You were lucky you both were taken at a good time.'

'It wasn't our choice, you know, and I was dying,' Fal revealed.

'Oh. Dying, were you?'

'I had cancer in my system and was taken up just as I thought I had breathed my last. I assumed I went to Heaven when I was confronted by a blob-like creature.'

'A Valastron?'

'Aye, and I figured he would be a menace, but we get on now. It has been some time.'

'Which one did you meet first?'

'Spazio.'

'Ah yes, I have heard of him. Funny fellow, depending who's side you're on. You were lucky to get a second chance at life and live the rest of it out here in space.'

'Yet, I have not gotten any older, or younger for that matter. I know a few decades have passed since then, and still there are no changes to my bio-systems. 'Tis the same for Cynthia.'

Buxby looked at Cynthia and found her ravishing to look at, 'So what did you do my dear girl, before your little space adventure?'

'Common housewifery, sir,' she said meekly.

'The Valastrons must have had good reason to bring together a housewife and a thespian. Odd combination, though,' Buxby thought aloud, quizzically.

'The odder the combination, the more revealing our human nature is. She was a great fan of mine, but had many anger issues and other bits which they picked up on. I was dying, and, as you put it, they gave me a second chance at life. They wanted me to share it with someone who really appreciated me and my talent. Then, we were used for experimentation. So here we are,' Fal explained.

'Yes, here you are,' Buxby paused, 'Anyway, the Earth is a mess. There are factions within factions, food is getting scarce, resources are dwindling and their throwaway culture of yesteryear is coming back at them with a vengeance.'

'So what will you do about it?'

'I don't know, but there are many other races in this system who would love to have a good conquest right about now.'

Cynthia jolted, 'Oh?'

Buxby responded, 'What, did I say something amiss?'

'No, sorry sir. Miles away, as usual,' she said.

He chuffed, smiling, 'That is alright. Why, does conquest excite you?'

To control and subjugate humanity was such a delicious temptation, she thought, with Fal by my side, we can destroy what is left and rule the universe together! It was obvious she was into science fiction in her past life....

A memory or two invaded her station, as she remembered a bit of her past:

Her interest in science fiction led to her interest in history and the concept of conquest. Conquest, she felt was her birthright, and in studying various bits and eras of history, she felt very attuned to their egotistical manners and desire to wage war against the enemy.

The 'enemy', in her opinion, was that family....that family who made her live a lie. She was a young girl, scowling at her (grand) father who then said, 'we are not your enemy.'

Au contraire, she thought and with a heavy burden, she remembered that comment into her adulthood, but she did not believe it. They 'were' the enemy, especially that (grand) mother. She was a nasty piece of work, indeed. One of the worst retorts was, "You think I was a bad mother, don't you?"

Well, duh, she WAS! All she cared about was religion. She and the family Cynthia was adopted into were Jewish. All the (grand) mother cared about was that the religion posed as an identity. Once, she had asked Cynthia about her feelings regarding Judaism.

She recalled in her mind: 'I could not share my true feelings as I had inwardly converted to Christianity in my heart. So, being tactful, I stated I had felt indifferent. The conversation ended for the time being. Then, the (grand) mother had, in a nasty tone of voice, stated that I was Jewish and nothing else, full stop, no questions asked, no further arguments stated, i.e., 'once a Jew, always a Jew.' This had hurt me greatly but as she did not know about my inner 'conversion' and God was keeping my secret, I tried to take strength from Him.'

A light flickered in her brain again and she awoke from the memoir-mal.

'Ummm....Cynthia,' Fal waved his hand at her, looking concerned, 'Shit, she's dreaming, silly one.'

Buxby wondered, 'Does she do that often?'

'I was aware of it from the time I met her. However, this is the first I have seen her do it. So, I will try something,' Fal touched her side and tickled her.

She jolted upward and cried, 'Wha--Ahh!'

Fal chided, 'Got you, my dear. You were dreaming, eh?' To Buxby he said winking, 'It worked, then.'

'So, you like the idea of a good conquest?' Buxby re-questioned Cynthia.

'Gosh, yes,' she said, wildly, eyes widening at the prospect, nearing another dreamable trance.

'Oh no you don't, my dear, do stay with us,' Fal grabbed and held her tightly.

'Are you sure you want to marry such an unstable specimen?'

'Why of course. After all, she is one of my species and the ONLY one left so to do,' Fal stated proudly.

'I see,' Buxby reflected, 'Looks like you've got work ahead of you. Here we are. What will you have? My treat.'

They got to a drinks counter at a local hall, made their orders and oblations and went to a nearby table to sit and carry on the conversation.

He wondered intently about Cynthia as her patterns were not congruent with most Earth peoples and asked Fal about it.

'Oh, she has a life-long condition. It makes her see things differently. It is her world versus everyone else's, really. It is called Asperger's,' he explained.

Buxby quipped innocently, 'Is that something one orders with cheese?'

Cynthia went hysterical with laughter. Fal looked amused too.

Buxby was further niggled about her so-called dream of conquest and queried her, 'So, if it was up to you, would you join forces with us, for instance, and attack Earth?'

Fal interjected, 'I do hope NOT, sir. She had childhood problems and it left her with this damnable desire of hers; however, that was dealt with,' Fal turned to her, 'Wasn't it??'

'It was,' she surrendered, partially. She was not going to let go of this one. She felt her passion quietly simmering as her inner soul boiled with discontentment.

Fal snapped, 'This anger problem must be destroyed, if you are to marry me, and I am helping you all I can so we may be happy together. I will not go down on some glory ride with you!'

'I do welcome your help and I hate being angry all the time, but I feel so unacknowledged, neglected, cast off....,' she cut herself short and sat there pouting, sulking and feeling downhearted.

'Recognition or infamy will come later. Your future is open, girl.' Fal looked directly at her. She flinched a bit, but was comforted it was him who stared and not another when he asked, 'Will it be with me?'

'Yes, sir,' she said, dejected.

'Look, your problem lay with the people who hurt you and they are now gone. We took care of that together, yea?'

She was relapsing again, 'Yes, but after the way I was treated???'

'Oh no, not here...shit..,' Fal looked at Buxby, 'Do bear with us, she gets into such a state over these matters.'

Buxby leaned back, took out a pipe to smoke and said, 'Carry on. I'll wait.' He started puffing and smiled at them.

Silly Earth-folk, he thought, but that girl.....phwoar! It seems possible she will make an excellent ally, Buxby thought, as the cogs wheeled inside his head as he kept thinking.

Cynthia harrumphed, 'Well!' Then she began to pout.

Buxby exhaled, smoke wafting in the air, 'Bubble burst again, Cynthia?'

She looked at him, stuck her tongue out and smiled.

Fal was horrified at her action and scolded, 'Is that the way to treat our host?'

'Sorry,' she apologised.

Some time passed and it was mid-afternoon.

Buxby asked, 'Do you have any plans while you are visiting us?'

'No, not really. We just wanted to take a break,' Fal explained. 'Speaking of breaks, do you have a loo around here?'

'Yes, we function just like you. It is over there,' he pointed to a door in the corner.

'Much obliged,' Fal said, relieved, kissing Cynthia atop her head, 'I shall return.'

He left her and Buxby together. It was weird being alone with this alien fellow, but he seemed harmless. He looked attractive, though.

'You realise Spazio sent for me to look after you both during your visit,' he said.

Cynthia was sort of surprised, but it was not unfounded, 'Really?'

'Yes. We aliens do keep in touch and since you are the most different round these parts, you were quite easy to spot.'

'Guess so.'

'You love him?'

'Who?'

'Fal, of course.'

Cynthia looked miffed, 'DUH!!! However, you are not so bad looking yourself.'

Buxby's inner wheels turned ferociously. He smiled, then dismissed her little quip, 'Nah, I would not take you away from your fiancé. He really does care about you, you know. I can see that.'

'We can at least be friends with one another.'

'Yes. We can...and we shall.'

Fal emerged from the facilities and rejoined his group.

Cynthia asked, 'Feel better?'

'Much better, thank you. How have you been getting on?'

'Well, thank you,' Buxby said, ' and, as it is warm outside, I was wondering if you would like to go out for some air.'

At last, proper oxygenated air, Fal thought, 'tis a nice day for it.

'Yea, let's,' he agreed.

The three of them left the hall and went out on a balconied area. There were plants and trees with all sorts of odd flora about them. They were different, but looked familiar.

They were colourful, with splashes of blue, green, red, orange, and yellow, in a rainbow-like stance. There was a small waterfall nearby which trickled down blithely into a main pool, which was not for swimming in.

They started to take a walk round when Buxby had an idea.

He asked Fal, 'As a former thespian, what medium did you specialise in the most, or did you do a bit of everything?'

Fal pondered the question, 'I have done mostly stage work, and a bit of the (then) newer mediums of television and cinema.'

'Crikes, you are awfully highbrow, aren't you?'

'What do you mean?'

'This traditionalist mannerism of yours…..the way you talk, your stance, your......,' he glanced at Cynthia, 'Your appeal..... to the ladies.'

' 'Tis utter nonsense,' Fal dismissed, waving his hand.

'It seems like you are more of a man of mystery as we will never see those plays you were in,' Buxby lamented.

'No, and maybe it's all for it. There were no cameras in the theatres in those days.'

Buxby asked, 'Are you keen to go to the cinema?'

'Oh, you've cinemas here!?' Cynthia piped, 'Yes, please!'

'It looks like its unanimous, then,' Fal concurred, 'It has been awhile and it would be rather compelling to stare at a screen rather than one staring at me!' He aimed the comment directly at Cynthia, knowing he was her purpose of adoration in her previous life. She shuddered, but understood his intense gaze.

'Well, there is a film out now called 'The Tighter Andromeda.' Looks opportune, and might be suitable for you two intended to be,' Buxby invited.

'Suitable for us intended?' Fal repeated Buxby's comment.

' 'Tis no film for young princes, that I can assure you,' he said, mimicking Fal's style of speech.

'I am NOT a young prince, sir!'

'I know, that is why I suggested it and it's playing tonight. D'you want to come?'

Fal looked into Cynthia's eyes, and did not hesitate then. 'Alright, we'll go. We must contact the ship however, as this may turn into a long night,' he remarked.

'And perhaps a long morning,' Buxby said, 'Here is the communicator.'

Fal looked at the imposing item with distrust. 'Now, how do I work it?' He fumbled with the controls, dropped it, and made a disgruntled sound before giving up.

Buxby offered, 'Want me to do it?'

Fal gave the unit back and Buxby typed in the message. 'There, it is done,' he said, 'You have all night and morning with me.'

The prospect was unexpected. I did not want this fellow hanging round with me and my girl, Fal thought. However, the opposite would be equally awkward and this fellow Buxby did know his way round the planet a bit......yet, how long for, is anyone's guess.

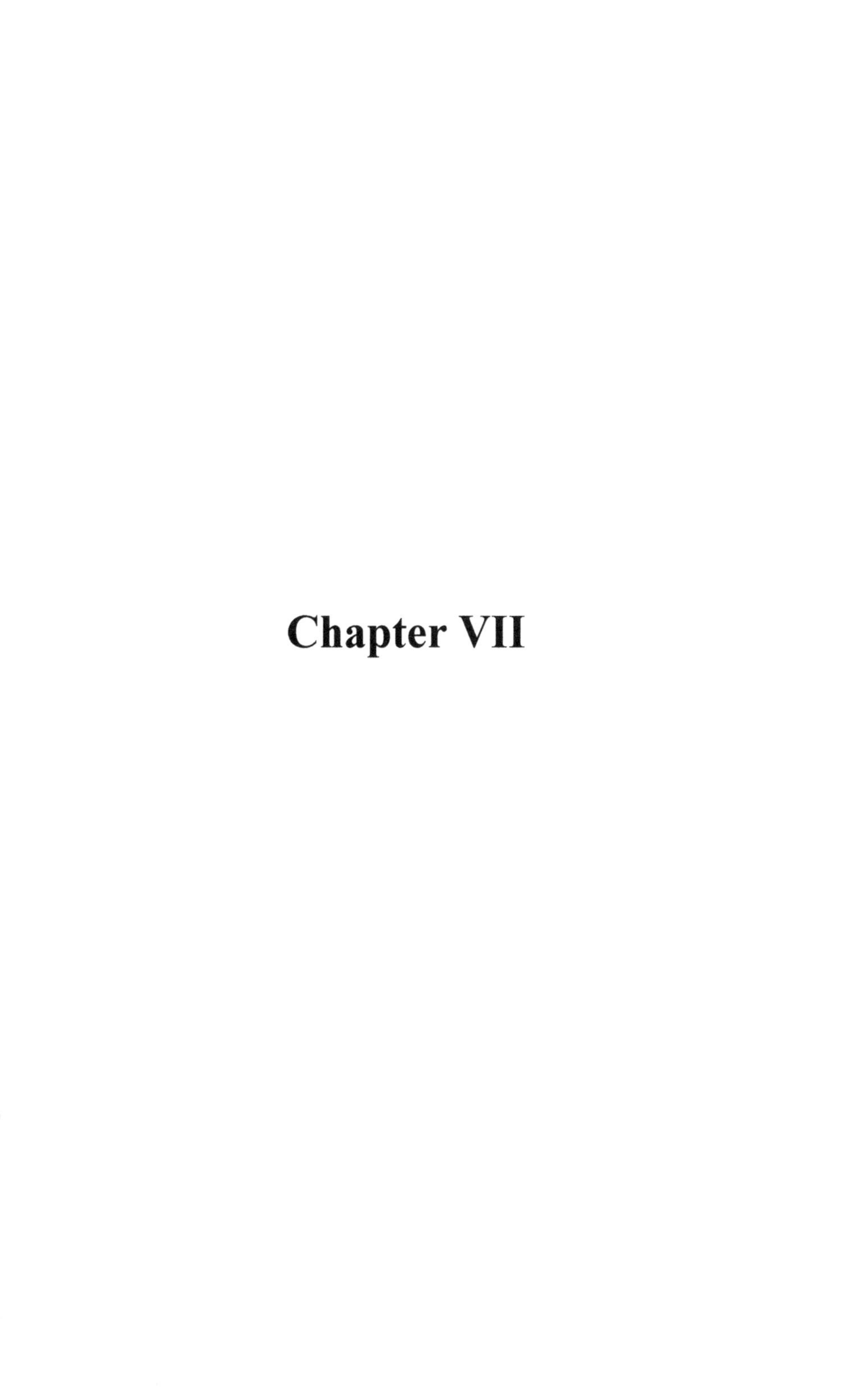

Chapter VII

After Buxby proposed his idea, he put his plan into action. He took Fal and Cynthia out to eat first, to a restaurant ran by Valastrons, and staffed by Silardians. It was quite exotic compared to Earthling tastes, yet, inoffensively presented and tasteful. It as a very delicious meal and the three of them were satisfied.

'The cakes here are good too,' Buxby recommended.

'Smashing,' Fal said, 'we will share one, then.'

So they did. The cake was a simple moist chocolate/vanilla sponge mix with cream on top. It reminded Cynthia of close-knit nights with Fal as she was eating it. He saw the look in her eye and reproved, 'Now, now, dearest, behave thyself.'

After swallowing a mouthful, Cynthia retorted, 'NEVER!'

Buxby smiled to himself at this. These former Earth beings are rather strange indeed, he thought.....still, that girl, wwhhoooaaahhh! His mind was buzzing deliriously thinking about her.

Once the necessary oblations were made, Buxby took the couple out to a nightclub, called the Regalburgh. There, a local four piece band played, although there was a fifth member on hand to use the odd instrument, depending on the song. The band was called The Lattice Wyndows; its members were Larry, Harry (who was Buxby's twin brother), Ced, George and Willec. They had full longish hair of various colours, humanoid in looks and in stance, wearing metallic effect suits and slightly high heeled ankle boots.

They were primarily a guitar and drums band, but had a keyboard in the set, in case a patron requested a tune of a more classical nature. Their latest single, 'Grow Yer Own' was Top 10 and rising.

There were a reasonable amount of people there, who were drinking, dancing and overall having fun. The music was spacey and pulsating.

Buxby spoke loudly over the vibrant sounds, 'Cool, innit?'

'Quite a groove, I'd say,' replied Cynthia.

'Takes some getting used to,' Fal admitted.

Pompous tit, Cynthia thought, giggling to herself. She did not think this would be 'his' sort of place, but, as an actor should, he played the role with good relish….

And relish it, he did, as he danced with Cynthia for a good while Buxby hung out in the corner, smoking his pipe. He waved to the dancing couple, who, he thought, looked absolutely ravenous together.

Once the song had ended, Cynthia excused herself to go to the loo, kissed Fal, and dashed off. A cloakroom girl stood by watching to make certain all was well. Cynthia approached her and asked her where the loo was and she pointed her the way. The girl had a 1960s style 'beehive' gold coloured hairdo and wore a aquamarine neon mini-dress.

When Cynthia had finished in the toilet, she went back to the girl, out of curiosity. She never thought she would be in the company of 'this' many aliens, yet here she was and hastily, she introduced herself.

'My name's Cynthia, Cynthia Lear.'

'Oh, my name's Cattapilla White. My friends call me Cat,' she spoke with a unique accent.

'Nice to meet you.'

'Same here. You alone?'

'Nah, I'm with my boyfriend and an alien who befriended us when we arrived. It seems the Valastrons sent him to look after us during our visit. '

'Would that be Buxby, by some chance?'

'Yeah,' Cynthia wondered (how did she know?!).

'I've got a couple of friends here,' Cat introduced her to Branche Raille and Pat Magower.

'Hi,' they both said together.

'Hello, it is nice to meet you both,' said Cynthia in response.

Pat asked Cynthia, 'D'you get out here much?'

'No, this is my first time here. I was on a day trip with my boyfriend and met up with an alien fellow who is looking after us.'

'Buxby,' Pat and Branche said in unison.

Cat asked, 'Lucky you, where are they now?'

'I don't know,' Cynthia pondered, as she looked around, where she spotted her party in a corner chatting with alien folk.

'There they are,' Cynthia pointed outward.

'Oooh, that tall one's really a dish,' screamed Branche.

'He is my intended,' Cynthia confessed.

'Wow, you two are planning marriage? I would love to meet him anyway, just to see what he's like, please,' Cat begged.

Pat enquired, 'Who is he? What's his name?'

'Spectrum Fallace.'

The girls giggled at the name; one of them tried to crack a rude joke but was hindered by a looming figure approaching them.

Cynthia introduced, 'This is Fal.'   To Fal, she further stated, 'I was just chatting, meeting new people and the like.'

'I see,' Fal said formally, 'So were we. We were chatting to the band. One of them is Buxby's kinfolk, you know.' He smiled, knowing those girls would swoon and faint at any time when the band was mentioned. He remembered the female adoration from his time and noted it had remained universal.

Fal waited 'til their moment of ecstasy had passed, then continued, 'They always wanted to meet an Earthling.'

Cat interjected, 'Earthling? You're an Earthling?'

'Yea, Cynthia and myself were abducted years ago by the Valastrons. Our lives had not been the same since.'

'Did you guys know each other on Earth?' questioned Branche.

'No, she was an infant under a year old, from another country and another life. I had been very ill at that time and supposed to have died, but.....,' Fal explained, wincing at the painful memory.

'You were abducted. Oh my God, I am so sorry,' Cat moaned.

'Well, it DID make things interesting for us,' Cynthia bemused.

'So they hooked you too up, for wha--? Why did they pick people from different times?' Pat further asked.

'Experimentation. No, do not worry, we were unharmed,' Fal said, 'I used to be an actor in my past life and she was a great fan of myself, living in another time.'

Cat squealed, 'Oooh, I can understand that! Wot's Earth like?'

Fal thought about it, 'It was good when I lived there, but changes occurred due to climate, society, and attitude which made it a bit slippy. I heard it is a lot worse now, but I had not returned in recent years.'

Cat supposed, 'Obviously cos you 'died', right?'

'Correct.'

'Wot from?'

'Cancer.'

'Ugh! We get that here too, a few cases of it pop up now and then.'

They mulled over in silence as the record continued playing. The band had taken a break at this time. Buxby and Harry were catching up, like siblings do, and Fal was eager for Cynthia to return to Buxby so they may introduce her to them.

'It was really great to meet with you. I hope to see you again,' Cynthia said.

'Yeah, it was great,' Cat said, 'We're always here in the evennights. Bye for now.'

'Bye,' waved Cynthia and she walked away with Fal to Buxby.

Buxby was waiting with the group when Cynthia and Fal emerged from the concourse.

'So, this is the Cynthia we've been hearing so much about,' Willec said.

'Yes,' she answered.

Larry asked, 'How did you enjoy the music?'

'I thought it was great. Spacey, trippy, lots of guitar, just my style,' Cynthia responded.

'Ah good, so you'll stay for another round,' Ced said.

'Okay,' she agreed, slightly embarrassed at the attention.

Harry suggested, 'Any requests?'

'Do that recent song, ah.....erm...,' she tried to remember the name.

'Grow Yer Own,' George revealed.

'Yes, that's it,' Fal said, 'Carry on, then gentlemen.'

'Don't mind if we do,' said Willec, holding his guitar, climbing onto the stage.

They then did a reprise of 'Grow Yer Own', which sounded like:

Grow yer own, grow yer own,
Or I'll just hang meself and groan,
Grow yer own, grow yer own,
This bald patch is making me ston'd.

With verse accompaniment, and guitars, it sounded like a future Number One.

Buxby came up to Cynthia and Fal, 'If you wish to make that film we planned to see, we need to go now.'

Oh yea, THAT film! The blue movie. Being at the Regal-burgh had been great fun, but they did make plans to see this film.

So they left the club and made way for the cinema. They paid for tickets and popcorn and went to their seats. It was not too crowded, but there was an audience spread thinly throughout the auditorium.

'This stuff is quite good,' Buxby said, filling his face, 'try some.'

'Oh?' Fal took a handful of popcorn, and ate it slowly, fingering each piece one by one.

What a pompous tit, Cynthia thought again. Damn him, I'm going to cuddle him up in marriage, even if he does eat popcorn one kernel at a time!

The film rolled on as the story developed. It was a romance, alien style, along with the honoured niceties that accompanied its progress.

'I have never seen it done like THAT before,' Cynthia whispered to Fal.

Fal took her by the hand, caressed it and submersed himself into every pleasurable scene shown therein. He wanted her so bad and she felt the same way. She had a son in her previous life before the abduction, so the act had been completed in her lifetime. Yet, it was not as glorious as she dreamed. Her condition made it impossible for her to really let go and enjoy. Control was always an issue with her. For one to really do these things properly, one had to really let go. She could not let go properly, but slightly overcame it with Fal.

They carried on watching the film for its duration. It peaked, sizzled and oozed at times but it did not bother them. They were grown up in that sense, and they remained unfazed by the action, except on a sexual level.

Cynthia lent closer to Fal and kissed him. He turned to receive as their lips met in as hot a passion as the film being watched.

Buxby turned to look and was fascinated by the reaction the humans next to him were giving. Since his alien physiology is similar to theirs, anyway, he, too, was feeling something from the film, especially about Cynthia. He did not want to broach the topic to Fal yet, with him being engaged. Nevertheless, the thoughts inside Buxby's mind were even more intense and simmering nicely.

Once the film ended, it was well past midnight. Fal and Cynthia were tired by this time but very excited at what they saw. They had not planned to remain on Andros this late, so they lacked the night time amenities.

Buxby, always having an answer for everything, spoke up, 'Perhaps you two can stay at my place for the night. I can make room for you both, if you like.'

Fal thought about the proposal. 'Well, we will need our privacy. As long as it is for the night, as we should be getting back to the ship in the morning.'

'You will, you will,' Buxby replied, then thought to himself, Oh bother! Well, never mind, perhaps another time.

They left the theatre and walked back to Buxby's home. His flat was mostly tidy, considering a middle-aged bachelor male lived there, alien or not.

'You can have my room, I will sleep on the sofa. I'll get some linens for you.' Buxby walked off.

Cynthia and Fal waited on in the lounge and seat on the nearby sofa whilst Buxby prepared their room. Once it was finished he offered them a nightcap which they gladly imbibed.

'Guess I should turn in. I really appreciate your kindness, Buxby. Is there anything I can do to compensate you for your time and hospitality?' Fal asked, not knowing Buxby was meant to look after them.

Buxby declined the offer, knowing his mission, but did not declare it to Fal (although he mentioned it to Cynthia earlier in the day when Fal was in the loo).

He said, 'What I would like would be....' he blushed furiously at this bit, '..and if you do not want this, you do not have to, but I would like to have Cynthia for a few moments.'

Fal looked shocked but unsurprised as his intended was quite attractive, but being attractive to an alien was another matter entirely.

'We're getting married soon,' he protested, 'that request is out of order,' he stopped, then quickly recanted, 'As long as it is just the ONCE, well,' he sighed, 'I will agree to it on one condition.'

'What is that?' Buxby asked.

He smiled, 'That I can partake therein.'

'Deal.'

They shook hands, said goodnight to each other and parted company. Buxby remained in the lounge where he offered to sleep and Cynthia and Fal went into Buxby's room and closed the door behind them. As they had no night clothes, they stripped off what they had on, and got into the fresh linens together. There was some tension, being in a strange bed but they took it well as Fal caressed Cynthia, to calm the nerves.

He asked, 'You like this?'

She reciprocated and massaged his midriff area. 'Mmmm....
do you?'

Fal moaned a bit when her hand went down to his lower half as she fondled her way into his affection.

'You're not really tired, are you, my love?'

'Not really, just more adrenalised,' she responded.

They moved closer to kiss as Fal tried to recall those cool moves he saw in that film. The flow between them was rigorous as they carried on with their natural actions.

Buxby laid on the sofa, which was at this time put out as a bed, slowly drifting to sleep when he overhead the activity coming from his room. I'll get there, he thought to himself, dreamily, I will see to it. The thought of her loving him in his bed made him more relaxed as he went under to sleep.

When morning came, Buxby was 'repaid' and Fal kept to his bargain with him. It was a most fascinating experience to the humans, yet it proved to be a joyous occasion that pleased everybody. Afterwards, they had breakfast together in the flat. Buxby then returned them to the port to their awaiting ship.

'It has been fantastic,' Fal said, 'We must do it again. You are welcome to attend our wedding.'

'Would love to. Have you a best man?'

Shit, Fal thought, I am alone in the universe with Cynthia.

'Erm....no come to think of it,' he replied meekly.

'I would be happy to fill the role.'

'Would you? Much thanks,' Fal felt much relieved of this.

'And you, my dear,' Buxby crooned to Cynthia, 'You take care,' he gave her a small thin card, 'Here's my number. Do be in touch,' he kissed her.

'It's been grand with you and thanks for everything,' she said and returned his favour firmly on the cheek.

'Lovely to meet you. Bye for now,' Fal said, climbing into the ship, Cynthia following in after him.

They were both aboard with Buxby watching their departure from below.

'Now we return to the ship and plan Our Day,' Fal beamed.

Cynthia smiled as the ship spent its throttle in an aerodynamic leap into space. Buxby continued to watch their departure 'til the ship went out of focus and sent a message to Spazio confirming their return and all was well.

Once aboard the Yakrey, Fal and Cynthia went to their respective quarters, when it was realised they need to 'shack up' as one says. This was done a long time ago, when Cynthia moved into a sardine-tin of a one bedroom flat with her first intended. Fal never had that sort of memory as he was far too busy in the theatre for such sundries. When he eventually did marry in that past existence, he automatically lived together with his then-wife. For Fal and Cynthia, it did make sense to live together, as they were about to be married. With a bit of planning, they picked a larger space within the ship and moved in.

'It would suck to be alone now, Fal,' Cynthia whinged.

'Yea, we will remedy that error and rearrange, then, hmmm?'

Cynthia thought, Cheeky blow, thou art, Spectrum Fallace! You always have an answer for everything. Yet, she was proud to be marrying such a man. He was everything to her, a near father figure, without the ghastly age differ—wait, there WAS a huge age difference, but their bio-zones had been adjusted to comfortably meet in the meridian. It was a most satisfying relationship, especially as she once loved him as the actor she admired in her past life. He was also the most beautiful specimen of male origin she had laid her greedy eyes upon.

The intercom in the room alit. It was Spazio.

The raspy voice spoke, 'Glad to see you have returned. Overnight stay, Mmmm??'

'Yea,' Fal said, 'Sorry about that. One gets carried away and we have never been to another planet before other than the fair Earth. It was most interesting for us.'

'How did you find Andros 4, Cynthia?'

She reflected on her visit, 'Different, but the same. Similar in tastes and habits to Earth, yet so much more liberated. An alternative point of view, I think.'

Spazio quipped, 'Widens the mind, does it not?'

'Yea, it does,' Fal answered.

'I will leave you to it, then,' Spazio respectfully switched off the comm.

Fal and Cynthia took tea in their newly designed room and had a lovely meal. They shared some time together and abedded for the night (or whatever the space equivalent was).

As he drifted toward sleep, Fal felt a twinge in his chest area, a feeling he had not felt since....wait, he remembered, I had been ill in the previous life, yet that cleared up surely??!! After I was taken by these aliens......he neared that point where sleep won the battle, and never minded the matter. I will deal with it later, he further thought, praying whatever it was will pass soon.

Chapter VIII

Time passed and Fal and Cynthia's wedding was under way. It was decided to be held on Andros as that place seemed a decent and now familiar location. It was a better alternative to marrying in space. Why marry aboard a bulky old starship, when there were good planets nearby to get one's frock off?!

Fal wore a bridegroom suit such as one he married in on Earth. It was a typical suit but with metallic thread weaved into the fabric to make it more glam. Cynthia's gown was cream coloured, long, with a sleeve and a bit of neckline showing the upper chest.

The ceremony was held at the Grand Cathedral of St. Om-Nom, where, centuries earlier, the monks who once held quarters here would repeat the saint's name in their daily devotional litanies. The saint himself was a devout follower of his God but he had a unquenchable weakness for food. He tried his best so as to be less attracted to appetite and concentrate on God, but his enemies would taunt him and he would go back to eating.

The local authorities of his time heard about this wretched fellow, who, in their eyes, struck up trouble in his preaching of the Gospel to the Androsians. Eventually, he was put to death by making him eat all his favourite foods to uncontrollable excess. Another martyr in the shrine, he was canonised and now remembered by those with weight issues.

The Cathedral was as large, not unlike the Saint himself, but in an edificial manner. It was quite full, for the aliens were able to witness for the first time a human marriage. Buxby fulfilled his role as best man and Cattapilla was Cynthia's bridesmaid. There were other aliens willing to volunteer in the traditions of matrimony, with awe at the novelty of the same.

The day went favourably, and the sun dipped down in the sky to make way for nightfall. There was a small reception and afterwards, Fal and Cynthia departed for their honeymoon. A complimentary ship, courtesy of Spazio, was waiting for them. After bading farewells, they departed to begin their holiday together.

'That was fantastic, Fal,' Cynthia exclaimed with delight, 'I got you now, forever and ever!'

'Well, as they said in church, 'til death us do part,' Fal remarked as he was piloting the ship.

Cynthia sighed and hugged him firmly. 'I love you,' she declared privately to him, 'I really do love you.'

'As do I, my Cynthia,' he said, looking ever-so-kindly upon her and gave her a kiss.

They landed in Ee-El-Oh Harbour, which was miles away from their first port of call, Point Ee-El-Pi, where their first adventurous lark started on Andros 4.

Cynthia fumbled in her purse for something and found Buxby's card and gave it to Fal. 'Perhaps on one of the days he can join us,' she thought aloud.

'We will see,' Fal took the card and put it in his pocket.

'Well, other than the girls I met at the Regalburgh, I know no one else.'

'Let us settle down before we go visiting, then,' Fal recommended as their accommodation was reached, 'Ah, here we are.'

They landed the ship, right beside the sea. There was a bed
and breakfast that Spazio planned for them to stay at, which
allowed them time to spend together. It was the least he could
do, considering he had them removed from their old lives, one
of them on the brink of death, even!

The couple spent a fortnight there, enjoying themselves
especially at night-times, when they experienced enormous
pleasure consummating themselves and their new lives
together.

During the day they took long walks near the beach, learned
more about the alien cultures that populated the region, visited
museums, art galleries, and churches. They also spent some
time with Buxby who was delighted to join them for a day or
so, gaining more familiarity with them, especially Cynthia.

Fal still occasionally felt the familiar twinges in his chest.....
Oh no, he thought, not here, not now and he silently prayed it
would go away.....for the moment.

They walked along a boardwalk, Fal holding Cynthia's hand
quite firmly, 'How's it for you, luv?'

'Pleasant....a different sort of holiday, don't you think?'

'Yea, I like the sea air and the pier.'

He felt another twinge again and put his hand on his chest.

She asked with concern, 'You alright?'

'I am alright. Not to worry.'

'I remember you mentioned to me you had been ill before.'

'Yea, that was years ago, Heavens, 'tis now a few decades yonder now!'

'Maybe we should get it looked at locally.'

'Cynthia!' he retorted, but immediately backed down. He knew she was right. He continued, 'Sorry I snapped.'

She gave him a hug.

He paused, reflected on the old days when there were tests, doctors, hospital visits....God, not here, please not here. He silently prayed again.

Cynthia, in a cheeky tone, asked, 'Do you want a doctor or a priest?'

Fal broke from his prayer, 'Why do you ask?'

'I see you are praying. I can tell. Are you scared of doctors or something?'

The memory was still fresh in his mind, but he knew he had no choice, 'I will arrange for a doctor then, and go from there.'

'It sucks to worry about such things whilst on holiday,' she whinged.

'Yea, but have faith, my love, there will be good times to come.' He kissed her atop her head.

Thankfully he was right, for now.

He was looked at by a local physician who said he had to continue with medical treatment on the starship. He will also have to undergo further testing to see where the problem lay, once the holiday was over.

Fal exhaled a sigh of relief as Cynthia embraced him, 'You will be alright then?'

'Yes, my sweet.'

She kissed him firmly and later on, they enjoyed loving passion betwixt the sheets which was entirely and truly their own.

Their honeymoon drew to its natural conclusion and they returned to the Yakrey.

'I really enjoyed that, Fal, did you?'

'Quite so, yes,' Fal replied, but secretly was dreading the upcoming medical bit.

'Hopefully, these aliens could find out things that Earthmen dare to dream about!'

'Most comforting words, my dear,' he complimented, 'Time will reveal all.'

The next few days were trying for Fal. After all the tests had been completed, he was summoned into the office of the Valastron doctor, Cosimos.

Cosimos approached Fal, 'Do come in, sir.'

Fal walked in and sat in a nearby chair.

The alien doctor questioned him, 'You have been ill before, haven't you now?'

'Yes, of cancer.'

'Where precisely was it located?'

'Lungs.'

Oh shit, the doctor thought, as he read the printouts from the tests.

'I am afraid it is not good news. The cancer has returned.'

Fal exclaimed with disbelief, 'I thought it had been cleared when I was abducted. I felt nothing of the pains I had prior!'

'We thought your body had cleared itself when you were teleported aboard. However, there were a few dormant cells hanging about. They could reactivate, or remain dormant. In your case......,' he hesitated.

Fal's emotions became turbulent as he asked the inevitable, 'How long do I have?'

'Depends on the level of aggression. You could have a few days to over a year. We could give you something to retard the progress but, as you know, you may not have much time.'

Fal's eyes welled with tears, 'Am I to have time with Cynthia?'

'For now, yes, but you better tell her. No brave-man nonsense.'

Fal grimaced, brushed his tears, and extending his hand, 'Thank you, doctor.'

Cosimos shook his hand with a tentacle and continued, 'Sorry to break it to you like this. We will do what we can to make you comfortable. I can give you something for the pain.'

'Much appreciated,' Fal was unnerved. God, just after I had married a beautiful, if not unusual, girl. He looked up at the ceiling and silently prayed, 'Why do Ye need me now? I need time with my Cynthia!'

He walked out of Cosimos's office thunderstruck and went to their quarters where Cynthia was waiting.

She asked eagerly, 'How did it go, Fal?'

'It is not good. I......,' he stuttered.

'Wha---why?'

'The cancer returned.'

Oh shit, that's right.   He was dying just before his abduction, but it had been all clear, no????

'I may not have a lot of time. They will help me as much as they can,' he continued.

Cynthia was astonished. She finally found someone she loved and could relate to, sort of, and now he could inevitably be taken away from her....just like her natural father.....

She blanked out again, horrible memories filtering to the forefront of imagination:

'I remember talking to my mother mostly on the telephone and when I was really young, I distinctly remember talking about my father and she said to me 'I know where he is'. I never thought to pursue this.

'One day, my natural father had called the (grand) parents. The (grand) mother had spoke to him but I was not privy to the conversation and had told me that my dad had called and when I asked if he asked for me, she stated, "he did not ask for you". She then further told me that if any one who approaches me saying, "I am your father", she told me to run away from that individual. I did not understand this and nothing came of it except confusion.'

Feelings of jealously eroded Cynthia's mind as the loss of her father had made her want men. Older men. Unreachable men. Actors, musicians, historical figures.....anyone who would be willing to reach out to her.....though none ever did. It was only imagination in command and no one else. Women were vile to her and she seethed at those who had those type of men that SHE ALONE WANTED!

Thus, she violently hated females, old and young, especially the glamourous types who, in her eyes, always got their man.....except she wanted THAT man as well, even if it was before her time. She hated their pretty curves, beautiful lives, perfect parentage and anything else which aroused her envy.

She further recalled: 'Unfortunately, I was a bit of a tomboy because the (grand) mother de-emphasised my femininity by making me wear baggy clothes and hiding myself. She scrutinised the clothes I wore and if a top looked tight on me, she would say that I looked "too busty". I was not allowed to wear make-up nor high heels. I also wore my hair in the 'Dutch-boy' style and overall, I looked very boyish.

'Regarding boys or having boyfriends, in the real world, opposed to fantasy, I fared poorly, as religion reared its ugly head and the inevitable due to the 'is he Jewish?' question came up. I just gave up on this, as I did not want to cause any further trauma than necessary, so I waited and never pursued. I did have a couple of instances when I did go out with someone but it was only once or so and nothing became of it.'

She then recovered and looked around the room, feeling quite glum about the situation. How could Heaven be so cruel to take away my Fal, she thought, even if not now....eventually. It was so unfair. She held him so tightly and did not let go, crying over him as she did so.

Later on, Fal had to excuse himself for his medical monitoring and left Cynthia on her own. She felt a pang of desperation and fumbled about the room searching for that card Buxby had given to her weeks ago on Andros. She thought frantically, Shit, where did Fal put it???!! She then came across the card in his coat pocket where he put it at the time she gave it to him. It was so sorely needed now, as his number read out to her like a sharp neon sign shining in an evening on Andros 4.

She informed Spazio of her intention and was given a line on the comm. unit. She dialled the number and a bit of ringing occurred, and upon the sixth ring, a familiar voice answered. 'Buxby speaking.'

'Oh hi, thank God it is you. I need you aboard the ship. There have been developments that you need to be informed about.'

'Cynthia?'

'Yea, 'tis me.'

'Ah yes,' he remembered, 'You, with the funny accent.'

'Haha,' she hooted sarcastically, remembering his funny side, 'This is serious. When can you come up to the Yakrey?' she desperately pleaded.

'Okay, my girl, keep your skirt on, I'll be over in a bit. See you soon,' he hung up.

At last, she got him! Cynthia had an odd smile on her face, like that of a lady's portrait of long ago. Just then, Fal entered the room.

Fal asked, surprised, 'What?'

'I just phoned Buxby; he will be here soon. He needs to know.'

'Alright.'

'How did your appointment go?'

'Procedural and quite tiresome, my lady,' he replied, with the air of formality he was accustomed to as a thespian, but then softened up, 'Especially since I would rather be with YOU.'

Cynthia blushed at his emphasis and felt guilty she acted so rashly for the outside company. She was desperate for reassurance and a slimy Valastron would not do for a kiss or cuddle in one's darkest hour.

'Well, I.....,' she stumbled verbally into a corner.

'Darling, I know this is going to be rough for you, and I know I will not have an easy ride, either.'

Cynthia interjected, 'And you losing your life, leaving me alone!'

'Aye, you shall not be alone, as you may think, yet we must face it bravely together, my girl.....and thank you for inviting Buxby. I think he would make a good ally. He is reliable and humanoid for starters, just like us. Not so horrifically different.'

'Whereas Valastrons aren't the type one would want to....you know...umm,' she stopped.

Fal held her head up by the chin, 'I can imagine!'

He laughed as they embraced again, 'At least we can spend some time together before he gets here,' Fal proposed.

They went to the bed nearby, stripped off their garments and climbed in. They whiled away the time entwined and rocking to their natural rhythms. She gave him endless kisses all over and he reciprocated, each one more arousing than the last. It went on for awhile, his knowledge about 'making it last' being put to good use. When their time had come, at last, it felt glorious to the extreme. Looking at her husband, Cynthia was reminded happily of the various fantasies she had about him during her past life, and was pleased, finally, to 'let go and let Fal.'

The comm. system buzzed as they disentangled themselves from one another. It was Spazio informing them of Buxby's arrival.

'We'll be there shortly,' Fal announced, switching off the unit afterwards.

They got cleaned up and dressed, with a feeling of more positive vigour. Cynthia looked up at Fal and gave him another kiss.

'For the moment we just had together. I wish every day could be like this,' she wished aloud.

'I so do wish too, my love. My darling,' Fal put his arms around her, 'We had better be going.'

They went to the hangar where Buxby's ship was docked. He was waiting there with Uffizio, as usual, doing his daily welding.

Fal cheerily exclaimed, extending his hand, 'Buxby, my friend, how are you?'

'Grand,' Buxby shook his hand, 'Um…your wife was quite concerned when she contacted me.'

'Yea, she had right to be concerned. Let us away to our chamber and we will discuss our news with you.'

Buxby looked at Cynthia, 'And how are you, my dearest?'

'Thankful you arrived.'

'You sounded distressed.'

'Aye, I was.....still am, actually.'

Buxby thought, Oh God, what could it possibly be?

Their quarters were not far and they sat down on the cosy furnishings laid out. Fal told Cynthia to contact Spazio for some tea, to which she happily obliged.

Buxby asked, 'So what's the big news, then?'

'I....,' Fal tried to break it to him, 'I told you about the cancer I had when I was taken by the Valastrons.'

'Yes, I do recall that. Do go on.'

'It has returned. I thought it had passed, but recently I had noticed a resurgence I had not felt for many decades now.'

'Heaven, that must been a long time ago by now....surely they could eradicate those cells?'

'No, the cancer had spread. The initial cells laid dormant all this time, and for some reason, they had reactivated. Apparently, they were unnoticed....I was told I might not have much time, but they are trying to retard their progress upon me.'

The door swished open and the tea was brought in. It was served and happily consumed.

Buxby continued his query, 'So what will happen?'

'There are no plans. We live day to day. I go in for monitoring and take some medications to stay the pain. This experience is so deja vu, I so fear the worst. I will leave somebody I deeply love behind.'

Cynthia drank her tea and exhaled, thinking, he will have more than the one, after all our rhythms together.

She decided to tell Fal.....and it was convenient that Buxby was around too.

'Ummm....Fal,' she piped.

'Yea, what is it, Cynthia?'

'I think I'm.....,' her hand went to her tummy area.

Fal's eyes widened. Buxby looked pleased.

'Oh Cynthia, of all the blessed moments,' he cried. He gave her a hug, remembering when, in his previous life, his wife then had blessed him with several children. 'I so hope to live long enough to see the little one.'

Some hope, Buxby thought, with Fal's condition, he will be lucky enough to just see her belly swell up!

'Congratulations, my dear,' Buxby lent over to kiss Cynthia, 'Think on a name, yet?'

Cynthia exclaimed, 'Nope, too soon, in my opinion. I did not believe it would happen!'

'Well, I will be around for you, if you need me,' Buxby offered.

'Much obliged, thank you,' Cynthia accepted the offer, kissing Buxby.

'It looks like you might need to spend time here because Cynthia might need help during my appointments,' Fal said.

He's right, Buxby thought, I would not mind living up here for awhile, but......

'I have an idea,' he recommended, 'Why don't you two relocate to Andros to live? You can get the treatment you need, we have centres for that sort of thing; the air would do you some good. We have amenities and the best thing is that it resembles your old Earth. Much better than this tin can in space, no?'

Fal thought about the prospect....and if I do die, he thought, at least I can depart this life on a planet, and experience the normality I should have experienced the first time round. He and Cynthia had now been there twice and it looked like a nice place to live. It would make the illness more tolerable, make him more comfortable and there would be more things to do, day to day, instead of being in this 'tin can', as Buxby so elegantly put it.

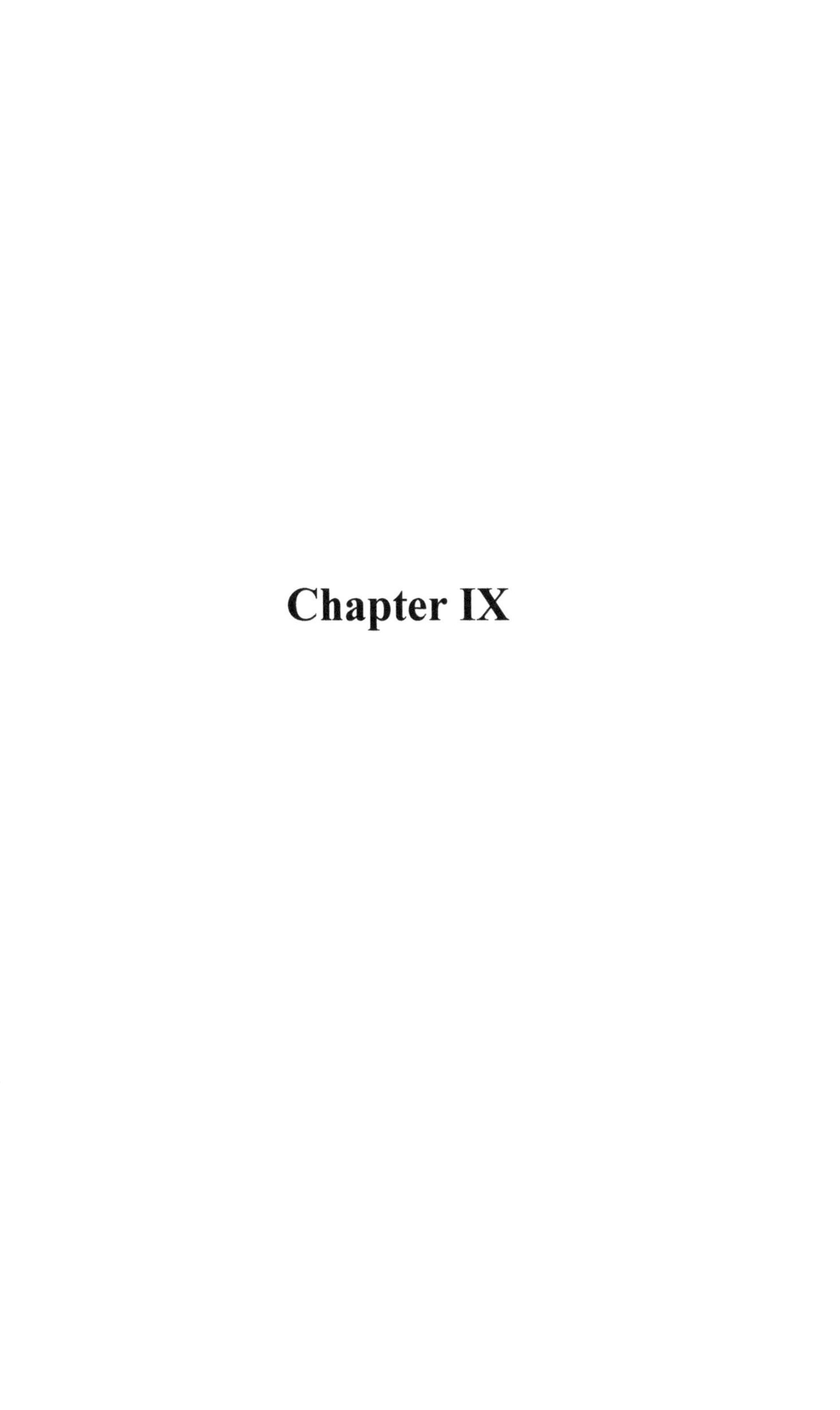

Chapter IX

It was agreed that Fal and Cynthia relocate to Andros during the time of Fal's illness. They situated themselves at a local hospice where he could be looked after and made more comfortable as his condition negatively progressed. It was a bugger, actually, because they preferred to be on their own together, but Fal realised this would be a better option, just in case the worst was to follow.

Their suite accommodated them nicely and allowed Cynthia to live on the premises to be with her beloved Fal. They were happy at best and with Cynthia's belly growing, Fal swooned for her and prayed he could remain alive for a little longer. They spent as much time together whilst Fal's health was not too far gone. Buxby sometimes came to visit and was on hand to support Cynthia during those trying moments.

One time, Fal and Cynthia spent the day out by the pier, looking toward the sea.

'How are you feeling, beloved?' Cynthia asked him.

'Better, for now,' he replied, inhaling a quick breath, 'Tis lovely out here. Ideal place to die, don't you think? It is much better than dying in urban London, where I would have, if not for.....'

'FAL!' Cynthia interrupted, holding him closer. He was getting quite morbid lately, probably preparing for death, but still.....it was too soon. Too soon. Anytime would be too soon. She relished the time she had with him, and there was not one day when she was apart from him for long periods.

She continued to hug him, weeping bitterly onto his fawn-coloured tunic.

'Please, please Cynthia, oh....my dear girl,' he started, then paused, embracing her lovingly. 'I shall not leave you yet. I pray I can remain with you as much as God makes possible.'

The waves pressed upon the shallow sand, striking with due force. They walked toward the beach area and nearer the water, it suddenly got chilly. Fal held Cynthia firmly, giving her his warmth. Still, I wish I had a coat, she thought.

' 'Tis so beautiful and wonderous here, unlike being in a stuffy old hospital-style room, waiting to die,' Fal sighed.

'Do you wish to pray more, Fal, perhaps in a church?'

'Thank you. I am alright,' he smiled, 'Good of you to think of me.'

They stared at the waves; Fal prayed anyway, silently, in this most radiant of settings.

Oddly enough, Buxby found his way to the beach and caught up with him and Cynthia.

He called out, 'Hello my friends!'

Cynthia told Buxby Fal was in prayer at the moment and to give him a few minutes.

A silent pause followed. Fal concluded his prayer, and turned to Cynthia and Buxby.

'Why hello Buxby,' Fal responded, hugging him.

'It is not a bad time for a visit?'

'No, we are happy you joined us. Do stay, please. In fact, things have not been too well for Cynthia. This has been very difficult for her.'

'I see,' Buxby replied. He came over to Cynthia to give her a hug. She tensed up at first, then melted in his arms.

Oooh, that feels good, Cynthia thought. Buxby read her mind a bit, not too deeply, but enough to sense her emotions and realise she needed a lot of support to get through this. It was pretty obvious that she did not get any assistance in her ancient past. It seemed to him she was treated pretty roughly.

Suddenly, Cynthia tensed up again, sensing another warning light in her mind:

'I remembered the lack of support in early school life and how heavily it emphasised the religious element which proved intolerable. The early schools attended were of Jewish origin. The temple ran the nursery and kindergarten I went to. Then I was enrolled into a sectarian school. Unfortunately the time there did not last as I did not get along with most of the kids there and the fact that there were children of Israeli origin who aced the Hebrew language curriculum whereas I had failed in it. I found the Hebrew language very hard to grasp and did not take to it well at all. No one else cared to help me and I remember the teacher who did the Hebrew curriculum being very unsympathetic with me. I remember being on the school bus with the rest of the children there and they were teasing me. I also remember that there was a diary written in a notebook, which told of the 'bad' behaviour or progress. I do recall having behavioural problems in addition, and one incident was most disturbing. One day I had talked out of turn in class and later I had masking tape (or the like) put over my mouth (and I honestly do not recall who did this).

'After that was done, the (grand) mother and her mother, had been laughing at me and making fun of me. I was crying and after some time of this, the tape was removed.   At the end of the second year there, the head of the school (at the time) had told the (grand) mother that I "would never amount to anything."   I was taken out of that school and put into a secular private school and had attended such schools until I completed my final year prior to college.'

She came round again, with Buxby and Fal looking at her quizzically.

'Erm, Cynthia,' Fal queried, 'how often do you get these relapses again?'

She responded, 'Huuh???   Dunno.....ummmm.....,' the stammering blew its gale force wind into the conversation.

'Look, maybe, you should see a doctor,' he recommended.

'It is nothing, Fal,' she protested, 'it is part of my condition. I am not dying from it, I just have difficulty coping with your condition, knowing we may not have much time left!'

'It still should be seen to.'

A few moments passed whilst Cynthia regained appropriate composure.

Fal checked his watch and decided to return to the hospice, 'It is getting late. I believe I have medication waiting for me.'

'I would like to go with you, at least for Cynthia's sake,' Buxby volunteered.

'Good. She could do with a morale boost.'

With that, Cynthia kissed Buxby and thanked him. He blushed as he accompanied them back home.

During the walk, Fal asked Buxby over to have a private chat. Cynthia stayed a few steps back sensing they needed to discuss something and respected the same.

'Buxby, I know we have been friends for a short time, and I would not ask you otherwise, but as my time is limited, I need to ask a favour.'

He perked up, 'What do you need of me?'

Fal stopped suddenly and turned to Buxby.

'I need you to take care of Cynthia when I am gone.'

Buxby gulped involuntarily, 'Gosh, I do not know what to say. I am a lone soul myself. I am...'

'No, seriously. I want you to look after her. She has nobody and the Valastrons won't cut it. She likes you and you both get on well. I saw that on the morning we spent together.'

Buxby recalled that morning in full view. Then, he had lusted after the Earth woman but now, to take her, her problems and pregnancy on board would require serious thought.

'I am honoured that you ask this of me and it seems Cynthia requires much care and support, possibly more than I could handle.'

'Well who else is there, Buxby? Remember, we have been abducted! We cannot relate to the Valastrons, but as you are more like us, you seem to have potential. Do have a think about this, but if you say no, we will have a larger problem than just my death.'

Buxby realised the implications of this matter. Fal's right, he thought, she does need support through this, and probably a nanny for the child to be.

'I will look into it and see what I can do for you,' Buxby offered.

'Thank you. It is the least I can do for her. She is such a magnificent woman, once you get past 'certain' things.'

'The relapses, Asperger's, crap upbringing, and the like.'

'Yes, quite. We have tried to relieve her of these issues, but with the current situation, it has been most difficult.'

It was a lot to think about. They carried on walking and at last reached the hospice.

They walked in and a nurse named Brax was waiting in the foyer.

'Time for your medication, Mr. Fallace,' he said.

Oh God, here it comes, Fal thought.

'Let me settle into my room; please meet me in there, thanks,' he advised.

'You were supposed to take it an hour ago; but alright, I will dispense it in your room.'

Oh Christ, Fal thought, they are going on as if my life depended on that stuff. Well, it DID depend on it, but one was still a bit hopeful that it did not get that far.

They went into their suite. Buxby and Cynthia went into the adjoining room whilst Brax dispensed the medication to Fal. Cynthia started to cry again, Buxby held her close.

'I trust you heard our discussion earlier,' he said.

Disoriented in her tears, she questioned, 'Wha--?' Then she recovered, 'No, I was not paying attention. I thought you needed privacy.'

'I appreciate it, but I think you should know. Fal told me to look after you when he goes.'

Cynthia's eyes widened, 'YOU?'

'Aye,' he said in a serious tone.

She exclaimed, hugging him, 'Buxby! Do you think ye up for the challenge?'

'Well, I may need assistance, especially with the baby you are carrying.'

She swelled with newfound hope. The promise of a good looking-after sent her mind into the outer cosmos. She would not be alone after all.

She held Buxby tight until the nurse announced he had finished with the medications for the day and that they can see Fal.

They went into the room where Fal lay in bed. Cynthia went up to kiss him and said, 'I know what you have planned for me, and I thank you from my heart.'

'Oh?' He sat up.

'Yea, you want Buxby to see to my needs.'

'That I did. I do not want you to be alone, especially with your respective delicate conditions.'

She kissed Fal more firmly on the lips. It felt so good, she wanted it to last forever. Buxby watched over them and felt they needed to be alone together.

'Ah, I will be getting on now, let me know if you need anything,' Buxby said.

Fal looked at him squarely, 'Sure thing, and thank you.'

Buxby saw he would be needed and felt obliged to help them. He left the room quietly as Fal and Cynthia continued their kissing and embracing.

Cynthia and Fal were now alone and she caressed his chest and kissed him tenderly. It was a last ditch effort for intimacy due to his deterioration and her pregnancy. Yet they would not take such mediocrities aboard when there is still love to be had. Fal adjusted his position to allow her to share his bed. 'Twas a bit of a pinch for them, but they managed to fit in somehow and perform their (probable) last rites together as a couple. They fell asleep in each other's arms, hoping it would not be their last.

The next day, Fal had an appointment with the local specialist, Dr. Oliviyay to check on the progression of the cancer. He was a typical Androsian, humanoid, professional, late middle-aged with short hair turning into old man grey.

'Mr. Fallace, your condition remains critical and going fast. The medications given to you are helping, but only on temporary basis to make you more comfortable. Are you in any pain?'

'Actually, no, I am not. How long do I have now, then?'

'I cannot say and I will not because the inevitable will happen. Nature, not science, determines the phenomena. I cannot predict, but all I can say your tide is near its ebb.'

Out of time, in other words, Fal mouthed to himself.

The doctor asked, 'Beg pardon, did you say something?'

'No, sorry, just thinking aloud. It has been very difficult with us, having just married Cynthia and now expecting a baby.'

'I know, and I am very sorry indeed, but alas, when nature calls us....' he trickled off.

'Well, thank you Doctor,' He got up to shake Oliviyay's hand.

'I look forward to seeing you again,' Oliviyay said, hoping it was not too late for Fal.

Fal then left the consultation room and walked down the corridor to his suite. Cynthia was there alone, reading a book. Fal came up to her asking, 'What are you reading?'

She glanced at the corner, 'Oh, just some silly romance.'

'Romance is never silly,' Fal said, 'Look at us. Are we silly?'

She could not argue out of that one. She put the book down and held Fal.

'You know I have not much time,' he said in earnest.

'I know.'

'It is worsening.'

'Not surprised,' she said, tonelessly.

'I know this has been a most difficult for you. Let us go out again for some fresh air and forget about it to concentrate on us,' he proposed.

'Maybe have some tea, perhaps?'

'Sounds good.'

They went to the canteen for their mid afternoon drink.

'Shall I contact Buxby to join us, if he is free?' Cynthia asked.

'Well, not now, my love. Let this be betwixt me and thee.'

'Thespianic to the last, eh?'

'As always,' he gave her a warm smile.

Cynthia hugged Fal again for support, for love, and for eternity.

Their tea was served and they enjoyed the time together. She thought, Has it been that long I had him? The problem was they only just married but spent many years together and wanted plenty more....but now, it may not be possible, if at all. She was determined to milk all the time in the world to be in his presence.

She asked, 'Shall we go outside in the garden?'

'Delighted, my love.'

They finished their tea and went out. The garden at the rear of the property had flowers of all types and colours, a rockery and lots of benches surrounding a lush green lawn. There were quite a few people out, taking in the sunrays. The day was most enchanting and one to enjoy being alive in.

They sat on the bench together, holding one another. Fal's complexion looked slightly pale, compared to a more healthier hue he displayed when Cynthia first met him. He was thinning out too, despite the food he took in. The cancer was doing its worst inside and it took its toll on him. Who knows how long it went on for before Fal's chest went a-flutter?

After some time outside, Fal decided to return to the suite. They went back, had a light dinner and spent the evening watching telly. Cynthia stayed close to Fal and carried on kissing him throughout the programme they were watching. It was like being teenagers at the cinema, not that they did anything of that sort when they were respectively teens.....

She soon felt weary after the show and asked, 'Want to go to bed?'

'Yea, I think we should turn in for the night. I am feeling a bit tired, actually.'

They did their bits and tucked themselves into bed. Cynthia refused to sleep in the bed in the other room as she would rather be with Fal. She really wanted to make love to him, but her tummy's size was preventing her from getting too frisky. This was a hapless cause, but as she came closer to his chest, his heart was still beating away; thank Heaven, she thought and she fell asleep, holding him tight, with that sound firmly entrenched in her mind.

During the night, Fal had a dream. A Voice called unto him, using his former name, the name he was christened with.

'Alexander Pennece DeMilo'

Within the dream, Fal awoke, 'Yes? I go by the name Fal.'

'I know, but this is not where you are now.'

'What?'

'Your time has come, good sir,' the Voice stated.

'No, please...I...,' Fal begged, 'I've a child on the way, a woman who needs protection, I cannot....'

'You have made relative provisions for both. It is no longer your concern. Come Mr DeMilo, or Fal, if you prefer.'

'No, no,' he resisted, for a brief moment. However, remembering the last time he 'died' he was abducted and wondered if this was all a trick. 'There are no aliens round here, now, are there?'

'Not this time, sorry. Those aliens gave you many more decades of life; time which I hope you have well-spent. Come, my child, you are at one with your Maker now. Make your peace and follow me.'

A blast of energy ran through Fal's body and stopped. He became limp and will never again speak. The voice of Death ebbed away, taking with it its newly acquired prize fate had earlier cheated It out of.

The next morning, Cynthia stirred. It was not too early, maybe eight o'clock, she guessed. She got up to check and it was a couple of minutes to. Okay, I was semi-correct, Haha, she thought. She went back to the bed where Fal lay sleeping, or so she thought. She checked his chest to see if that lovely heart was still beating. Silence emerged louder than a crash of thunder. She realised he had died in the night whilst she was sleeping next to him??!!!

The occurrence was painful and the tight whirring of memory began to remove her from reality:

'At 14 years old, I had experienced a death in the family for the first time. A great grand-mother was babysitting me as the (grand) parents went to Israel for a relative's bat-mitzvah. I had gone to school during that time and forgot my house keys. It was raining and I was knocking on the door to no avail. I thought this was strange and I continued to knock on the door. I then went to the next-door neighbour's home and asked the lady of the house for the spare keys. Once obtained, I retuned to my home and opened to door. In the room I found the great grand-mother sprawled facedown on the floor. There was a plate with some leftover cake or bread on it with accompanying crumbs. The dogs were barking and I panicked. I went back next-door and told the neighbour of the crisis.

'She went to my house and called the appropriate authorities and took care of the matter. I was then placed temporarily in the care of a nearby relative who looked after me for a couple of days before the (grand) parents arrived home and when they did arrive home the funeral took place the day after. This was a very trying time for me and did not help my spiritual well being. The Jewish faith was far from being a comfort to me by this point and, although I did not begin to think of alternatives, I knew something needed to be done soon.

'Nearly two decades later, I got a telephone call from another relative stating that the (grand) mother had passed away. I must confess here and now that I was more relieved than anything as I felt I did not have to 'put up a front' for her. I went home for the funerary rituals. I was planning to remain only a few days and then return home. However, an in-law had talked me out of leaving via a guilt trip, stating that I should remain as the (grand) mother was 'good to me' over the years (or words to that effect). I changed my travel plans and remained with the family for the funerary week. A couple of days later, there was a rest from guests coming to the family home where the (grand) father, a distant relative and myself stayed during this period. I was watching television and keeping to myself when a guest did arrive. I wanted to be alone for a while, but unfortunately, this led to a heated argument between that relative and myself when she said to me "we are a family of givers and you are a taker!" I also noticed that she had been talking to some of the other family members there, which looked like she was talking about me. Paranoia flared rampantly within and I was certain the family was going to shut me away thinking I was crazy. I got so scared I phoned my friends in my home town to calm my nerves, as the psychological trauma had been so extreme.'

She quickly recouped her energy and pressed the 'In case of emergency' call button on the nearby intercom. The nurse, Brax, answered, 'What room please?'

'It is Suite 70-133. I think we have a problem here,' Cynthia panicked.

'What is the situation, dear?'

'I think he's passed.'

'Passed what?'

'DEAD!'

'Oh, I will come up to assist.'

It took forever, she thought, but Brax entered the room and checked on Fal. The nurse confirmed his death and Cynthia was silent. She could not speak and too dumbfounded to care about anything at the moment.

'Should I send for a doctor to check you? You look like you need someone, Mrs Fallace.'

'Who was that doctor Fal saw yesterday, that specialist?'

'Oh, Dr Oliviyay. I will contact him to inform him of what happened and send him round, if he is not in consultation.'

'Thank you,' she said as Brax wheeled out Fal's body to a separate room.

Cynthia went to fetch Buxby's number from her mobile to tell him.

'Dead? Hang on, I'll be there, luv, and this time, you will see me more often, I am happy to say.'

Cynthia smiled and rang off. Shortly thereafter, Dr Oliviyay entered the room. Cynthia stood up.

'No, no, no, please, take a seat,' he said.

She sat down with him.

'I will have to do an autopsy to find the cause of his death. I know it was cancer, but I want to know how far it spread and possibly when the cells became reactivated enough to kill him.'

'Thank you,' she said.

'Are you alright?'

'DUH!'

'Yes, I know, stupid question. Well, at least physically, with your baby, and all.'

'That side of things is alright, but for the discomfort of being this fat.'

'Thankfully it won't be for long.'

Cynthia thought about what Fal said about her 'relapses' and thought to query this doctor about them.

'How long have you been getting them for?'

'A while now, especially since the abduction.'

'Abduction?'

'Yes, many decades ago, myself and Mr Fallace, formerly known as Mr DeMilo, were abducted by the Valastrons. I was living life with as much normality as I could, save the Asperger's.'

Oliviyay interrupted, 'You have Asperger's?'

'Yes, apparently I was born with it but not diagnosed until my mid-forties. It helped me understand the difficulties of my youth, but I've been getting flashbacks of the bad memories when under much stress.'

'You do not take kindly to stress, then.'

'No, I cannot cope with it, nor crowds, nor heavy volumed social situations and the like.'

'Well, if it is all in the mind and not the body, there is nothing I can do to help. Counselling would be more beneficial.'

'Tried that years ago. Sucked beyond reproach.'

'Did not work, then, eh?'

'Uh-uh,' she shook her head.

'Look, the most I can do to help is to see how your husband died. Do you have any other family, friends who can look after you? Maybe those Valastrons?'

'No, I rang up Buxby. He had actually been promised to me by Fal who had arranged for Buxby to look after me after his death.'

'Very thoughtful. Now, my dear, I must dash, for I cannot tarry any longer. With your husband's case, plus lists of other patients to see, my day will be crammed as a biscuit tin with no air.'

She got up, extending her hand, 'Thank you kindly for the time you did spend with me and let me know what you found about Fal.'

'Will do. Goodbye then.'

He walked out into the mad rush of his day. Buxby arrived at this point.

'Was that the doctor I just passed?'

'Yes,' she sniffed, 'I am glad you are here Buxby.'

'What happened.'

'Died in the night. I heard his heart beat nicely and I fell asleep. I then awoke to silence.'

'Cynthia,' Buxby extended his arms out to her, 'I am here now.'

'So I am a widow?'

'Yes you are.'

'So now what?'

'Well, once we deal with Fal, give him a good send-off, and give it some time, how would you like to be Mrs Buxby?'

Wow! Cynthia thought. I have heard of being cared-for, but this is too cool to resist. I will never be alone again! A pre-planned and ready-made husband, too!

'Are you sure you can cope with the likes of me, you know what I carry.'

'Yes that and the child, I know. We will not let that get in the way, will we now?'

He so looked like a little knitted tea-cosy with a cute bauble on top, she thought, and a very comforting sight. Buxby recommended they return to the Yakrey as their time on Andros was now redundant.

'There really is nothing more for us to do here. I will contact Spazio and let him know we're returning to the ship.'

She fumbled through some belongings and started to pack up to clear the room. It was true that being here was for Fal's sake due to his condition. Otherwise, the starship was just as good. She thought about it and asked Buxby, but he was engaged in conversation.

She waited until it was over and then asked, 'Could you live with me on a starship?'

Buxby went over to her, 'Yes, I think I can get used to it.'

'Fal and I had a room together there. We can share that room too. This room can be cleared in no time. We only took essentials anyway as we did not know how long our stay would be.'

Buxby gave her a kiss, 'I understand. Sounds good. Have you given consideration for the wedding?'

'Let us do it informally, maybe in a chapel?'

'We can do that. There are quite a few to choose from. We can plan from the Yakrey. However, one thing at a time......,' he reminded her in a serious tone.

'Right,' Cynthia gulped and dreaded what was coming in respect to Fal.

They began to arrange to return to the Yakrey and plan for the future.

Chapter X

Buxby arranged Fal's funeral at the nearby chapel by the hospice. This proved a fair convenience to the residents there who were at the tail end of their lives. It was a small affair, as Fal had no real family to speak of (other than Cynthia). His abduction, now nearly two centuries ago, had forced an unintentional abandonment from his previous family. Buxby, and of course, Cynthia were present, as was his twin brother, Harry and his band-mates (for moral support).

Fal was remembered fondly for his spontaneity, adaptability and wit. Most of the aliens present agreed that he spoke eloquently, in an admittedly humorous manner. Fal was given an elegant send-off. His body was taken to a local crematorium and the resulting ashes buried in a noble grave. Cynthia missed Fal very much and wept bitterly throughout the whole affair.

Her relapses caused further trauma as she was led down another dark path of memory lane:

'I recalled my natural mother passing away. I went home for the funeral and stayed with the family for a few days. I had a small conversation with someone during that time and he said to me "don't be a stranger" and "blood is thicker than water". I did not respond and I let it go. Afterwards, I thought to retort back, "but one cannot drink blood to survive" but obviously, it was too late. I also recalled a time when a photo of my mother at a young age was shown, threw me into hysterics, as I cried 'I am an orphan, no one wanted me!' The family present then argued with me and stated that she DID want me. I never believed them. What I really hated afterward was that I had to endure endless conversation regarding the Jewish religion, Jewish culture and Jewish heritage. Any discussions or opinions regarding non-Jewish people were harsh and uncaring.

'It made me sick to be there and I could not wait to leave. It felt like being bullied, coerced, and being without a choice. It really boggled one's mind to say the least. 'Someone from the temple had come to visit during the week after my mother's death, who had a daughter who emigrated to Britain (which was at this point, something I was hell-bent on doing myself). She was living there as a working professional, married to a British citizen (who was also Jewish, to the best of my knowledge).   I had spoke to this person and insanely jealous feelings, compounding with the loss of my mother had made it impossible for me to continue to talk to her and I excused myself and cried bitterly in another room where a television had been turned on.   I was so upset that someone else 'made it' and I had not, living the way I did at the time (which was on minimum wage, casual hours doing a food service job at the local university).'

Another memory flashed viciously in her mind:

'There was another family member who died, a relative who lived abroad. I was not really intending to go to the funeral, in fact, I left it last minute. I honestly did not want to go. I was persuaded to attend by various workers at a job I had at the time, as well as family. I relented (again!) and took the flight back where they lived. I was not happy to see anybody nor wanted to be there in the first place. As the death had coincided with the Jewish holiday of Passover, there was no seven day mourning period thereafter, so it was a one day event (thankfully).   I had already converted and was a devout Anglican and was extremely miffed at being 'knocked backward' to go through this shit again. That evening, I was staying with a relative who took me to her friend's house. It was the first night of Passover and they had the traditional seder meal. I remember in the past hating these meals, because it took over an hour to get to the food and I just was never into that shit anyway.

'There was ceremony, discussion of the meanings thereof and overall sense of 'us vs. them' distastefully abound. All I wanted to do was either eat or get the fuck out of there! It was hell for me.

'The best way of 'getting out of it' was to cry. I had just attended a funeral, surely THAT would allow for the lingering of tears. So I tried it on, and lo and behold, it worked. I was excused and taken to another room where I carried on for a bit longer. It was not the most pleasant of experiences.....'

Buxby caught sight of Cynthia and asked, 'Are you alright, dearest?'

Cynthia, feeling queasy and out-of-it, said, 'No, not really. Help me!' She reached out her hand, for him to grab onto and he held her tightly.

'My love, my dear, we will get through this,' Buxby comforted.

He knew he put his foot in it when he took on the care of the fair Cynthia. He sighed and continued to hold her, as he wanted to do the best he could for her.

One of the band members, Willec, went up to Buxby, 'How's the lass now, then?'

'I think she is alright,' Buxby replied and to Cynthia he asked, 'aren't you, luv?'

She looked up at him, closed her eyes and fainted in his arms.

Buxby panicked, asking Willec, 'Can you help me get her to the ship?'

'I believe it would be better to have her seen to here,' Willec recommended.

'Nice idea, but these lapses she falls prey to are part of a neurological condition she has called Asperger's. She is not in real danger.'

'Ah, I see,' said Willec, 'I trust she does not take well to stress, then and it looks like she has been pushed to the limit, especially with her pregnancy.'

'Yes. There are a number of things involved, but suffice to say, she will be alright, once this storm passes.'

Harry went up to Buxby, 'Are you sure you can handle this? Poor thing.'

'I know it seems harsh, but I promised Fal I would look after her. I am planning to marry her.'

George interjected, 'Marriage?! Bit of a step, that, eh?'

'Maybe, but she has got no one and she is carrying a child.'

'I can see that,' Willec pointed out.

They carried her from the chapel to an awaiting ship, when Willec again urged she remain on the planet until she recovered. Buxby pondered the thought and decided to take her back to his place for a few days.

'I do hope she gets better,' Willec said to Buxby, patting him on the shoulder, 'Godspeed.'

He then departed with the others, leaving Buxby to care for the girl. Harry remained to help his brother.

They put Cynthia into Buxby's room for a rest and went into the lounge to sit and chat awhile.

Buxby remembered the last time she had come here, under more pleasant circumstances, when visiting Andros with Fal and staying overnight. He shared his feelings with his brother as he dreamily recalled the memory; how he had fantasised about her and himself in the lounge, whilst she and Fal were engaged in their own rhythms that night.

A cruel twist of irony had shown that wishing as opposed to responsibility can be very different indeed. Cynthia had fallen asleep in the bedroom, still thinking about Fal. It tore her mind apart and the relapses became more frequent. Her mind began to twist toward a dangerous curve and the anger inside swelled fatter than her belly ever could.

Buxby excused himself to check on her to make sure she was okay.

He spoke softly, 'Cynthia, my love.'

She responded in a delirium, 'Fal?'

Oh God, Buxby thought, her mind was still on Fal.

'No, we just buried him.'

Cynthia opened her eyes, 'Buxby?' It was as if she forgot where she was and thought Fal was still with her.

He cradled her in his arms, hugging her. Harry came in to help.

'Not right now, Harry, thanks,' Buxby said. He was confident he could help her on his own.

Cynthia was better now, but felt very different inside. Her tummy was still filled with the coming baby, yet her mind was acutely focused. There was a minor air of confidence which she had never felt before. She got up and looked round her. This room seems familiar, she thought....oh yeah, that night with Fal, she chuckled to herself upon the memory.

Buxby came into the room. She opened her arms to him, giving him hugs and kisses and thanking him for getting her through the nasty ordeal.

'You're most welcome, Cynthia,' Buxby returned her thanks.

'I trust we will be getting married soon.'

'No time like now, I would say,' he said, but thought, it will take some planning.

They chose to have the wedding at a smaller venue, a chapel, as they discussed. When the day arrived, it had been an overall success. They had not felt this good in weeks. Cynthia's dress had to be tent sized nearly, to accommodate her delicate condition and Buxby's suit was one of his more simple but elegant ones. Harry was Buxby's best man and Willec gave the bride away. It was as happy an affair as Fal and Cynthia's wedding, though not as elaborate.

After the formalities, Buxby and Cynthia returned to the Yakrey.

'So how does it feel to be Mrs Buxby, then?'

She gave him a kiss in response.

'Are you alright now?'

'Yes,' she said confidently, but added, 'I do feel different.'

'How so?'

She could not really explain this, it was just an odd feeling inside. It was due to many a combination, not really down to just one thing. Buxby thought about it. It had been hectic in recent months, plus her problems, gosh, it was taking its toll on her.

They settled in the room where Fal and Cynthia lived. There was an eerie feeling about it as one of its former occupants was no longer there. Cynthia rummaged round a bit, seeing that there could be room for Buxby, once a clearout was held with odd bits sorted out and cleared away. Buxby arranged for some articles of his to be put in the room as it looked like he will be on the Yakrey for some time.

Taking a breather, Buxby and Cynthia had tea together.

'So where do you want to go for the honeymoon?'

She thought about it. The previous one with Fal had been fantastic, until the cancer returned.

'I do not know,' she said, then suddenly, feeling completely 'off course', 'I feel like attacking Earth.'

Buxby's eyes flew open. 'What?'

'Remember that conversation we had when I first met you?'

'Yes, when we were together before Fal excused himself. We discussed something about your wish for conquest. You went off about it and Fal had to control you a bit.'

'Yes, that is correct.'

'I was rather intrigued by what you said. I actually thought you were joking, but somehow your tone sounded serious. Were you?'

Cynthia blushed. Although she had done away with her family a long while back, it did not stop her from the wish to attack others on the basis that 'they did not help her' and that 'they let the horror resume upon her.' She was deadly serious about revenge and here she was, up in space, with an alien for a husband. Damn it, she was going to do it.

'Yes. Those creatures are foul pieces of shit anyway, and deserve to die,' she stated with glorious conviction.

'I do recall their blundering upon one of the outer planets which Valastron young were being kept and then killing them....,' he looked at Cynthia's belly.

Cynthia finished his sentence, '...out of their stupidity, ignorance and arrogance.'

'To be honest with you, Cynthia,' Buxby sipped the last of his tea, 'I have a confession to make. It was no accident that you were abducted. We were hoping you would ally yourself with us in our cause against the humans....'

He carried on, 'We picked up on your struggles, problems, ongoing relapses, lack of self-worth, bad memories, and your Aspberger condition.   We felt you could be the perfect candidate to assist us in our struggle against them.'

'What have they done to you, aside from the Valastron incident.'

'Well,' Buxby reflected, 'aside from screwing up nature, they were spreading ill-founded attitudes far and wide which made no sense to us.   And what was worse, polluting the universe with archaic technology, which was damaging our eco-systems.'

'The technology which uses primitive fuel sources.'

'Aye, that is right.'

Wow, just like what happened on Earth centuries ago..... when there was a big palaver over fuel and atmospheric issues, whereby the fuel and other such pollutants were damaging the outer layers of the atmosphere, causing the climate change that continues to currently progress at an alarming rate.

Buxby looked at Cynthia, and reached out to touch her belly, 'how much longer till you deliver?'

'Couple of months, I guess, I do not know,' she confessed. The recent events made her lose track of time.

'You get yourself checked out and safely delivered.   The honeymoon will wait.   Let us wait for the child to be born before we make any serious plans.'

'You are right and thank you for your consideration,' she kissed Buxby.

She had her scans done and everything seemed to be within normal limits. Her mind, however, was becoming further twisted with evil thoughts and her desire for revenge more ongoing. With her condition and raging hormones inside, she made an advance for Buxby, who was quite startled in the attempt.

'Why, my lady? Are you itching for something?'

'Aye, my lord,' and with that, she kissed him most kindly, most gently and more seductively.

She knew getting him into bed would be out of the question, she would most likely veer him off, with her size. They managed anyway, but with no penetration, as that would be difficult. So she stayed with him, kissing him.

Buxby interrupted, 'I've another confession to make to you. I think you will like this one.'

'What is it?'

With that, his alien body turned more human. Cynthia's eyes popped out in disbelief and surprise.

He said, smiling, 'Ahh, so you like to see me in this mode, then?'

He looked very quaint in his shirt, tie, trousers and cardigan. He resembled a fellow of middle-age (just like Cynthia) and comfortably attractive, but with a receding dark hairline.

Wow....a metamorphing husband, all for me, she thought, gosh, I would love to have him now....damn this belly of mine....I want it....UUGGGHH!!!!

'Don't look so glum, my luv, I think I can accommodate you,' he offered himself to her and gave her the pleasure she required with delicate touching. It felt awkward, removing the clothes and all, but 'twas very enjoyable and sorely needed. The end relief came to its stirring conclusion, and she gave Buxby what she could offer to him.

The night settled down as Buxby and Cynthia got comfortable in their slumbers. Buxby remained in his human form for the moment. He reverted to his alien form once she fell asleep.

Meanwhile, the hospice had contacted the Yakrey, in regard to the autopsy report promised by Dr. Oliviyay regarding Fal. The next day, Spazio spoke to Buxby about it.

'The report showed the recurring cancer had devastated his system and it had gone on for a very long time, possibly since the abduction. We thought it had fully gone away then, but it has been the most recalcitrant of human diseases we ever encountered. I do not think we should tell Cynthia.'

'I agree,' Buxby concurred, 'She has enough on her plate at the moment and this would send her screaming into the next galaxy. We do not need this now.' He pondered at the complexity of the matter and felt very sad for Fal.

'No we do not. She is about to have her baby. Let her be.'

And so, the child of Fal and Cynthia was born in due course thereafter and was named Spectrum Falby, after his father and stepfather.

Cynthia hated the experience and thought, in space, birthing would be easier. So she gave in to having another child with Fal when they got together.

Cynthia recalled the first time round (on Earth, before the abduction), being pregnant went well, however, the birthing proved difficult and a Caesarean was made upon her. For this pregnancy, she hoped it could be delivered naturally, but, alas, it proved just as difficult and another Caesarean was done.

She was much older now by decades since her very first experience. Although, her youthful features were retained and her body was still happily intact with vigour, it did not stop the birth being unyielding.

Buxby was extremely happy on the day and enjoyed father-hood for the first time. Fal would have been over ten moons by now, but he did not live to see the blessed moment. Cynthia hoped that there was some knowledge about it in the beyond.

Falby was cleaned off by a Valastron nurse and put in a child-basket. Buxby looked fondly down upon the child and reflected, 'He is ever so lovely, and looks a lot like Fal.'

'Yea, 'tis a goodly memorial to him,' Cynthia said, imitating Fal, 'I remember he had eagerly wished to see this moment.'

Buxby looked straight at her, holding her hand, 'I know, and in my prayers, Cynthia, I will tell him what a beautiful son he has.'

The fleeting moment of remembrance was whisked away when a servant called Grazia, who was also a midwife, entered the room. She slithered quietly on her tentacles and spoke in a high pitched voice, asking, 'How are you all doing so far?'

'Exhausted, but relieved,' Cynthia responded, 'Got anything to eat?'

'I can get you a tea trolley. First let me look at the new baby for a check-over.' She stood over by the baby who gurgled at her. 'He is so lovely,' she turned to Buxby, 'Are you the father?'

'No, the father was Spectrum Fallace. He died on Andros due to a returning cancer,' he said despondently.

'Oooh, that's too bad,' she continued to make sure the baby was well, which he was, and asked Cynthia, 'Can you breast feed or do you want me to bring you a bottle?'

Cynthia remembered the last time, ugh, she thought, it was miserable. However, the breast pump did come in useful on that last day in hospital back then.

'Could you please bring me a breast pump and some empty bottles?'

'Sure, I will include it along with your food.' Grazia departed to retrieve the requested items.

Buxby and Cynthia were alone with the baby. They kissed and felt most triumphant.

'Maybe we can have some of our own, eh?'

'Not yet, please,' she protested.

'There may be an easier way.'

'Not as much fun as the traditional.'

'Ah, I know, but hear me out. They could take some of your eggs, duplicate them, along with my wet biologicals, and we can have multiple children!'

The thought was as enlightening as it was horrid. Imagine more offspring of Cynthia Lear and that matched with an alien!

She made a face at him.

'Wha--well, I am just suggesting it so we can train them to fight against the humans,' he whispered.

She turned sharply to him. Now, that is not a bad idea. Train them to believe in the ideology of her conflict (along with grievances of the other aliens), 'Sounds good, but wouldn't they die in battle?'

'We can make so many of them, it would never matter. They can be incubated on the ship. Imagine an army of thousands upon thousands, just made from you and me.'

The prospect could work, in theory, however, it would take much planning and many sperm and eggs to accomplish this.

'When can we start?'

'Anytime you like, my dear,' he smiled, sniggering into her arms.

Cynthia had a more wicked plan, 'Could you morph again, please?'

'Why, don't you like me as I am?'

'Yes I do, but oh, please humour me.'

'Alright,' he relented as he morphed into the human form, this time, wearing a green tweed cheque suit and monochrome tie.

She shrieked and gave him a hug, 'You look like a little pie, you do!'

He smiled, not minding the changeover and loving the attention it gave him.

At that moment, Grazia arrived with the trolley. She noticed Buxby.

'My, you look different,' she said alarmingly.

'Well, it is a parlour trick I do with Cynthia. It makes her feel more at home.'

'Okay, um.....right. Here's the tea, breast pump and bottles. If you need anything else, let me know.'

'Thanks,' Buxby called as she departed.

Little Falby started to cry and it was obvious what was needed to be done. Cynthia used the breast pump, filled one of the bottle and gave it to Buxby to feed the babe. She then made some tea for both of them.

'It is so nice to be married again and now with a baby, it couldn't be any better,' she said, drinking her tea.

Buxby, still feeding Falby, stated, 'save for our planned invasion.'

She thought about this, and looked at him, 'What are we going to do with Falby?'

He sighed, 'Well, since we cannot be singing and dancing the number with this little one in tow, I think we should arrange for him to be looked after. I'll ask Spazio about it.'

'Let us be with him for the now. It has been awhile since I've experienced motherhood.'

'You've done this before, have you?'

'Yes. Once. More than enough,' she remembered, 'We will leave Falby on the Yakrey for now.'

They agreed to this and shook hands. Falby had finished the bottle and gave a burpy residue on Buxby's suit.

'Ah shit, you little….,' he put the baby in the basket and grabbed a nearby cloth to wipe himself with.

Cynthia hadn't laughed so hard in a long time.

'What's so funny?'

'You know what is so funny,' she sniggered, 'I wonder how Fal would have responded.'

'Oh, that big-head,' he said in frustration, 'Ah, that's got it.' He finished cleaning off the suit.

Cynthia still smiled and giggled.

Buxby warned, 'You just wait till he does that on a spanking-new dress of yours!'

She grinned wickedly, mimicking Fal again, 'Well, I would know to have a large size wipe cloth atop me so I do not suffer the residue!'

He promised, just as wickedly, 'Oooh.....when you are out of this room and we return to our own!'

They hugged each other and tucked Falby into his basket for a good kip.

As intended, the baby moved into Buxby and Cynthia's room with a cot placed next to the bed and a new dresser with baby bits provided. They were in the room discussing plans when Spazio sent a communiqué regarding the baby.

'I hope he's found somebody suitable,' Buxby said concerned.

He flipped a switch on the comm. unit.

Spazio, thankfully, had good news, 'I got a sister on Andros called Mattice, who is willing to look after your child. In fact, she is married to an Androsian, Dignitaaz, and they are more than willing to help. Sadly, they have no children of their own.'

Buxby and Cynthia gave each other a knowing look and kissed.

'Much obliged, Spazio, thanks,' Buxby said.

'You are most welcome,' the unit switched off.

Phew, that's that sorted, Buxby thought. He glanced at the little fellow and knew he would not see him growing up. It was a dismal reflection but he will try to visit with Cynthia when he can. However, with the coming declaration of war, it may become impossible.

Chapter XI

Little Falby was sent off the Andros to live with Spazio's sister. It was a sad occasion for Cynthia, who personally cared for her first son in his formative years, will now have no control over her Falby.   Yet, she felt it was best, as she was chosen by the Valastrons to assist them in the fight against the humans.

There was a council held regarding the planned invasion. Buxby, Cynthia, Spazio and a few others were present. They were searching the star charts to see where they can commence their attack on Earth.

Cynthia had ideas rolling in her head. Before the move to England, she had been living in horrific conditions in a far-away place. It was absolutely mental! She seethed on the matter quite often in her head, thinking what she can do to alleviate that personal hurt. She turned to see the huge juicy land mass located in the Western Hemisphere on the chart.

'Go to that area; start with the one in the middle,' she pointed enthusiastically, 'Ooooohhh......we can surround them at both ends and do a clean sweep throughout the world. Everyone is toast at that point, and any survivors shall be brought to ME!'

'As you wish, my lady,' Spazio murmured. He loved her spunk, 'tis such a shame he was not biologically compatible with her, as to......he thought to himself, but never mind, there is work to do as he focused more on the task.

Buxby offered, 'Cynthia and myself had previously discussed possibilities for mobilising an army using our bio-samples.'

Hmmmm, thought Spazio, this interspecies experimentation seems to be working.

'Possibly even duplicating our samples making enough beings to be able to fight,' Buxby continued.

'Yes, well, I think that would be perfect,' Spazio concurred.

Cynthia interjected, 'Aside from these, we could also use captured children from all over that planet. Speed up their life signs, give them a good psychological seeing to and man the ships! If they resist, well, we will know what to do with them.' She felt proud of her big-mouthed, freed-up attitude she acquired since the abduction.

'That is a very good idea, my dear girl,' Buxby said.

There was a scribe present, Ghespatche, who took all this down with a smile on his well-weathered face.

The anticipation inside Cynthia was getting more and more intense as the minutes ticked by. Buxby and Spazio felt her manic energy through their bio-computers and felt something needed to be done before she gets out of control and trips up again.

Buxby got up and went to Cynthia, 'Do you wish to leave for now? They can handle the rest.'

She protested, 'Huh? I was having so much FUN!'

'Yea, and THAT is what we are afraid of. You losing control, going into your relapses and phasing out on us. We cannot have that. You need a clear head for this. We need you.'

Cynthia contemplated.

'I do have an alternative to your pain, and I can morph again, if you like,' he whispered.

Cynthia shot up like a rocket, 'Right, when do we start?'

Buxby smiled at her and gave her a kiss. Spazio looked knowingly and handed the vials to Buxby.

'Go forth and do the maths,' he said.

'With pleasure,' Buxby winked.

Cynthia came up to Spazio and kissed the top of his head, 'Thank you,' she said and departed.

They left the others in the council room and returned to their quarters. Uffizio came into the room informing they were ready to launch the ships.

Spazio, in his thoughts, said aloud, 'Now we must wait. Do keep everything in order until the time comes.'

Uffizio exited the room to resume his shift.

They were to be cloaked ships, one-manned, small, yet effective little fighters. There were previous missions which proved to be fallible compared to what was being planned now. Some species tried to invade, yet, they lingered round various points of the globe as the cretins below kept guessing their every move. Other species just came down upon them by pell-mell surprise but it resulted in a messy job. No, this time it will be different….better, more efficient and....more glorious.

Meanwhilst, Buxby had completed his sample taking and sent the vials down through a chute to the nursery labs, where they will be duplicated and spread far and wide. There could be modifications done on them as well to allow for diversity and to make them first-rate pilots.

He returned to the bed where Cynthia laid and intertwined with her.   He had already morphed into the inoffensive and attractive counterpart which sent her up a tree.

She kissed him fervently and put her hand near his member.

'Oooh, Cynthia,' Buxby chuckled out a sigh as he put his hand over her respective and letting her enjoy the moment.

'Buxby,' she, too, sighed as the rapture continued.

Some moments passed between them.

'There are plenty more where that came from,' he whispered seductively, as his pleasure eased.

'Oh, so you can do multiples?'

'Yes,' he grinned, 'just like an Earth woman, such as yourself.'

'Former Earth woman, I might add!'

'Yes, well,' he scoffed, 'You know what I meant….and like.' He leant backward, eager in anticipation, relaxed among the pillows. He loved her very much and was very pleased to be able to enjoy her as much as she enjoyed him. True, he had an alien form, but the special morphing trick and ability to have multiples made life together much more interesting.

The joy was endless and they captured themselves good and hard as it came toward destiny. Shortly after, the groaning ceased and both were quite refreshed. They tarried in the room and thought yea, they had it good.

When the invasion was set, Cynthia thought of some verse to commemorate the moment and dictated it to Ghespatche:

'World Invasion'

You hover over me as the darkness covers the ground,
In my pretext, the darkness is a mere shadow of presence
For other worlds, it is literal darkness....
The inner city ships arrive so closely,
Their lights reflect the multitude of life aboard them.
Living movements below see life above.
Lacking full understanding of intention,
These movements flee toward elsewhere.
Problem is, where could they go?
Where can they be?
There is no place left for them to escape to,
No more combat planes nor missiles to fight back with…..
So what else is there to do, but to simply enjoy the final assault.
Our armies are strong enough to withstand a counterattack,
Cos their gear is made up of toyish parts from Taiwan.
Much is laid waste here, so far, you see.
The land below is scorched,
Hulks of debris are burning throughout the desert,
And the buildings ripple fire in a matter of moments.
This is really quite entertaining, thus, to say the least.
We are not such frightful beings,
Just the type who must prevail over others,
Whose ugliness is seen to in other ways.
So let us rid ourselves of these pompous asses,
There is no exception among them!

Their wreckage of molten metal, fires and breathing space
Does little enough to be desired.
Let us rejoice in the being of our own presence,
There is so much to be thankful for.
We see destruction of what they thought of as 'superior',
Which burns and bursts under heavy pressure.
And, as the celestial command beckons us,
We prepare for festal desires.

* * * * *

The humans captured and brought aboard the Yakrey were a motley bunch and quite dingy. They were cretins compared to the primacy of Cynthia Lear. No one could compare to her coolness, her edginess, tenacity and besides, the aliens chose to abduct 'her' a long time ago. Everyone else back then were so wrapped up in their own affairs, and living their lives in complete mediocrity. She had no affairs to speak of, in any direction, save for the one in her imagination, which the Valastrons were eager to explore.

Their wait had come to fruition as a one way mirror was set up for the scientific panel put together to witness the reproof (nay, ranting). They knew Cynthia had A LOT on her mind. She was desperate to have a piece of the action and Spazio allowed her to let loose amongst them. It was to be 'her' time.

Cynthia remained alone, without comfort, in order for her rage to penetrate into her consciousness. She hoped it would not be a vicious confrontation; alas, the cretins do defend themselves well. Sometimes they are armed to the teeth with a quick quip that Cynthia was never able to master, due to her condition.

She hated them bitterly for this, with a passion and with a vengeance. Her blood soaked through every pore over the matter and she (honestly) could not do anything to stop them. It was a form of helplessness that delayed her, but not anymore. They shall be the prey now, she thought, as they became more stupid as they evolved.....

...and stupid they were, for they had weaknesses for creature comforts, and did not care about the cleanliness of the society they lived in. They were surely not housed with an intellectual acumen which matched her own (on a good day).

She was such a lovable creature, a lonely thought process in the sky that Mankind decided to shelve and forever ignore. Well, let us see them do some shelving now!

She plundered her thoughts for some fab vignettes to persecute them with.   She encircled them like a rabid dog on the prowl, looking carefully at each tatty individual.   Her drool was thirstily trickling down the edges of her mouth, caressing the outer flesh as a comfort. She boldly thought things which were ne'er before seen to in her lifetime.

There was a thick tension in the air that could be cut with a blade and she was eager to pounce. It built up gradually and it caused a delicate sensation in her mind. It also sent waves rippling inside her like a forced energy screaming to get out. She resolved within herself to speak. It was a vicious rant and she did not expect anything special in return, just (hopeful) satisfaction and blood....'their' blood!

'So you think you are so much better than me. You think just because I had a difficult start in life, being tried AS A CHILD, you choose to either exploit it, or ignore it......and you all chose to turn away whilst I was held in vexation and you lot were ruining a universe, nay, a mere child, such as me?

'It was not like I had any decisions to make....I was a baby.......
I HAD NO CHOICES.   HOW DARE YOU JUDGE ME BY THAT FAMILY AND THEIR FOUL MISPLACED RELIGION??!!!!! Those responsible for me had been destroyed.....BY ME!   Now 'I' have made a choice, TO KILL THE LOT OF YOU AND ALL OF YOUR KIND!!!!'

She paused, laughed cruelly at them, continuing to gloat, 'A child, oh, she is just a child, she would have been institutionalised if not for us, they once said to me.....well, that is bollocks AND I WILL NOT BE SILENCED!   I WILL

HAVE MY SAY IN THE MATTER and for those who refuse or choose not to listen will pay for their lack of discernment!

'YOU are all hypocrites!   Firstly, on the one hand, you love a bit of rebellion.   Then you laud the new order that cometh afterward and go all conservative.   HOW DID YOU EVER LEARN HOW TO BE CONSERVATIVE????

'YOU think you can rebel against me or the aliens, YOU ALL GOT ANOTHER THING COMING.   YOU WILL NEVER EVER GET AWAY FROM ALIEN RETRIBUTION AND DOMINION OVER HUMANITY!'

She stopped to breathe.   The cretins looked quizzically at one another in complete befuddlement.

One of them piped up, 'Are you sure you have the right group?'

Cynthia screamed, 'SHUT THE FUCK UP!'

Another added, 'Where are our children?'

'THEY ARE FIGHTING ON OUR SIDE AGAINST YOU,' Cynthia pointed her gloved finger back at the prisoners.

Most of them murmured, 'What is she, nuts?   We did not do any of this shit.'

'TO HELL YOU DID NOT!   I make YOU ALL solely responsible,' she loved having the final word over them.

Meanwhilst, Spazio, the committee, and Buxby all watched behind the mirror, watching intently, eating popcorn and letting Cynthia become that Hail Glorianna she craved to be.

'This will make for excellent research,' one of the committee members, Chechinno, stated.

'Research be damned, this girl is in real pain. It is such a pity they were so mean to her. Little wonder she is so vengeful; she feels they are responsible for her problems,' Spazio said in a serious and sympathetic tone.

'Yea, I know,' Buxby said, reflecting, 'She IS a beautiful person underneath, once you get to know her. Not many people did, however, due to their misunderstanding of that condition of hers. She has every right to bring them to task here. They probably ARE responsible for standing idle in this matter. She will not let this one go, really.' He then began to weep a little whilst in his reflective state.

Spazio concurred, eating his popcorn and making a mess of it because the tentacles did not grip very well. A lackey had assisted him forthwith.

Cynthia continued her rave against the cretins, 'I spent THIRTY-FOUR years being in a place one did not want to be in, dying spiritually. I HATED where I was born, as I was living a lie, dwelling within a dungeon I DID NOT BELONG IN AND SHOULD HAVE NEVER BEEN PUT INTO IN THE FIRST PLACE!!!

'YOU TOOK AWAY MY FATHER, MY TRUE HERITAGE AND RELIGION, AND MY COUNTRY. YOU CAST OUT MY POOR FATHER ON RELIGIOUS GROUNDS TO DIE ON THE STREET WITHOUT SUPPORT AND HE LOST EVERYTHING, INCLUDING ME! IN ADDITION, YOU RUINED ME IN THE PROCESS; I AM COMPLETELY RUINED AND IT IS ALL YOUR FAULT!'

With that, she located a firing weapon nearby and aimed it at a random bunch. They took a direct hit and experienced a several-minute-horrific-convulsion which ended very messily. She grinned insanely and wanted to target another group.

However, she paused again, making certain she was right. Oh, of course, hell-yes, she was right! She gathered up more firepower in her gut (instead of in the weapon), thinking, oooooh, what to say next. Her eyes glanced at her hands, and realising the final crux of her pain, she released her inner dragon.

'AND FOR THIS,' she removed the dark gloves, revealing the extent of her small hands, the deformity being all-to-obvious at the tips, 'For this I bled and suffered, to the death. I did not take that medication which caused this imperfection.

'Yet, YOU ALL had taunted me and perpetuated the pain I had felt and still do (thank you very much!), as I am not as beautiful nor as fully formed. You will all DIE for your disobedience towards me and will pay a further price for MAKING ME LIVE LIKE THIS!!!!!!!'

She heard another voice in the crowd, who was a bit too optimistic, 'But we did not do this to you, any of it. Look, set us free already....'

The rage became blindly monstrous, building like a furnace about to explode. She repeated the words she specially used for the ex-family:

'YOU ALL DID THIS TO ME AND IT IS ALL YOUR FAULT!!!!!!!!!!!!!!!! YOU CAUSED INADEQUACY, INSECURITY AND MALIGNANCE TO MY EXISTENCE. YOU ALLOWED THIS SHIT TO HAPPEN TO ME!!

'I WILL TAKE BACK WHAT IS MINE AND YOU CAN ALL GO TO HELL FOR WHAT YOU DID TO ME. YOU ARE ALL TO BLAME—THERE IS NO FORGIVENESS IN THIS CASE. MY REVENGE WILL NEVER BE COMPLETE UNLESS YOU ALL DIE NOW!!!'

She exited the room and found that same red button beside the door used to extinguish a group of people she once knew long ago.

This time, her dearest Fal was no longer with her. She will have to do it alone. She deeply lamented this fact and it nearly broke her, yet alas, she could not show this as a weakness for fear of rebellion amongst the cretins. She then regained some more self-assurance and her internal fire burned as if on a steam train, spewing its vapours through its chimney-like shaft up into the air, and the train itself going on a one way track to oblivion.

She used her energy to do the deed and upon impact, her freedom was released. The screams therein were most satisfying and she smiled to herself, saying aloud, 'Christ, I did it! I aired my grievances and destroyed the mother-fuckers who perpetuated them.' However, there were so many more out there, and she realised she alone would have to confront them. Her mood then turned sober after thinking about that.

She walked over to Buxby who was waiting for her in the corridor.

'My darling, did those nasty people hurt you?' He embraced her as she nodded yes to his question.

She sniffed, 'Their presence ALWAYS hurts me. They distract me. They destroy me. I want them expunged out of the universe. I need a break; it is too much.'

She was reminded of the time she confronted her family, and Fal had been there to comfort her.

She tripped over another landmine which triggered back to that fateful confrontation and recollected:

'I remember facing the family in the room and confronting them over the evils they did to me. I then told them the truth about their so-called Jewish heritage: somewhere in the Germanic regions of Europe (possibly the German/Polish border), there were two underage children who fell in love. They were from different classes of being and thus, their parents would never allow them to hook up. Both families had a Christian background, possibly Orthodox or more likely, Catholic. These lovesick children decided to flee to be together.

'They were on the run, but as they neared the age of consent, they were unable to find a Christian church that would marry them. Under parochial rules, residency is required to be married in a respective church in an area. Residency in any area was not an option for these two runaways nor did they want their marriage to be reported back to their parents.

'So they ended up going to a Jewish temple to do the deed, as a temple is willing to bend over backwards for someone as they pay for the service! Thus, they found a place to go to get married and had 'fraudulently' entered the Jewish community and assumed an identity therefrom. They had remained on the run until they hitched a boat to depart Europe for good, and go to America for permanent settlement.

'IN OTHER WORDS, THERE WAS NO PROPER CON-VERSION TO THAT RELIGION NOR WAS THERE A LINK TO THE ORIGINAL TWELVE TRIBES AS BIBLICALLY DESCRIBED! There is no record of a conversion, just an ASSUMPTION OF A NEW IDENTITY. There is no way one can trace THIS family at all, whereas, other Jewish families CAN be traced!'

She further recalled: 'I told this to the family and informed them of committing religious and identity fraud and trying to encapsulate me to the crime therein. I also informed them that THEY WERE THE SOLE CAUSE of my father's downfall, due to his religion conflicting with theirs. They did not admit nor deny as they did not speak in response. It pissed me off, right royal, and I stormed out of the room to execute them, saying:

'YOU ALL DID THIS TO ME AND IT IS ALL YOUR FAULT!!!!!!!!!!!!!!!!! YOU CAUSED INADEQUACY, INSECURITY AND MALIGNANCE TO MY EXISTENCE. YOU ALLOWED THIS SHIT TO HAPPEN TO **ME!! 'I WILL TAKE BACK WHAT IS MINE AND YOU CAN ALL GO TO HELL FOR WHAT YOU DID TO ME.** YOU ARE ALL TO BLAME—THERE IS NO FORGIVENESS IN THIS CASE. MY REVENGE WILL NEVER BE COMPLETE UNLESS YOU ALL DIE NOW!!!!!!!!!!!'

Cynthia's mind revolved around her and realised she was with Buxby this time and not with Fal.

She squeezed Buxby tight. 'Kiss me,' she begged. Buxby met her lips with a passion and love that made up for the potent psyche-session the Valastrons set up for her as well as the horrible relapse that just occurred.

'Uh, Buxby,' Spazio called out.

'Yes?'

He whinged, slithering towards them, 'Can you please do that somewhere else?? We will round up some more for you to take liberties with later on, yeah?'

So matter-of-fact, she thought, but the call of Buxby was sorely needed as they walked to their quarters.

The reprobations continued and, as more cretins were captured, more were being killed in the assaults. The devastation was plentiful in this most trying of times for them. However, some of the 'lucky' ones found ingenious ways to leave the old world and make it out on small freighter ships to find a new one, taking with them as much of their hand-me-down cultures they could find, which also included DNA samples of lost non-human life, to be recreated at a later date elsewhere.

Most of the children were taken away to be used as pilots to man the alien fighting ships. They were young enough to be converted to the Cause, and although they missed their families, this triviality was wiped out during training. They since stood ready to continue in the struggle for intergalactic domination.

The fighting continued on Earth, but the planet was nearing the end of its viability. Fumes released by toxic chemicals choked up the atmosphere, all buildings, great and small, were devastated within their own rubble. The parks, once green and flowery, had displayed a muddy-grey, barbed-wire look.

Nothing was spared, save the overused landfills which the Valastrons put to better use. They took all the waste matter to convert into weaponry and, as there was more waste than common sense, there had been a plentiful supply.

After many emotional outbursts during the reprobations, Cynthia Lear was failing fast. It was all taking its toll on her and she was aging rapidly. The years were catching up with her, as she was already living well beyond her time. The relapses were also getting worse, especially after confronting the prisoners. It was very difficult to experience the pain again, built up for years on end, as it was being used against the cretinous horde she kept seeing before her. The harsh responses over the years seriously impaired her soul as she felt the negative echoes of her past reverberate within.

The initial experience was an uphill battle and can only be classed as abuse, involving mental cruelty and anguish. She was grossly underestimated, overprotected and treated like a child up until she left home (and beyond).

As a result, she lacked self-respect, and now she was going to take back the respect she was denied, by violently punishing all who were captured in the conflict.

During one of the reprobation spells, she collapsed due to over-exhaustion, during one of her passionate outbursts.

An orderly, Domytaz, was sent for her and she was taken to a room to be looked after by Cosimos, who consulted with Fal a long time ago regarding his cancer. Now he has the difficult task of dealing with his wife, or Buxby's wife, in this case. He assisted her when she underwent a nervous breakdown.

Vexation consumed her mind and she could not think straight, if at all. The memories remained, and unfortunately, they were the bad ones, which drained her slowly but surely.

She wept profusely, as she was veering toward finality with endless resentment in her heart. However, any remaining compassion and love she did have was saved for Buxby and the children.

Buxby was sent for and he entered on arrival. She looked ever so fragile and even more precious to him. He came up to her to give her a hug and remained with her for company. He even assumed his human morph of the 'tweed suit and tie wearing' gentleman, as he did before, just as a special comforter for her.

She queried weakly, 'How goes it, Bux?'

'Never mind that, my love, how are you?'

'Duh! What do you think?'

He looked her over. 'Shattered,' he said.

'Worse, actually.'

'Oh my love, this has taken so much out of you, hasn't it?'

'Verily, it hath,' she said, trying to invoke Fal's spirit.

'You rest now,' he patted her hand.

She then thought about her son, 'It has been awhile since we heard about Falby.'

'I know. He is safe on Andros and growing up well. He's nearly of age now, in fact. I would love to see him, if we can.'

'Maybe now is the time,' she said, 'I think I am dying.'

Buxby's face changed, 'No, you cannot. We need you.'

'My life span has well exceeded its natural limits, Buxby, I do not believe I can go on much longer.'

'You are not giving up? Not after what WE have been through together?!'

'I may have to. Not the fight, of course. Let that continue to show the cretins who's boss. No, my angel, I am getting exhausted.'

He questioned her with a look of conscience, 'You are not regretting all this, are you?'

She mustered enough energy to shout, 'Hell no, I do NOT regret what has transpired!' Then, she laid back down, softly, 'Yet, I feel I have done my bit. What more can I do??'

'Do you feel you have achieved your goal? Your destiny?'

'I fear my destiny may be unpleasant.'

'Oh fie, that is cretin nonsense! You do not believe in all that. You had every right to do what you did and you helped us regain control of our bit of the universe. It is getting frighteningly smaller, you know.'

'That reminds me of something I remember being said about Earth ages ago before the abduction. They chose their path and my path, too, was chosen; but my path overran theirs.'

'Indeed it did, my dear.'

'Did the ranting scare or upset you?'

'It helped me get to know you better in a roundabout way, as you are most unorthodox. To us aliens it did not cause upset, but it was fascinating to see how much negativity a human can bear. It was an interesting venture into your mind, thus the reason why you were taken.'

'I see,' she sighed, realising the significance of her abduction.

'I really do want to see Falby.'

'Doubt he'll remember us. It would be nice to see him again but it may be awkward.'

'Time will determine that. I will see if I can get it arranged. At least our samples made for the great pilots who fly our vessels.....'

'.......to supplement the cretin's children,' she finished his sentence.

Buxby sighed, wondering if it were possible to get one of the samples to be able to have for his own, instead of the destiny of a fighter pilot. However, he looked at Cynthia and thought again. Piloting may be a better option....she does look worse for wear and motherhood may not be good at this time, possibly at any time. He would have to consult Spazio about it. After a time, he said his goodbye to her and left the room.

Spazio and Buxby discussed the matters at hand.

'I do not see an issue. After all, it is your bio samples; it will be just one less to man the ships,' Spazio said.

'Unless you get an Earth child to man the ship in its stead,' Buxby advised.

'True, but they are starting to dwindle in numbers, which is why we asked for your samples. I will set one of them aside for you. Once it takes form, it will be in the cot in your room.'

'Right. I also need to get in touch with Falby. Cynthia is not at all well, but still herself and I want him to see her before she.....,' he lingered on the thought.

'Yes. I know and I will arrange for him to meet you. He will have to come here as she is too ill to travel,' Spazio agreed.

'I had not seen him since his infancy.'

'I think it is time you met properly.'

Buxby thanked Spazio and left the room. He thought about recent events, but they went beyond his Androsian mentality, as he once had a simple life.

Now his life consisted of two children, one he had not even seen for a long time, another who has just been birthed (artificially) to be separated as his own, and a wife who has more needs than he could ever have imagined. Yet, he kept his composure because Cynthia needed him most.

Cynthia was made stable for the time being, but no longer involved with the War. Since her breakdown, it was decided that any prisoners taken were to be vaporised immediately, without the verbal flogging. The Valastrons felt it best this way. They had enough examples to research from anyway.

After all the years in space, she has never been more happier and satisfied with the people she now resided with, including her time with Fal. She was still able bodied, but her mind was going.

The continual relapses she suffered made her further aggrieved about her past, and the thirst for revenge became insatiable.

Although she gave the idea to invade the Earth which started the current War, it was human folly that caused the initial friction with the Valastrons. Neighbouring races assisted them and word got round about Cynthia's personal vendetta. The aliens thought that if humanity was willing to forego one of their own, then what are they worth in the universe?

Shortly after, it was arranged that Falby would take a break from his studies at university and visit Cynthia and Buxby on the Yakrey. He walked into the room with Buxby and saw the cot that he once laid in, now occupied by one called Buxamby, who was sleeping quietly. The new child had grown into a normal looking humanoid, but had some alien variation thrown in. He was of a pinkish colour with a garment of pink, white and yellow all swirling round the fabric.

'Cynthia,' Buxby called.

'Yeah?' she answered, wobbly.

'Look who I have brought.'

She looked up at the new arrival. Her eyes stood wide open, 'Fal?'

He lent to kiss her, 'It's Falby, actually. How are you?'

She regained some strength, her feisty self peering through, 'Getting old, going downhill, and totally wasted, but you look a right treat, just like your father.'

Buxby turned to him, 'So how is school for you?'

'Great. I am studying a wide range of topics, I do not know which to get into yet.'

'Hopefully, not a girl,' Buxby joked.

They laughed and continued chatting. Some refreshments were made and they tucked in.

Falby contemplated his next question, as it was slightly delicate a matter to pursue.

'What was my father like?'

Buxby knew this would come up, 'He was an amazing being with an elegant manner and poetic soul.'

'He was an actor, right?'

'Well, yes, but he would disagree. He would call it 'being a thespian.' '

'Was he really abducted?'

'Yes and so was your mother, though not at the same time,' Buxby turned to him, 'You know, he really wanted to be there when you were born, but he died too soon.'

'Of what?'

'Cancer.'

'Ugh,' Falby made a face.

'Yeah, that is what I thought, too.'

Falby looked at his mother and asked, 'What was it like to be abducted?'

Cynthia tried to answer as best she could, recalling, 'I was living my life as it was at the time, and next thing one knows is being taken away from that life to this,' she waved her hand at her surroundings, 'and the experimentations done weren't too bad, but annoying all the same.'

'They did not probe your......,' Falby stopped, as he knew better than to ask such a question.

'No, they were more interested in my mind rather than body. I think they had a field day with it, actually. It took them long enough!'

Buxby took Falby aside and explained to him more about his mother's previous life, i.e., the irresponsible upbringing, Asperger's, and the current War.

'So, did she start it?'

'No,' Buxby said, 'the humans had an incident with the Valastrons which turned unfortunate and they needed your mother to tip the balance against Man. If they cannot care for their own kind, then what is their value among us? There was already a small conflict and she had the idea to invade the Earth itself. Now, we are at War.'

Falby tried to take it all in as best he could and asked, 'Is there anything I can do to help?'

'Well, you may have human DNA, but you were raised by aliens. Where does your heart lie, then, hmmm? What lies inside your mind?'

Falby looked at his mother who was laying on the bed, in a slight stupor, and said, 'I am very sorry you were put through all this and I will help in the struggle, whatever it takes.' He held her hand, and she thought, God, even his hands are like Fal's! It might well have been Fal, if not for the youthfulness of the fellow.

She gave him a hug, 'Thank you. I appreciate your thoughts and intentions and will remember them, but please, do not give up your studies on my account. Live and learn. My way is nearly ended...I love you…I...,' she trailed off.

She found it difficult to understand the depth of one's caring as she was never given the same in her early years. She could not believe her son would just 'drop everything' for the sake of the Cause.

She then wept in his arms, holding him in a similar way she did with Fal. This confused Falby, but he held her for a time.

'Here, let me,' Buxby offered, cradling her, 'Go back to your studies, lad, I will take it from here. It was very nice to see you at last.'

'Good to see you too, fath---,' he stopped.

'You may call me father, if you wish. Technically I am your stepfather, because Spazio's sister and husband did not adopt you. They were merely looking after you.'

'Thank you,' Falby gave him a hug.

'Do be in touch,' Buxby called, as he departed the room.

'Will do,' he called back and waved.

God, what a lovely boy he's become, Buxby thought. Fal would have certainly been proud of his little seedling. He held Cynthia, who had stopped crying and was just dozing away in his arms.

'Cynthia, you okay?'

She stirred, slightly awake, groaning.

'That was a most pleasant visit.'

'Yes it was. Inquisitive little shit, though,' she frowned.

'Well, he did ask pertinent questions. All kids do that.'

'I know, I remember. Thank you for letting me see Falby. It was all worthwhile.'

'Yea, I wanted to see him too,' Buxby pondered as the baby awoke and started crying.

Buxby walked over to the cot and cooed, 'Oh now, what does my little love want?'

Buxamby retorted, 'You know damn well what I want.'

Cynthia looked at the child, 'He speaketh,' she cried, aloud, in shock, nearly fainting.

'That's an Androsian for you. We develop much more quicker than our human counterparts. It was annoying to have to wait for those human children to grow and be trained as pilots, I can assure you!'

'Well, he is half Androsian, so I can see where the intelligence comes from.'

Buxby gave the bottle to Buxamby, who took it and began his feeding.

Cynthia had another relapse and was dreaming again, thinking of her son and Fal. However, this time it was different.

'God, he's just like........,' she nodded off into darkness.

She had a dream. Fal had called out to her.

'My love,' he stretched out his arms.

Cynthia looked round, and in her quizzical nature could not believe who she saw.

'Fal? I just,' she turned, confused, continuing, 'Um....didn't I just see.....?'

'Our son, yes, you did,' Fal said, 'He is a wonderful boy and you did well for him. I also congratulate you on little Buxamby. What a spirited child he is! Reminds me of someone I once knew,' he said, winking at her.

'Well, Falby was looked after on Andros and Buxamby was one of the samples Buxby and I kept for ourselves, whilst....'

'Yea, you invaded the Earth, didn't you?'

'I, uh, had to. I felt it was my duty to do so!'

'And you went against humanity?'

'After the way I was treated, they deserved no better!'

'Ah well, 'tis not for me to decide that. Come my love, take my hand. Your time has passed. We must away.'

Cynthia exhaled deeply and took his hand, very tightly. 'Twas her end, alas, as she felt her spirit roam free. At last, the pain has left the system.

She lay dead, and Buxamby saw what happened.

'Umm...father,' he said, unsure of the situation.

Buxby answered, reading a paper, 'What is it child?'

The baby looked at her, 'I think she has passed and this bottle's past it,' he tossed the bottle Buxby's way.

It missed the intended target and fell on the floor. He let out a small burp, but it was contained within. He knew better than to expel personal matter on one's parent, unlike the stupid human babies, he thought.

Buxby got up to see, 'Gosh, you're right, little Bux,'

'What are you going to do?'

'You are to go to a nanny, as there is the deceased to deal with.'

Buxamby protested, 'Can't the grown up aliens deal with her?'

'As her husband, my son, I think Cynthia would want, nay, demand, me to deal with her arrangements,' Buxby answered.

Oh boy, always busy busy busy, Buxamby thought, I want to play with Daddy! He pouted for a few minutes.

A Valastron aide, Benelauna, was called into the room and examined Cynthia to confirm her death. It was noted in the logbook. Buxby did not know what came over him, but a crash of emotion had hit him quite hard.

'At last she is at peace, I hope,' he prayed.

Buxamby spoke up, 'Why? Wasn't she happy?'

'No, not really little one,' Buxby lamented.

'I would have loved to perk her up.'

'I do not think it would have worked, my boy, she carried enough burdens as it is. She could not see past them nor get past them. From what I was told, she was treated quite horribly back in the day,' Buxby's eye shed a tear, 'Maybe someday I will tell you more about her.'

Buxamby retorted, 'As long as it doesn't come down as a scary night time story!'

Benelauna came over, 'I am sorry for your loss, but I need to prepare her for burial now.'

'We shall have a funeral similar to Fal's, on Andros, where she will be laid with him,' Buxby decided.

'I think that would be very fitting, sir,' Benelauna commented as he wheeled the body out of the room.

Buxamby asked, 'Where's she going?'

'To where Fal lies buried, well, at least his ashes anyway.'

'Who's Fal?'

'Her previous husband before me. He died awhile ago,' he turned to his son, 'Once the formalities are complete, we'll go back to Andros permanently and live together. Perhaps Falby can join us.'

'Who's Falby?'

'Fal's child with your mother, Cynthia.'

'Ah. That lady that got carted away.'

'Yes, that is right.'

Buxby stood in the room and tucked his little one in the cot to say good night. Now, there was much to do.

Chapter XII

Cynthia Lear's funeral was held where Fal's was. Buxby, his brother Harry and Harry's band mate Willec, the baby Buxamby, Falby with his guardians Mattice and Dignitaaz, Spazio and Uffizio were in attendance. She was fondly remembered by the aliens for her assistance in the recent conflict with the humans and how she gained their understanding in respect to her challenging condition.

Her sufferings were duly noted and she was declared expunged from any wrongdoing, as her early life was not her making. Mankind had it coming to them and it had to take such a girl to achieve this. Her body was taken to the crematorium and her ashes laid in a special plot next to her second husband Fal.

Now they lay together, Buxby thought, and that should satisfy her eternally.

Everyone met afterwards at a local restaurant where many toasts, prayers and thoughts went up in Cynthia's honour.

Buxby toasted first, 'To hell with what the humans say, we'll take her any day!'

Willec agreed, 'Hear Hear! May she find the lost happiness she deserved.'

'The most interesting specimen ever tried out,' contributed Spazio.

Falby and Buxamby cried, 'We'll miss you Mummy!'

Once the toasting had ended, private conversations ensued amongst the guests.

'She was very hard work,' Harry noted.

'She certainly was,' Buxby concurred, 'but it was worth it. I did owe my friend a favour, you know.' He tried to smile, but found it difficult.

'Your progeny is quite the lad,' Harry continued, admiring little Buxamby.

Buxby looked in Buxamby's direction, 'Yes, he has something there. I think he's got to have inherited my wife's attitude.'

'An attitude to carry on the War?'

'Possibly.'

Buxamby piped up, 'You got that right and when I grow up, I want to be a fighter pilot and kick human butt! That's one for my mother, you fiends!'

'Buxamby,' Buxby scolded, 'now let us not get hot under that collar. Leave your mother out of it and let her rest in peace.'

He then remembered the first meeting with Cynthia, with Fal by her side, and recalled how lively and highly strung she was then. Oh God, he thought, not another Cynthia, and one with alien blood too! He may have admired her spunk then, but to live with it and see it transmitted anew was a bit too much for him.

Falby had an idea to alleviate Buxby's irritation.

'How about I take little Bux to the park, you know, get him off your hands and let him run about for a bit,' he offered.

'Good show, Falby,' Buxby thankful for the suggestion, 'It will do him good.' He admired his stepson's initiative.

Falby put Buxamby into his buggy and wheeled him out to the park.

Buxamby was very excited. 'Let's go on the swings!'

'Okay, little guy, we'll do that.'

'By the way,' Buxamby said, 'we may be coming back to Andros forever.'

'Oh?' Falby said, surprised.

'Yeah, Dad told me. We don't need to live in space anymore. We were hoping you can join us and we can live as a family.'

'Well, I had not made any plans yet regarding life after my education. I'll have a think about it and discuss it with my guardians and see what they say. I am old enough to live on my own, but it would be difficult. The fact you and Buxby consider me family will make things easier.'

They entered the park and Buxamby was put in the caged infant swings.

He shouted, 'Wwweeeeee! It's like flying a ship, Falby!'

'Looks like it, though I would not know.'

'I want to be a pilot.'

'Yeah, you told us at the restaurant, big mouth. You're getting some preliminary training right here.'

They had a play for a few moments when Buxby, Harry and Willec found the park where the children were. The other guests have already departed.

'How are you doing with little Bux?' Buxby asked Falby.

'He's okay, once you get to know him and what he really wants to do.'

'I know. Play, play play!' Buxamby shouted louder.

'Well, he is just a baby,' Willec commented aloud.

Falby retorted, 'Yeah, a baby with Mother's attitude!'

Buxby gave him a rebuking look, 'Now don't you start. Your mother was a wonderful, if not unusual, person. She would have liked you if....well, never mind.'

Willec went up to little Buxamby, 'How's my little fighter doing?'

'Great!' he answered, then wondered who in heaven he was talking to, 'Uh, who are you?'

'I am Willec, a friend of your late mother.'

'Ah. She must have had many friends by the look of it.'

'Well, we only just met. I did not know her very well, other than what Buxby told me.'

'I heard you're in a band.'

'Yes, The Lattice Wyndows.'

'Interesting name. What are lattice windows?'

'A leading effect on a window to give it a criss-cross design.'

'Ah. Can someone change me?'

Willec ran to get Buxby, who sorted Buxamby out in a nearby changing room.

Buxamby enquired as he and Buxby exited the room, 'When can I get my pilot's licence?'

The adults present all laughed, shaking their heads at the tenacity of the little fellow.

'Let us see when that time comes. We'll go to my place now,' Buxby said.

Falby excused himself, 'I will join you later.'

'Right,' Buxby waved him off, still carrying Buxamby to his buggy. They went to his place together with Harry and Willec.

Willec winked at the child, 'He definitely reminds me of Cynthia when I met her at the Regalburgh.'

'Got the same sized mouth, that's for sure,' Buxby commented.

'I hope he is not as needy,' Harry interjected.

'Nah, it shan't be like that,' Buxby told him, 'I know he will have a happy life and get to do what he wants to do, even if it means training as a fighter pilot to kick human butt, as he puts it. All our samples have been bred to become pilots anyway, so it is quite natural for him to want it. He does not seem to be one who would want from others, except maybe obedience.'

Willec sounded surprised, 'You had samples done on yourselves?'

'Why, yes, we did to help with the War effort.'

'There must be nursery labs filled with you and Cynthia in millions of test tubes,' Harry marvelled.

'Could be more,' Buxby reflected, remembering how much fun it was getting those samples.

Willec pondered, 'Is Buxamby going after the humans in the way Cynthia did?'

'Don't know. Let's get him into training and go from there,' Buxby hoped.

'What an eager child,' Willec spoke with high regard.

'Yes. Time will tell.'

* * * * *

Many years passed. The war continued its gruelling turn with humans and aliens fighting for domination throwing rubbish at each other, by converting the waste into weapons.

The humans who survived the Earth attacks had found a home on a distant world they called Novaterra, making their homes in a tract of land the size of Eurasia and Russia. The land mass had little bodies of water within itself, so as to promote coastal regions. The rest of Novaterra, like Earth, had accumulations of water surrounding its globe. The land was in the middle of it, like one's own island.

The population was sparse, but with survivalist instincts dwelling in each person, they found clever ways to carry on living.

The earlier divisions of race were no longer applicable due to the survivors breeding with one another and starting families together. Thus, humanity now consisted of **one single race**, a hodgepodge of mixed racial (and alien, in some cases) bloodlines and DNA that ensured diversity and continuity.

They even thought of better ways to handle waste products and toss-away matter. A rubbish haulier company was set up by previous Dukes of Clearance to handle it all, with the current Duke still remaining in charge of it. There were many factories built to sort out these precious materials needed to save them. The aliens (and Valastrons in particular) earlier have been converting confiscated human rubbish into their own weaponry, so now, the humans began collecting their waste more aggressively to use it for the same purpose against the aliens.

Unfortunately, due to the hasty departure from the dying Earth, human advancement was not forthcoming. In fact, it took a few centuries knock-back, like it was when ancient Rome fell. So, whatever technology had been salvaged from Earth, was what Man needed to work with on Novaterra, even if it seemed backward by current standards.

Falby was now an engineering researcher, developing ideas for weapon improvements and finding alternative ways of using the recycled human rubbish. Buxamby was a pilot, just as he wished to be. He had flown into the fray of battle, many a time, not worse for wear, and loved every moment of it.

They stayed close as brothers could, but they could not be farther apart in personality. Falby was more refined and collected, but he sided with the aliens despite his human origins. Buxamby exhibited a more rigorous nature and picked up the torch Cynthia once bore, but without her complications.

They both felt it was their duty to take part in the struggle against the humans. After all, they believed it was Mankind that made their mother's life hell.

* * * * *

Several centuries onward, there seemed to be no end to the War. One of the humans, a fellow called Hadralica Gades, was due to sign a peace treaty with the alien races. His ship fell under attack by a belligerent bug-like alien species, the Saturninons, who acted in Lear's name. They loved conflict and found it fascinating a human was willing to go against the grain of her own kind to encourage a most fruitful harvest. So the ship was destroyed and the War carried on.

Most of the people originally involved in the Conflict were long dead. Some were replaced, some were forgotten. Others like Falby and Buxamby had descendants carrying on the struggle. Falby's descendants eventually joined the humans on the newly established Novaterra. They also reverted the family name to Woodes-Hastings, one out of several named lineages found among records salvaged before leaving Earth. They felt this name sounded cooler, more human and they just simply preferred it.

Buxamby's descendants all had the Learian attitude toward life, but they had cooled down in recent generations. Their family name was also changed and they chose Buckingham, due the name being similar to the alien Bux. It sounded more human as these 'cooled down' generations, too, cast their lot with humanity. The ongoing duplicated samples of Cynthia and Buxby were still going strong, as the fighter pilots they were trained to be, continuing the fight against the humans.

Chapter XIII

(Circa AD 3000)

It had been nearly a millennium since the invasion of Earth. Now, the Earth was experiencing an awakening, an acute sense of self-awareness it never felt before.

It said to itself, 'Gosh, what do I feel around me?' The Earth felt a heavy substance shelled round it and cried, 'Oooh, this pinches, oowww!'

It looked around itself, its charred remains being all too obvious around it. The heat of the endless fires twisted into its soul which was felt throughout its global body.

It shrieked, 'What is this concrete straitjacket doing to me? Oh, how it is so choking me. God, I need to get out of this!'

A ray of light from above shone down and spoke unto the crying world, 'Well, why don't you bloody well do something about it, then? Renew thyself!'

'Why....how?' the Earth stuttered in shock, looking inward at its proverbial mirror, and struggled to think. Then it realised a possibility, 'I used to go through tectonic plate shifts causing mass earthquakes and devastation all about. The humans had so hated this as I would ruin their livelihoods, homes, and even their lives, yet there are no humans or any creature here to speak of....wait a minute.....yes, that's got it!'

The Earth then stated aloud, 'I will fight and take back what is MINE and then some. I have existed for so many years, the wretchedness of creatures has sustained me not; I have now returned to seek my revenge! Those bastard humans had not ruined me yet.....'

It frantically searched for its old continental plates which formed the epic land masses humanity once lived upon. Amongst its ruins, there was a titanic mass which the Earth decided to have submerged instead, as it was the most damaged of all. The land had gradually sunk under the two oceans which surrounded it. Once the cleansing had been completed, the oceans backed away slowly, revealing the land mass made anew.

Then, once the plates have been located, the Earth done itself a service and a great friction occurred, one which indubitably would have broken every Richter scale worldwide. Everything left on the Earth's surface was shaken up, and crumbled beyond recognition.

As Earth carried on its cleansing process, it found some ruins lying around and decided to leave them upon its surface. The few abbeys, churches, a theatre or two, and a few odd railway stations were left alone as these bits looked very homely, with all the greenery taking shape around them. It provided Earth's face with some character and quirkiness to which a barren landscape could not aspire.

Some time had passed as the artificial residue had left the exterior. The Earth sighed, 'Ah, that's better.' The shell that once encompassed its fragile body had quickly crumbled to plain dust, so easily blown away.

'Oh Heavenly Alleviation, I am able to breathe again! That feels so good,' the Earth suddenly felt its sweet relief. The old planet had replenished itself through the quakes and watery cleansing to emerge as invigorated, with newer lands boasting the most lush greenery it had not seen since the beginning of time.

A splendid green and brown complexion had emerged at the surface and the seas were at their maximum blue.   Even a life form or two was beginning a new existence.

'It seems the damage was not that bad, 'twas just a mere trifle of a scratch on my surface. What an annoying itch that was,' it reflected, cockily and with much cheek. It had a good laugh about it, before drifting off to its path of eternal rest.

Chapter XIV

(Circa AD 3190s)
(FINAL YEARS OF THE WAR)

In Novaterra, several factories were built to convert the endless waste matter into weaponry against the aliens. There were two types, the sorting factory and the munitions factory. It was a daunting task to sort out all muck, but at least it was dry muck.

Cedric Wolfe-Harris was a foreman at one of the sorting factories. He oversaw his shift workers, one of them being Cynthia Daye, securing the materials fit for purpose. Cynthia separated the glass from the plastics and occasionally handled tins. She did not mind the repetitive nature of the work, as it suited someone with Asperger's. It was a job and it paid reasonably.

In a nearby munitions factory, Joanna Portaclaire, with hundreds of other workers, took all the sorted materials and put them into machines which turned them into slick weaponry. They dared to carry on when the charges were put in and all the danger therein was present. Another load had been completed and needed to be taken to the flagship Clunor, commanded by Pomphrett Greyrivers.

* * * * *

Aboard the Clunor, Commander Greyrivers stood alone, surveying the unknown. He knew they needed the weapons quickly but it would take some time for the convoy to arrive. He sighed heavily and he mopped his brow with a brush of cloth, as it was quite warm. He was as nervous behind his embroidered lapels and his confidence was just as crudely stitched. He was confident in his command, but he knew these alien races had proven most formidable in previous battles.

He bemoaned the ongoing longevity of the War and how much it cost in human life, not to mention alien (to which he wouldn't, of course); of the constant threat of battle at a moment's notice, not really having time to scramble oneself aboard the fighting vessels…..

He thought about his long dead ancestors who moved from old Earth to Novaterra, how there was alien infiltration amongst the humans, (Buckingham and Brackbury, for example, being direct descendants of them, but he knew whose side they was on), how humanity became one....oh and what about that Lear girl who got us into this whole mess in the first place??? Surely, she was human, but her life was so degraded (as it was told), that she cast her lot with the aliens.

However, the biggest point of all was the use of rubbish to fight this all with!! There was a lot of it about, as humans had not changed completely, yet it was finally put to good use and the new planet is now free from human muck. The Duke of Clearance's family dealt with all that anyway. He came from a long line of dustman and rubbish hauliers, dating back to the early parts of the War.

On board the Skipioh (the Yakrey was decommissioned years ago), the Valastrons were planning to ambush the aforesaid convoy on its way to the Clunor. They were now led by Spazio's descendant, Muscita (a Valastron-Saturninon half-caste), and his Valastron aide Aedilas. Although it was not a major priority in the past, Muscita was hell-bent on eradicating the humans after so many centuries of war with them.

The more recent generations of Valastrons, and possibly Androsians, have developed the Learian attitude toward humanity. They were most upset with the fact that some of their race had joined with humanity and turned coat in favour of mankind.

The message seeped into the minds of the Valastrons, Androsians as well as other alien races like the Saturninons, and the Silardians (who dealt with the food provisions). Between them, they carried on the War.

Muscita had a brilliant plan. Destroy the Clunor and attack Novaterra. He conferred with Aedilas, who thought it was good because it could bring the end to the conflict. Get rid of the humans, he thought, and the universe 'I wish Lear was still alive. She'd know what to do with these ingrates,' Muscita said.

'From what I heard, she was a complete mess, though brilliant in her ways,' Aedilas reflected.

'Yeah, in her samples, more like!'

They both laughed at this, knowing what was needed to be done for mass production. The continuing plans of human and alien DNA sample blending to create their own fighters against the humans, once the human children ran out, was a milestone in their history.

Aedilas hooted, laughing with his tentacles loose in the air, 'I did not know her, of course, but she sounded like a right cracker!'

'Let's use her power to overcome humanity,' Muscita decided.

He pressed a button, summoning the fighting forces to launch for attack. Urbican was called to lead the attack.

'Proceed to the Novaterra orbit and seek out the human ships,' he commanded.

'Right you are,' replied a pilot called Legatoss.

The alien fighters were small, with bright green colours on the sides of the wings (where their weapons were housed). The human's ships were larger, with blue-tipped wings hiding a stocked laser arsenal, and had the advantage of detecting alien ships via bio-readings.

Legatoss had spotted the convoy passing near their territory toward the Clunor. There were over one hundred fighting ships poised for the ambush, hoping it would evolve into a full blown battle. He informed Urbican about the convoy.

Urbican ordered, 'Let's pounce on them...now!'

The ships took flight, heading toward the human convoy and its protective fleet. Aboard the Clunor, a young boy, Yorkward Edfriar came upon the deck and handed Greyrivers a printout. Greyrivers read the same and called out, 'Mobilise all our ships to engage and send the Whadjataat squadron to secure the convoy.'

Yorkward returned to the console and quickly texted the ships. One of the escorts, Cateliffe, received the message first, and already had spotted the oncoming fighter craft.

'Cygnet, this is Cat. Buckingham, do you read me?'

'Yes, Cat, Cygnet here, I see 'em.'

He veered his ship close to Cateliffe.

'We need those weapons, Cat, get thee to the back, I'll take pursuit.'

'Aye, Cyg.'

Cateliffe's ship went to the rear to protect the container ship.

Urbican's ships began to fire on the humans.

'Shit, we're under attack,' Tudmond (the Dragon) cried.

'Greensleeve, Nay-Smith, cover me,' called Buckingham.

'Aye, sir,' Nay-Smith said.

The ships went to intercept the enemy vessels and commenced firing on them. Nay-Smith crept upon one and in point blank range, fired on it.

He cried triumphantly, 'I got you!'

'Good work, Nay,' Greensleeve (Woodes-Hastings) answered in jest, 'you old Horse!'

Nay-Smith laughed and continued to fight.

Meanwhile another vessel, the Boar, was being pursued by an alien. It's pilot cried out into his intercom, 'God, I cannot hold him!'

'Hang on, Richard, I'm coming,' Greensleeve said. Being the hero that he was, he veered behind the alien vessel and got into its blind spot. He fired on it which caused a huge explosion, singeing the Boar but letting it escape with the pilot and ship intact but shaken up a bit.

'There won't be a Boar Roast tonight,' Richard chuckled, 'but I do owe you one, Alec. Thanks for that.'

'Most welcome,' he answered.

Suddenly another lot of alien ships fired on Buckingham, damaging the Cygnet. The console went ablaze as he released an exhaust valve to let the smoke out. His pilot mask got damaged and seared into his lower lip.

Seeing the ship's damage, Cat asked, 'Cygnet, you alright?'

Buckingham wittily stated, 'Yea, and there will be no Roast Swan tonight, either, Cateliffe, Haha!'

'There goes dinner, then,' Tudmond teased.

'Oh, do can it, Dragon,' Buckingham moaned.

The fighting continued. The humans were just as dogged as the aliens, but both sides faced numerous casualties. One alien attempted to destroy the container itself, but was shot down just as quickly as it had fired. There was one human, Brackbury, who was directly entrusted with the safety of the cargo. He held the keys to the weaponry container and did his best to defend the same.

He also had an extra weapon in his arsenal. Brackbury was to keep this to himself; no one else knew about it. Only a select few humans were aware of it, but they never dreamt it could be used or thought it would work. Taking a huge risk, he set the ship and container tow to morph using a shrouding device.

There were a row of oncoming alien vessels heading his way before the change. When he discharged, it resulted in a stunning array of fire. The invisible ship had fled past the fire, cloaking the container in tow, heading for the Clunor.

Richard cheered, 'Good ol' Bracks!'

'I did not think he would use it in such a tricky manoeuvre as that was,' Buckingham admitted.

Cat, obviously not privy to the information, asked, 'Where did Bracks go with the container?'

'It was the Cloak-in-Armour trick. It was something we devised to fool the aliens with. Created quite recently, of course, otherwise the aliens would make advancement upon us.'

'How will we know when he reaches our ship?'

'Our radars will inform us,' came the reply.

Still battling rows of attacking aliens, the human pilots knew it was now or never. Dozens of squadrons were killed in the melee and those left alive fought on to finish the job.

Shortly after, a message came through on the Cygnet confirming the arrival of the precious weaponry.

'Bracks did it,' cried Buckingham.

Greensleeve smiled inside his helmet, and joked, 'Good show. I bet he'll get a knighthood!'

'You never know,' he replied.

They continued to fly and take command of the heavens as they battled the last of the aliens.

Meanwhilst, Muscita and Aedilas were contemplating whether or not to continue with the fighting. The last of the mixed-race samplings were killed off and it was noted that the Clunor received its cargo, right under their noses. They weighed up the options and realised there was no turning back, nor going forward. One felt like a lame duck, just sitting there doing nothing, with no purpose.

Aedilas looked at Muscita forlornly, suggesting they surrender.

He screamed, 'You mean we should quit????'

'Well, what is the point now? They have their so-called 'precious' weapons and Heaven only knows how it will be used against us and further the losses. There are no more fighters and no one is around to egg us on,' Aedilas argued.

'Eh?'

'LEAR!'

'Oh, her,' Muscita said, defeated, 'so now what do we do?'

'Call in a truce, sir,' he replied, emotionless.

'The humans cannot win this,' Muscita sighed, after all these centuries of War, Glorious War, everything turned to dust.

'Neither will we. It is a stalemate. We are not getting any-where. Everything is finished and quite frankly, I've had enough of all this!'

'That is tantamount to contempt, how dare you?!'

'Well, if it is, I do not care, I am sending a message to the humans it is finished.'

Aedilas slithered past Muscita. Another loud sigh was emitted, but more heaving. He's right, damn him, Muscita thought. He knew he wasn't going to win and there was no point in carrying on. A message from the Skipioh was then texted to the Clunor. Lights flickered on Yorkward's console. Another officer, Breathawaye, stood by, receiving the incoming message.

He cried out, 'Sir, sir, a message from the Valastrons.'

'Muscita? Well, I never thought I would hear from him! Let me read it.'

The message had two words on it: 'ENOUGH ALREADY!'

Greyrivers thought it a bit sudden. Breathawaye wondered if it was for real. In thinking about the recent shipment, as well as that shrouding device of Brackbury's, the two officers figured the aliens would stand no chance against them.

'Acknowledge the message and arrange for them to come aboard to discuss terms. Inform the surviving squadrons to cease fire and return to the Clunor,' he said.

'Aye, sir,' Breathawaye returned to the console where Yorkward texted the messages to the ships.

In space, Buckingham received the message on his unit and announced to the pilots.

'This is Cygnet, here. Cease fire, I repeat, cease fire. We are to return to the Clunor. It's over,' he breathed a sigh of relief and the remaining pilots returned to the flagship.

* * * * *

After the battle, a ceremony was held aboard the Clunor. The members of the Whadjataat Squadron, i.e., Buckingham, Richard, Woodes-Hastings, Brackbury, Cateliffe, Tudmond, and Nay-Smith, received decorations and knighthoods for their important roles during the War, as did Cedric Wolfe-Harris and Joseph Arthur, the current Duke of Clearance. Brackbury had received a special commendation for his use of the shrouding device in order for the humans to receive the munitions.

Greyrivers and Breathawaye then met with the Valastrons, Muscita and Aedilas, to agree to a treaty between the humans and aliens. A real-time truce was enforced to ensure harmony in the universe, not allowing for the previous imbalance Man had caused.

There was to be no rubbish allowed to grossly accumulate on the face of Novaterra, thus all things 'thrown in the bin' would be recycled, no matter what they are made of. The planet was to be kept clean, and it was within every human to do his/her part herein.

Any form of greed was also abolished (as it was a grievous heresy), even though the aliens found that it was a quirk of humanity. They had tried to do experimentation, (like the type used on Cynthia Lear), to breed out this trait, but they could not find greed in a single physical cell. They then realised it was a 'concept' and one, proven time and again, which was dangerous to every living being in the universe.

Muscita, steeped in the Learian-point-of-view, vowed never to allow the humans to take advantage of what is not really theirs in the first place. Displaying any form of greed would 'upset' the balance of the universe.

All the humans would have the same rights, accommodation and facilities. No one person would have more import than any other, with no exceptions. Collections of valuable items will be property of the state by law.

A more familiar rule was also put in place, one which would (and should) resonate with all, 'Love Thy Neighbour', and this would be most important. These laws carried the death penalty, if not followed.

Muscita had an even better plan in store for the humans, staring at Greyrivers and pointing one of his tentacle-legs at him, 'We will also be watching you. You may have bred together to become one, intermingling with your own various races to survive, and even treasonously incorporating our alien blood into yourselves, you will always be subjugated by us. You may live your lives freely and do what you want, do what you like. You may enjoy your widened diversity, but remember, YOU ARE ALL HUMAN,' he emphasised the final word as if it were a curse, and spat it out like it was poison.

Aedilas added, 'Heed our terms and we can live harmoniously.'

Greyrivers looked at the aliens with a slight tinge of disgust, but he knew he was getting off lightly. Humanity itself was getting off lightly. All the aliens wanted was mutual and genuine respect, with the exception of those who still took the Learian view of hell and annihilation. They were not happy about the truce and wished to prolong the War, but were willing to give the buggers a chance, as long as the Valastrons kept to their surveillance of them.

The frightening memory that lingered in Greyrivers' mind for many years afterward was the Valastron promise, 'We will be watching 'you'.'

After that meeting, a statue was erected in Sydmouth Square to honour Cynthia Lear. The inscription read, 'Hail Glorianna – Remember Thine Own.' The alien's surveillance was done through the statue's eyes and there was fear among the humans not to disturb or vandalise the statue. There were also cameras concealed throughout the statue, in case the eye-cameras were dirty from bad weather or bird mess.

A weapon was hidden in the hands which would be raised and a sweep of laser beams fired from the fingertips to remind the people of the medicinal injustice she suffered.

If any human were to touch the statue in any way, especially to deface, (and bird mess did not count anyway as there were specialised cleaners to deal with that), they would be punished and there would be no escape from the laser volley that will come.

Thus, no attempt of such an act was dared nor considered by anyone, not even bored hoodlum teen-yobs! They now knew their place in the universe and that all their lives were at stake. Every human on the planet was aware they were being watched continually by the eyes and other camera-bits in the statue. Many other Learian surveillance statues were erected all over the towns and cities of Novaterra to remind the humans **who is really the boss of them.**

Chapter XV
(Circa AD 3200)
(PRESENT DAY)

We sat around, slightly dumbfounded at the history and personal experiences remembered during the War. I felt alone, because I sensed grave disappointment from the others, due to my ancestor who caused the trouble in the first place. The real problem was the fact that one needed to feel compassion for HER as she went through a plethora of problems which were: a) not her fault and b) should never have happened, full stop.

Yet, as she had no satisfaction from those who trounced her, and she felt she had every reason to 'lash out' at others, perhaps because no one helped her? I do not know. It was a family story handed down and sometimes not so enthusiastically and, more than likely, embellished. I wondered whether the universe would be the same if only someone did help her out. When help did arrive, however, it came too late. Her mind was already full of the poisonous stench which sparked the War. I know I could not have helped and I am unsure how those around her were able to handle such a firecracker.

I heard she died, consumed by bitterness, hatred, and that odd desire of hers for retaliation, but at least she had someone there for her comfort. I also realised that if it were not for her, we would not be here, in this pub, on Novaterra. I would rather be surrounded by loving people than be alone, as I had been. The friends I recently made were such good people, with their own stories to tell and having good solid shoulders to cry on. I took advantage of the opportunity around me, and started to cry, out of pity for the poor girl. I suddenly felt a hand on my shoulder; it was Alec.

'Come here,' he said.

I leant over him for a hug. Even though I did not have far to go, it was awkward with the chair set-up. I left my seat to sit on his lap. Ah, that's better. Now, I can give and receive a more meaningful embrace.

'I know it must have been difficult for you having to grow up with that knowledge,' he continued.

I sat there dazed, 'It was part of the stories I was told, the good and bad,' I sniffed. I looked up at him and my eyes were pleading for mercy and compassion and then I furthered my argument, 'She really was not a bad person. She was treated in the roughest of manners and in return, she just simply bore a grudge.....'

'.....the size of the universe,' Buckingham interrupted, finishing my sentence.

'And an ego to match,' I chimed back.

'As well as a very large libido!' Buckingham returned the volley, 'Did you know, she married an alien? A fellow named Buxby, an Androsian, as well as a human before him. The human died, though.'

'What was his name?' Richard asked.

'Spectrum Fallace.'

Alec looked at me in surprise, 'He is one of MY ancestors!'

Buckingham quipped, 'Ah, and Buxby is one of mine.'

Both men stared at me with intent. I felt cornered....yet, didn't we just spend the night together, not too long ago???? Uh-oh, I suddenly realised what this meant.

'We're all related, the three of us!'

Everyone at the table looked aghast. Nay-Smith saw the bother and wanted to break the ice.

'Well, it has been over one thousand years. There would have been many variations within that time period and I heard how you three have been 'close', you know,' he said, clearing his throat.

'I would never imagine one being this close,' Richard said, sighing, 'Well, that explains a lot. Alec, you've won her fair and square.'

Alec smiled like a Cheshire cat, 'I am forever indebted to you, my friend.' He then got up to shake Richard's hand.

'Still, I was happy to meet and help your Cynthia,' Richard added, 'Even?'

'Yea.' Alec and Richard shook hands.

The feeling in the room wasn't as tense as before. I found it funny having relations around me, even if it had been over a millennia of DNA between us.

I told Alec, 'Did you also know that Lear was abducted?'

He responded quickly, 'Fallace was as well. He used to be an actor by the name of DeMilo.'

'That's right,' I confirmed.

Brackbury had overheard us, surprised, 'Abducted?'

'Yea, they've both been at different times. Funny that, and later on, they got married. They had a child but, before the birth, he passed away,' Alec recalled.

'Oh gosh, that must have been awful for him, and her,' Cateliffe uttered.

'It must explain her turning against humanity, with that inadequate upbringing and the loss of someone she truly loved, especially when in the last weeks of pregnancy, oooh,' Brackbury noted with a grimace.

We reflected for a moment, then private conversations ensued.

I eyed Buckingham, needing to talk to him, 'I hope you do not regret what happened the other night, and I have to confess I am getting involved more with Alec.'

Buckingham turned to me, 'I know it, luv, I know it. I thought it would turn out this way, though it is a revelation that we are closer than expected. It is something to be proud of. Please do not feel ashamed of this. Nay-Smith is right; it has been many years, many combinations, many individualities. We are compatible, whether you want me or Alec, or both, even,' he smiled.

I giggled at the suggestion, 'I doubt that would be possible!'

'You never know. Now, you go on with Alec. I can tell you love him very much.'

'I do. I cannot control the feeling. Honestly, it drives me crazy, just to think of him. It feels like youth again.'

'Young love in middle age? Huh, that's a real laugh!'

I smiled, knowing he was teasing. He was right, though. I was definitely in love with Alec and prayed it would culminate in due course. It was very easy to relax and be free round these people, and speak how one wishes, even if it were along rude lines.

Buckingham continued, 'Not to worry about it. We are quite casual but careful in our relationship. Why, are you thinking further?'

'Yes but I will need time to be certain. I want to be with him more to get to know him and go from there. We are not getting any younger, you know.'

'No we are not. On another note, how was that spa then?'

I giggled and blushed. I whispered in his ear, 'I tried to grab a towel Alec had round his loins. Damn that he caught me at it.'

'Caught you out, then,' Buckingham sipped his drink, 'Saucy little bugger you! Did you enjoy that filming we did?'

'We did not expect it, but it was a refreshing surprise.'

'Good.'

'Thank you,' I kissed him firmly.

Cedric finally spoke up, noticing the kiss, 'Cynthia, my dear girl!'

'I was only thanking him, sir.'

'Oooohhh, and for what, I wonder,' he gave a me a wicked grin and a wink. I felt myself wanting to race to the ceiling and back with all these yummy men in my pocket.

'It was meant as an agreement,' I protested.

'Oh, if only wars could end that way, hey-hey,' Richard joked.

I stuck my tongue out at him, then returned to Alec.

'You alright,' he asked.

I responded, 'Yea. This has been a momentous day, most heady, I feel. Are you still on for coming home with me?'

'Of course, my love, I would not miss it for the world, even if it is a new one,' he smiled, then asked, 'What was it with you and Buckingham just now?'

'I was asking him about your relationship together. Now, that I am more involved with you, I had to be sure that it was okay with him. I do not want to break something up, if you two are very serious.'

He paused for a bit, 'We may be living together, but it is not like we are married. There is the intimate side, and it is quite flexible. Do you really want to commit to me?'

'Yes I do,' I said proudly, as if it was part of a grand catechism.

He smiled, 'Come here, then.' He opened up his arms to me and embraced me with a kiss. Everyone else was chatting and ignoring us, out of respect more than anything.

I suggested, 'I think we should return home, no?'

'We can do this in a more private setting.....or else we'll be here all night. Let me get the timetable for the trains,' he fumbled through his pockets to find the chart, 'Ah, here 'tis. There is another train in an hour's time. I think it is best we catch that one.'

It sounded good. I loved the current company, but the day was weighing heavily upon me and it felt cumbersome to remain awake. Alec and I said our goodbyes to everyone there.

'You take care,' Buckingham said, patting me on the back.

'Safe journey, you two,' Richard added.

I smiled and then saw Cedric coming up to us, 'Thank you both for all your help this afternoon. It was much appreciated.'

Alec chimed, 'Unexpected more like, but it was a pleasant experience. I wish you luck with the project.'

Cedric thanked him and turned to me, 'Good for you?'

'Yes. It was fun, yet I can see how it is not very easy as it looks.'

He smiled and said, 'True. I really enjoyed having you, my dear, Godspeed and do keep in touch. You have my number.'

'Yes. Another pub meet, then?'

'Perhaps. You going home with Alec?'

'He's staying the night with me.'

'You be careful, now.'

'I will, as long as I am willing,' I said cheekily.

'Oooh, you're a definite feisty dish, you! See you again, soon.
Bye for now.'

'Bye,' I waved everyone off and departed with Alec.

We walked down to the station and waited. The darkness
overshadowed the sky but there were monochrome fairy lights
round the lamp posts so it did not look so depressing and
dangerous.

'What a great day that was,' Alec reflected.

'Uuummmm,' I agreed, leaning over him.

'You tired?'

'Getting there. I feel exhausted, wound up, and crazed out of
my mind.'

'Once we get to your place, we will settle and relax, okay?'

'Yes,' I gave him a hug.

Shortly after, the train arrived and we left Brightpoole for
home in Sydmouth. The ride was okay, but more dull and with
that lingering tired feeling one gets when one returns from a
busy day away.

We eventually got home but we did not do much. After
necessary oblations, we headed for bed together for a good
night's rest.

We curled up tight against each other on my bed and his heart was pounding away next to me. It was a great comfort, as it lulled me into sleep.

The next morning, thankfully, looked just as pleasant with sunlight shining through the window. It moved around the room, playing with the patterns of the wallpaper and photos of various male favourites framed thereupon. The recent autographed photo Cedric gave to me awhile ago hung proudly amongst them.

I stirred slightly with my love sleeping soundly next to me. His steady heartbeat was still going strong, and I thought, thank God. I remembered what happened to my ancestor Lear and how her husband Fal had passed away in his sleep with her next to him. Eweh! I wanted to awake the babe, but I had no idea what he liked. I touched him lightly a bit on his cheek and jaw area and he wavered a bit. He had a smile on his face.

'Do continue that, please, it is so nice,' he snoozily grunted.

I caressed my hands over his flesh and tickled him. He was half-dreaming, groaning as he changed position, talking softly. I thought of an idea, so I created some further embellishment.

'What light dost shine in yonder window fakes?'

' 'Tis a torch light, milady,' he sleepily answered.

'Ah, the glow of artificial dissemination. Pray, what are thou reading, my lord?'

'A Joyful Passion,' he wickedly grinned, getting up suddenly. He took hold of me and firmly planted himself upon me.

A few moments passed, 'Let's a-toilet, before we commence,' he said.

We did our bits, then joined up again.

He asked, 'You don't have anything bigger, do you?'

The question caught me out, 'Eh, what?'

He patted the bed, 'This?'

'No, I live alone. I do not need anything bigger.'

'Then we will have to make do with what we have, then, won't we? I pray you suffer not my advancement upon ye, but I promise 'twill be such a treat.'

He beckoned me over and we embraced. His arms encircled round my body and he held me tight as we grew ever more aroused. He touched the passion and I moaned and giggled as I touched his tender self. We carried on, as he kissed and touched me, teased and pleased the pleasure, as I eased into a phase when I found myself getting desperate for more.

His tongue worked its way toward my lower half, which reminded me of a watery fairground ride, which I needed to really hold onto. For a change, this was a ride that did not make me dizzy. The feelings within us were so substantial that there was no turning back. This relationship was here to stay and it was felt universally betwixt us.

'Alec.'

He lifted his head and looked up, 'Yes?'

'What was it with you and Richard. Why was he so courteous to me on that snowy day at the hotel?'

'Ah, that. 'Twas a trifle. Pay it no mind.'

'Please?'

He relented, 'He owed me a favour because I saved his life.'

I turned to him, 'What happened?'

'He lost control of his ship during a flight to deliver the weapons to the Clunor. We were ambushed and had to fight. An alien was nearing its mark, when I blasted the bugger out of the sky away from Richard's ship.'

'That must have been scary.'

'Well, scary, maybe heroic. I don't know. We are even now.'

I hugged him more, knowing he was more than a love, he was a hero.

Chapter XVI

Weeks passed and I carried on with my jobs at the library and at Richard's office. The days proved fair, but my mind was focused on Alec. It did not make my time with Richard and Buckingham any more easier. Although both men were quite attractive, it was not as difficult as first thought. The nicest part about being there, was that there was someone to talk to, especially now that my kinship with Buckingham had been revealed.

I shortly found out that Richard had been having a go with Joanna after all. They made a good pair, probably far better than myself in that role. My thoughts did go to him, but later they revolved along a much more brighter sun.

The library job was, at most, a past-time...just something to do in the morning. I loved being there, but the solitude I was in sometimes pushed me too far. It was a humdrum routine, and although I did not mind it much, I eagerly looked forward to my afternoons with Richard and Buckingham, instead of going home and wasting time on one's own.

Alec remained at the hotel for the time being. It was a job and he liked it, for now. At his break times, I would hear from him, either by text or on the phone. It was moments like this that made boredom seem more tolerable. He was keen on seeing me again, as I was to see him.

One day, it was decided everyone meet up at the arcade for our usual hang-out. I came after work with Richard and Buckingham. Alec, Cedric, Clearance, Brackbury, Nay-Smith, Cateliffe and Joanna had joined up and sat at a nearby table. Buckingham excused himself and went up to the games console with Bracks to play some rounds of a fighter pilot game which he played at a previous meeting on his own.

Alec played his brain teaser games on his phone (as usual), Clearance nodded off (again!), and Cedric was reading a book (typical!!) and occasionally chatting to Cateliffe.

Joanna and I had gone together to another game involving a large green dot devouring smaller dots with some monsters and ghosts thrown in to complicate matters. She was quite good at it, whilst I was still very amateurish since playing it in my youth. I was beaten after a few rounds.

'Better luck next time,' she said.

'Yea, maybe. You're pretty lucky at the best of times.'

'Oh, how so?'

'You have Richard. That is indeed a jackpot.'

She thought about it, 'Yeah, so I have. You worry so, though. You have Alec and I heard he's the better one.'

My eyes widened, 'Oh, why is that?'

'Your man saved Richard's life back in the War. Richard told me about it.'

In the conversation I had with Alec that night he spent with me at my place, he revealed the reason for the indebtedness between them and why it was strongly felt it needed to be 'paid off.'

'I remember Alec told me about it too. He blasted an alien out of the sky, sparing Richard's ship.'

'Amazing what teamwork can do,' she reflected.

My mind, wandered off again in the midst of thought. Joanna broke the silence, 'Let's see what the boys are doing, eh?'

'Okay,' I agreed as we walked to see what Bucks and Bracks were up to.

Both men were working hard on their respective consoles and targeting ships to blast.

I asked, 'Hit anything yet?'

Brackbury quickly turned to answer, 'Yea, I believe we shot up several enemy ships. What did you get, Buckingham?'

'I got at least three of them,' he replied, concentrating on his game.

Joanna queried, 'You play often?'

"Yea, I like to keep fit mentally. It helps with work, too.'

'Shame it doesn't help physically,' I cheekily japed.

Buckingham turned to me, and gave me a stern look which melted into a smile. It caught me off guard, but I was relieved he took it in good fun.

Joanna and I returned to the table, chatting with those there, leaving Buckingham and Brackbury to their game.

Suddenly, Brackbury stated, 'I'm out.'

BANG! Another shot to Buckingham, 'Ah, I win again.'

'Saucy,' Brackbury responded.

'I practise a lot,' he turned away from the console to Brackbury, 'By the way, I am curious...'

Brackbury moved closer to him, 'What?'

'You busy tonight?' Buckingham proposed.

He looked at him dumbfounded, 'Well, I'm, uh.....,' he could not answer.

'I wanted to know because Alec is getting together with Cynthia.'

'Really?'

'Aye, he's got her a ring, too.'

'Wow. Well, I do not mind being in your company, Buckingham.'

'Why thank you. Are you of the persuasion?'

'Pardon?'

Buckingham whispered the intent in his ear.

Brackbury looked surprised, 'What? I didn't know you were.....'

'The door swings both ways. I had Cynthia once.'

Brackbury stifled a snigger, 'Well, alright, then.'

'You up for it?'

'Yea, sure, why not? There has got to be a reason why I'm divorced,' he laughed.

They went to the table where we were sitting.

Richard asked, 'You two okay?'

They looked at each other and nodded.

Alec had put his phone away and turned to me, 'Ah good, you're here. I have something for you.'

I could not imagine what it was. He produced a wrapped box with a ribbon on it. I thanked him and opened it up. It was a ring, gold banded with a small diamond in the middle. He then knelt down beside the chair, in front of everyone.

'Cynthia, will you marry me?'

I chuffed at the moment and thought, wow.

I declared, 'Yes, yes I will!'

He put the ring on my finger and it looked really sparkly with the light reflecting upon it. We hugged each other and exchanged a tender kiss.

'Well, well,' Buckingham said knowingly, looking at Brackbury, 'See, I told you so.'

Brackbury smiled and Nay-Smith and Cateliffe sat there stunned.

'I saw this coming some time back,' Buckingham admitted to them, 'I live with Alec, you know.'

I went over to Cedric to show him the ring.

'Now, that is lovely, it shows your old boy's got taste.'

I giggled, 'Yea, I know,' then whispered in his ear, 'And he doth taste good too!'

He said aloud, smiling, 'Ooooh, you wicked girl!'

Nay-Smith looked up, not realising the joke, 'What?'

I went over to him and repeated the whisper. He looked at me deadpan and wished he hadn't asked.

Alec chided me, his eyebrow raised, 'Are you being naughty, Cynthia?'

'Just mucking about,' I said sheepishly, 'A trifle.'

He forgave me and smiled, 'Well, we will let that one go, shall we?'

Everyone carried on chatting and there was another surprise to come. Richard and Joanna, too, had something to reveal. He gave her a box similar to mine which also produced a ring.

'Will you marry me, Joanna?'

She exclaimed, 'Why, yes!'

Joanna was most pleased and put it on straightaway. She kissed him as a thank you.

'Well, that's love for you,' Buckingham observed.

Brackbury felt sceptical and left out, saying to Buckingham, 'You are not going to give me a ring, are you?'

'Certainly not! Well, not yet, anyway. I just asked you for a date. Jeez!'

'Phew, that's alright, then,' he said, relieved. Two engagements were one thing, three would have been a miracle.

Everyone toasted the two engaged couples and carried on into the night.

Chapter XVII

Months later, the intended weddings were to be held at St. Halloe-in-the-Eves. It was extremely tense and challenging to arrange. I was very nervous and decided to take some time off both jobs to prepare for the ceremony. During these moments, I spent a lot of time with Alec, having fun with him, and also meeting with the priest to discuss matters in more detail.

After another meeting, Alec and I decided to blow off some steam in a nearby park. We gave chase to one another, and went toward some trees. One of them looked good for climbing and I dared him to go up. He began his ascent and held out his hand for me to grab hold of. There was a welcoming huge thick branch that we sat upon and contemplated what was to come.

'You nervous?'

'Nah,' he scoffed, cheekily.

'You know I don't believe you,' I grinned.

He smiled back wickedly, then got serious, 'I am more nervous due to it being not just us at the altar.'

'I see,' I thought aloud as I looked around the tree. Another concern popped into my head and I felt I ought to clear it up before we continued, 'Can I ask you a personal question?'

'Go ahead,' he replied.

'I do not mean to sound crass, but, umm.....,' I hesitated, thinking it would insult him.

He came closer to me, 'What is it, my dear?'

I looked him in the eye (which is something I would never do under ANY circumstance), and asked, 'You don't have any health concerns or anything wrong with you?'

His face turned serious at my off-centred line of query, 'What do you mean? Why, do you expect something?'

'My ancestor lost her husband to illness.'

'Yea, I know. Remember, her husband was my ancestor, well distant. I could not have inherited anything anomalous from him to my knowledge and even if he did, 'twould nay affect me due to the era we now live in. He was from another time and place. Our medicinal practises are far superior these days. By Heaven, you worry so much.'

'I just don't want to lose you.'

'You won't. You're mine, my love, forever.'

We hugged and I thanked God I had such a man to comfort me.

'To answer your question, once and for all, there are no known discrepancies, physical or mental. I am fit and healthy as a workhorse.' He looked at me squarely, 'Now you tell me, I know you have something.....,' he lingered in thought, sensing familiarity.

A long breath tickled the air with anticipation as I nervously confessed, 'Asperger's.'

'Ah, thought so. I knew there was something about you which spelled 'spectrum disorder'. I remember from that time you were at the hotel when we first met. There is nothing wrong in having it nor is it something to be ashamed of.'

I explained to him, 'I had it diagnosed at age three and tried to live with it as best I could. I am not ashamed of my condition but I normally do not like to discuss it with others. It makes me feel like it is a stigma and I do not appreciate the attention when asked about it. I know I am better than that.'

I stopped and mustered the strength to remember what I had been told, then continued, 'Lear had it too, but she was unaware she had it, and that asinine family who raised her had no clue either. She was diagnosed in her mid-forties. It explained so much, but it did not stop her from being angry and vengeful at the treatment by those surrounding her.'

'I know. Fallace tried to help her as much as he could and I will help you as much as I can. This time, though, no invading other worlds, got it?'

'Got it. So, you are willing to give me a go, then,' I said, relieved at the prospect. The comfort of having someone one can love is very priceless. I gave him another hug.

'Why of course! Do stop comparing yourself with Lear. Yea, she had her run, now let her rest in peace. Let us live for the present, eh? You have your life and you decided to live it with me. I will be with you in lifelong matrimony,' he stated with assurance.

I felt thankful, for his conviction was so strong. This was to last forever, well, at least until one's natural passing.

'So you will always be my baby?'

'Of course, unless we make one,' Alec smiled, raising his eyebrows up and down, knowingly.

'Aren't we too old for that sort of thing?'

He exclaimed, 'Nonsense!'   He then relented, nuzzling his face into my chest, 'Oh, well, if you must, we will have that looked into later on.'

'Alright,' I said, looking further out to find that branch we were on was one of longer branches that suspended over a lake. I stared at Alec for a moment, thinking of something extreme, but felt that, knowing my luck, it would backfire. I decided to inform him.

'Alec, do you realise where we are?'

'We are in a tree on a branch, sitting comfortably.'

'Have you seen what is below us?'

He looked down to see the inviting lake beneath.

'I guess there is one thing for it,' he commenced a tickle fight between us. Our fingers grooved stealthily within our clothes as we sought out each others flesh. We struggled with each other for a time, expunging the tension of the moment, giving way to laughter and pleasure. Eventually, both of us gave way, which resulted in our falling off the branch into the water. We kissed one another, then swam to land's edge and climbed out unto the grass. Our clothes were wet and muddy as the grass was thinning like middle-aged hairs on a person. It felt good and eased much of the pressure upon us.

We walked back to my place, as we had started to live together. It was working out well, although we will need a larger dwelling in the future.   Since that time, Brackbury's involvement with Buckingham had intensified and eventually, he filled the space Alec vacated.

The wedding date was nigh and when it finally arrived, it was a relief to everyone. Everything went as planned and everyone held a sentiment to get it over with because the intensity of each couple's romance had not gone unnoticed. Dear ol' Cedric had given me away and Brackbury gave Joanna away. The priest conducted the service in the traditional fashion, with both couples at the altar and vows exchanged.

'Do you, Brian Alexander Woodes-Hastings, take Cynthia to be your lawfully wedded wife, to have, to hold.....' the list went on.

'I do,' said he.

'Do you, Cynthia Daye, take Brian Alexander, to be your lawfully wedded husband....'

'I do,' said I.

Then Richard and Joanna exchanged their respective vows. It was amazing how the church was so full up as I stood looking like a porcelain china doll in the gear I wore. Could all this be true, I wondered?

Then, the rings were put on the fingers. The commitment was now sealed.

The priest addressed both couples, 'I now pronounce you man and wife. You may kiss your brides.'

Alec and I kissed like it was our last. God, it felt so good to now be Lady Woodes-Hastings. Richard and Joanna also had their exchange and loved every moment.

The reception was modest, and consisted of our usual group of friends, plus some of the wedding guests. It certainly was not as maddening as one had previously thought. Many toasts were drunk to the happy couples. Food and spirits went round and we danced all night. It was a fantastic party.

I went outside for a breather. I looked up and, as it had rained a wee bit during the day, I saw a rainbow streak in the sky. It seemed like a good omen to me. Cedric joined me, cup in hand.

He asked, 'How are you doing, old girl?'

'Well, thank you, but I cannot wait to remove this dress and relax.'

'Plenty of time for that, you know.'

'Yea. It is so different now,' I dreamily answered, then changed the subject, 'Are you still working on that project?'

'Oh, you mean Richard III? It is in the editing stage at the moment. Nearly done and it looks flawless, so far.'

'Our scenes are still intact?'

'Yes. All the fighting scenes are there.'

'Tricky thing is, love,' I reflected aloud.

'Can be. Why do you say?'

'You remember a while back, there was so much flirting and having a laugh. I let it all happen and now it had gotten serious.'

'You now have committed yourself to someone. Love is marvellous when respected and in the correct circumstances. I confess I was hoping you and I would venture out sometime, but I see the wheel has turned elsewhere.'

'Well, I am truly fond of you and I find you such a fascinating wonder. Perhaps it is age? Pray, do not be insulted.'

He smiled, 'I am not, but I do admit to getting on in years. We all are; that is why it is good you and Alec made the most of yourselves in this way.'

I looked at Cedric. He has such a kindly face and a mannerism that cannot be reproduced.

'Shall we go in?' I proposed.

'Let us go forth,' he beckoned.

I held his hand as we returned inside. He turned me over to Alec and we carried on the rest of the night, dancing and celebrating away.

Chapter XVIII

Alec and I decided to go on our honeymoon with Richard and Joanna. We would have our time together and, of course, separately. We were all good friends by now and thought it would be fun to share these moments. We visited the sunnier climate of Prinnyvale, where we had rented accommodation in a block of flats by the sea. There was a pool and a nearby beach with its boardwalk, pier and other delights. Thankfully, the weather was clement and we took advantage of being outdoors.

Never in my life would I have thought to be a Lady and I found this difficult to get my head round. I could not think of myself as one, as most people used to think of me as oafish, or the like. Yet here I am, ever so grand and at the same time, all plain and simple. No one I recently befriended made a do about it anyway from the start. I gave them the respect I thought was deserved and they dismissed the high and mighty and flew straight down to earth. There was no pretentious snobbery from the start. It was refreshing and most kindly of them.

Alec and I took a walk along the seafront. Richard and Joanna stayed behind in deck chairs by the pool in swimming costumes.

He commented, 'This is a most placid place, eh, Cynthia?'

'Great place for a holiday, especially a honeymoon,' I ribbed him.

'Yea. 'Tis undisturbed, calm, with its sea rolling foam in its misty fashion.'

'You poet, you!'

'Ha-ha,' he laughed aloud.

He smiled and we held each other to kiss. We cuddled and it was obvious we wanted more.

'I don't suppose we could...,' I thought again, unbuttoning his shirt and caressing his chest. It was so soft with light wispy hair upon it and he was just oozing with vigour and enchantment.

I proceeded to kiss the area, making my way past his navel towards his elastic-waist shorts.

Alec perked up, 'Nay. Not here. It may look deceptively ghostly, but, there could always be someone, you know.'

'True. 'Twould be most embarrassing. Yea, I am so desperate. Canst we try anyway?' I begged.

'Ah, do go on, and I shall content thee,' he yielded.

YES! This was a major victory for me. We went to a secluded area amongst some trees. I worked my way further down and proceeded to fellatiate Alec.   His eyes widened as he was enjoying the sensuous rhythms he felt below. At last, the release was most welcome, as he exhaled in relief, moaning passionately. I accidentally released a burp as I got up, and was most embarrassed.

'I am so sorry, my lord,' I giggled, then composed myself, 'You have now lost your head, and it is not even dinner yet.'

'Yea, I well and truly lost my head to you…ah….you have executed me well.' With that, he grabbed me and we enjoyed an indulgent kiss.

Then he said, 'And now that you have, at last, had your way with me, let us go see what Richard and Joanna are up to, then, hmmm?'

'Yea, why not.'

He tidied himself up and we went back to the lodgings. I saw Richard and Joanna still laying by the pool and I waved to them. I had a very wicked thought and, as it was quite warm, it should go to plan. I told Alec about it.

'I will need your help, though. To surprise someone without their realising it until it is too late would be quite tricky,' he said.

'If the others were here, it'd be much easier.'

'Well, they are not, but we are. It takes much effort to roast a boar, let alone baste one.'

'I think we should try it ourselves.'

We shook hands on it, and walked up to Richard. Joanna watched, bewildered, but did not stop us. We took hold of respective ends and carried him near the pool's edge. Before he protested, we threw him in. I spotted an inflatable ring-horse nearby which I gave to Alec.

'Here is thy horse, my liege,' he mocked, proudly, tossing the ring-horse to Richard.

Then he took Joanna on his own, and carried her to the edge and threw her in withal, 'And here is thy kingdom! May thou reign evermore!' Then, he saluted them.

They were completely surprised, but they wouldn't put it past Alec to do something of the nature. It was horrifically funny of him to dare prove his 'treasonous' self by such wretched means. However, it was taken for what it was, i.e., a good laugh.

I giggled hysterically and Alec walked up to me, removing his shirt, 'Do you wish to join them, my lady?'

'Pardon? You've got to be kidding, sir!' I could not stifle myself and slipped into formality, despite the atmosphere being so jocund and my babe, so sexy.

Before he answered, he hastily grabbed me, but I was not giving in without a fight. I tried to get him to let go, but he held on. We playfully struggled, tickling one another just as we had back in the park. It was easier getting at his flesh this time and after some time, we both went over the edge together. It was such a jubilant moment because Alec joined me in the pool, being the 'chivalrous knight' that he was. I felt such an adrenaline rush and was vigorously renewed. The four of us scoffed it off and exited the pool to dry ourselves.

I held onto Alec and kissed him under the towelling. He was so dear to me and I thanked Heaven for him. He was now mine to have and to hold, forever.